BLUFFING FOR BEGINNERS

A GOOD LIFE NOVEL

MERREN TAIT

LOLA PUBLICATIONS

Lola Publications. Raglan, New Zealand.

Print ISBN: 978-0-473-53098-3

Large print ISBN: 978-0-47355523-8

Cover design by Bailey McGinn.

Author photo by Eleanor Gee.

www.merrentait.com

ALSO BY MERREN TAIT

The Good Life series

The Year of the Fox

The Misdeeds of Sadie Quinn

Odd Girl Roar

The Amateur's Guide to the Art of Running Away: A novella

Britlandia series

Real Life and Other Disasters

Romance is Dead

PART 1

CHAPTER ONE

NOW. **Ruatapu Island, New Zealand**

"No! Jesus, no. You can have it, Em, I'm out."

Warren, the (apparently temporary) love of my life, couldn't have walked backwards from our new life together with more haste. He waved his hands out in front of him, palms outwards, and retreated towards our newly acquired utility vehicle. Before him, capturing his gaze like a fearsome Gorgon, stood the house we had bought sight unseen from the other side of the Tasman Sea.

I turned, hands on hips, from him to the house and back again. "Come on. You can't be serious."

He looked at me then, the whites of his widened eyes matching the pallor of his face.

"Babe," I said gently, "it just needs a bit of work. It'll be fine."

Through the scraggly foliage of what remained of a front garden, the house revealed itself in all its glorious dilapidation, a state that was not evident in the carefully staged photographs on the real estate website. The weatherboards were cracked and missing entirely in the odd place, the roof sagged in one corner, and what had looked like a lovely moss-green paint job was, in fact, moss. A whole wall supporting a vibrant and very damp ecosystem.

"It's fucked, Em. It's completely fucked. *We're* completely fucked." He'd backed himself up against the ute and with a slack-mouthed focus on the house, blindly groped for the driver's door handle.

"No, we're not. It's just an unexpected challenge. We can cope with it. Warren," I cooed, trying to get him to look at me again, "it'll be alright."

Warren, it appeared, did not agree with me. He'd found the handle and started to open the door.

"We're doing this," I said more firmly, moving towards him. "This is what we wanted. We've given up so much to be here. You need to give it a go."

"I don't. I really don't. I'm going back." He scrambled into the cab and buckled himself in, the seatbelt framing the soft round of his belly.

I pulled my shoulder-length red hair into a bunch behind my head and exhaled through pursed lips. Then I dropped my hand and said in the sing-song voice of condescension, "You're not going back to Melbourne. We just got here. Come on, let's go and have a look inside. I bet the view's incredible from the back."

"I can't...I can't..." He shook his head, his wide eyes still fixed on the building. He reached for the keys in the ignition.

"Warren!" I said sharply, my patience failing. "Snap out of it. You're having a panic attack. Look at me, Warren."

He kept stock-still, but his eyes dragged themselves away from the spectre of the house and focused on me.

"Take some deep breaths. Deeeeep breaths. In through the nose, out through the mouth."

His eyes remained locked on mine as he turned the key.

"Fuck's sake. What are you doing? Think about it." *I* took the deep breath. "Just stop and think it through. We've made a massive commitment to be here," I said more softly, "to get some balance back in our lives. Work part time, play part time." Through the open window I placed my hand on his arm and smiled reassuringly at him. "We're a team. We can make this work, and we have more than enough money to put this house right."

"You could come with me," he said through a weak smile.

"No." I shook my head and said with the reasoned calmness of a confident mother, "I'm not going, and neither are you."

He was quiet for a moment, then he blinked. "I'm sorry, Em, I need to get off this island." He put the ute into reverse and backed out of the driveway onto the road. I ran after it, grabbing the driver's door at the window slot.

"Warren, stop! This is crazy." He didn't look at me as he thrust the ute into first gear and accelerated forward, throwing up a shower of gravel and leaving me coughing in his dusty wake. "Warren! WARREN!" I punctuated his name with a single, throatrending scream. "You coward," I hollered at the ute's disappearing bumper. "Why don't you grow a big, hairy, luscious vagina? You...shitarse, you shitarsehole!" Just like my choice in men, effective swearing wasn't my strong suit. It didn't matter. He couldn't hear any of it.

The ute rounded a corner and disappeared behind a curtain of fern fronds, and my abuse dissipated into the indifferent island air.

Warren had deserted me with nothing. Not my suitcase, nor my handbag, not even a key to the sodding house. I was stranded on the bush-clad fringes of an island 250 kilometres from the mainland. If I didn't manage to intercept Warren before the ferry left again this afternoon, I would be sans everything for another week until the ferry returned.

CHAPTER TWO

BEFORE. **Melbourne, Australia**

You may well wonder how a couple of crisp, thirty-something urban folk found themselves radically shifting axis. Change was a notion that crept in, oozing its way between the gaps in the weatherboards of our inner-city townhouse. We'd been content for years in our lifestyle choice, but clearly one of us had forgotten to put the draft-stop against the front door.

WARREN WAS a portfolio manager for an investment company. I was an investment analyst at the same firm. We averaged ten-hour days, offsetting our hard work with social engagements that were pursued with the same level of dedication.

Monday was Beginning of the Working Week

Commiseration Day – dinner and a movie. Occasionally, it was date night, but more often than not we were joined by at least one friend or colleague. Activity spend: anywhere between $130 and $180.

Tuesday was Culture Day – exhibition openings, plays, arts festivals, and anything we felt might better ourselves intellectually or help in our transformation into well-rounded people of culture. The evening always concluded with dinner and drinks at a salubrious and/or new and trendy restaurant or bar. Activity spend: upwards of $200.

Wednesday was Hump Day – hump as in the middle of the week, though as Hump Day tended to also be Down-time Day (bottle of nice wine, takeaways and a Netflix binge), a hump of the other sort was not always out of the question. Activity spend: $60.

Thursday was Guilt Day – a trip to the gym (Bikram Yoga for me, lane swimming for Warren), followed by dinner at an on-trend vegan restaurant and virgin cocktails at a rooftop bar. Activity spend: at least $170.

Friday was, of course, Thank Fuck it's Friday Day – a tapas bar and an e-induced danceathon at a gig or night club. Activity spend: no less than $250.

The weekends were invariably spent nursing hangovers, having lengthy brunches, shopping and drinking more.

We didn't cook, we didn't host, and we didn't

save. And neither did anybody else in our career-hungry, high-energy group of friends. We led a life fuelled by adrenaline and an unsaid motto: work hard, play hard, live hard.

It was never going to be sustainable.

CHAPTER THREE

NOW. Ruatapu Island

I turned around frantically on the spot, not sure how to begin the recovery operation. The fact was, with a five hundred-strong population scattered over its three hundred-square kilometres, my chances of thumbing a lift on Ruatapu's metal roads were marginal to none. I had three hours with which to cover seventeen mostly hilly klicks. If I kept up a steady run, I should be able to make it.

I pulled my skirt against my legs and looked down at my ballet flats, cursing my willingness to be bondservant to "pretty" instead of "practical". My all-terrain footwear with GEL cushioned soles and floating arches were currently speeding their way back to Port Keulemans.

Of course, it's not every day that you're abandoned on an island in the outer reaches of national territory, but nevertheless, I should have been prepared for the inevitability of betrayal. Given the speed with which my father exited my life (some minutes after I'd made my presence known), it was only a matter of time before the pattern of desertion that I apparently attracted presented itself.

I had a vision of ripping Warren's spine out of his back, popping it out like a zip and proffering it to him, dripping, globules of gore glistening on the vertebrae. "See, Warren," I'd say to him, "this is what it looks like. It's rather useful. You might want to apply it sometime soon." Another scream rose from the pit of my stomach and erupted deep and guttural, the howl echoing across the valley and silencing the birdsong.

In the sudden quiet, things came back into focus. A letterbox was set into the ground a few metres from where I stood. It did not belong to our property.

I wiped my face with the back of my hands and swallowed twice to ease the rawness in my throat. Beside the letterbox was a path leading into a thicket of feijoa trees, and beyond that I could make out the dark shape of a house. I took a last look up the empty road and pushed through the trees.

On the other side was a bungalow the mirror image of ours, twinned in dereliction. I hoped the state of the house was more an indication of benign neglect than one of inoccupancy.

In the darkened entranceway, the textured glass of the front door revealed a light on inside. I knocked, waited a few seconds, knocked harder. Nothing. "Hello? Is anybody home?"

No response.

With a boldness born of desperation, I made my way around the side of the house. As I passed a window, I thought I detected a movement within, but it was so fleeting I couldn't be sure. I paused. "Hello? Hello! I'm your new neighbour. I could really do with some help..."

Silence.

I resumed my course on the rough path and rounded the corner towards the back door.

A trio of easels arranged in triptych formation stood on a covered patio, their empty canvases facing the backyard bush. Brushes and tubes of paint were arranged neatly at their feet, a set for each painting. Turning, I started at my reflection in a set of French doors and moved closer to peer through the gap left by a pair of partially closed curtains. As I raised my hand to knock, a cat shot out the cat flap at my feet. I had a good inkling the cat's name was not in fact "Fuck", and indeed, it didn't halt to acknowledge my ungracious greeting, choosing instead to scramble up a nearby tree to watch unblinkingly as I tried to avert disaster.

My leap backwards at the point of issuing my expletive had sent me stumbling into the closest easel.

In my attempt to catch the falling canvas and avoid tripping over the legs of the easel while in full, unbalanced motion, I lost my footing and landed backwards on the paving stones, the canvas cradled against my front. My breath left me with a *whoosh*, and I sucked uselessly at the air in rasping groans.

When my lungs finally recovered the ability to inflate, I sat up, pulling the canvas off my chest. It was far from empty. A pencil sketch of a bird filled most of the frame, and a single dark-green brush stroke swept down the back of its neck. I looked down at my t-shirt. A curved green line smiled up at me. "Huh."

I hastily stood up, uprighted the stand, jammed the smudged canvas back on the easel's ledge, and ran back to the door, the percussive force of my knocks shaking the key from its hole on the other side. I watched it fall, wincing as it hit the floorboards. "Come on. Please! I know you're in there – your painting's still wet." I peered through the glass, wiping the fog of my breath away with my hand. "Look, I'm completely harmless. I'm just...I've got a bit of a problem, and I really, badly need your help." The house continued to taunt me with its silence. "Oh, come on!" I rattled the unyielding handle, shaking the door in its frame. "Please!"

Defeated, I turned slowly, stifling a sob. A distorted pair of barn-style garage doors waved at me from across the weed-ridden back lawn. I wiped my eyes on the shoulders of my ruined t-shirt, took a deep breath, and stalked towards them, yanking one open wide enough for me to squeeze through. There, spotlit in a shaft of dancing dust motes, sat a faded blue HR Holden.

I gasped, my hands moving instinctively, running over the square bonnet. I peered at the registration certificate. 1966. "You're a beauty," I whispered into its dulled paintwork.

After a quick glance towards the gap in the garage doors, I tried the passenger door. It opened heavily, creaking on its hinges. I climbed in, breathed in the mustiness, and slid across the cracked leather into the driver's seat. No keys. I got out, opened the garage doors as wide as they could go and called to the house, "I'm just going to borrow your car. Don't worry, I'll bring it back. It's in perfectly safe hands."

CHAPTER FOUR

BEFORE. **Melbourne**

Around the time I turned thirty, something fundamental shifted within me. At first it was physical – I simply couldn't keep up with our lifestyle anymore. I wasn't getting enough sleep, and I began to pick up every virus that winged its way through the crisp, recycled office air. But I didn't stop. I had work deadlines and projects, and I couldn't possibly fit a day of bed rest into my schedule.

And then, inevitably, it became mental. I didn't *want* to keep living the way we did. The catch was that Warren loved it and it was what all our friends did, and I didn't want to alienate myself. So, I behaved as if I was still up for it but started feigning headaches and bad PMT. I enrolled in night classes but went home to sleep instead. On the days when those excuses became worn and threadbare, I relied on caffeine. I started averaging nine cups a day.

On the weekends, I'd take myself off to the city art gallery and spend hours studying the techniques, following the brush strokes and dabs of the master painters. I wasn't interested in other media. I breathed in the oils – colours so rich you could roll them around on your tongue, taste their depth, their texture. The gallery became my refuge.

But it wasn't enough.

WHEN THE SHOWER plug hole blocked every time I washed my hair, I knew it was time to go to the doctor.

The tally of ailments was impressive: liver function well below normal, high blood pressure, erratic menstruation, iron and B12 deficiency, insomnia, hair loss. I didn't need the doctor to tell me I needed a lifestyle change if I didn't want to become a bald, sallow, medical time bomb. I just wasn't sure how I was going to pull it off.

Inspiration hit when the house next door sold for $1.2 million. It was bigger than ours and worth more, but I knew ours wouldn't be far behind. I got the house valued without telling Warren.

Warren and I had been together since I was eighteen and he was twenty-one. We bought our first house when *I* was twenty-one for around the median house price that year – $355,000. Eleven years later, it was worth an eye-watering $950,000. With a mortgage of roughly $241,000 we could potentially come out the other side with $700,000 cash in hand – enough to semi-retire on if we bought something else on the cheap.

It took me two weeks of extensive searching to find the house on Ruatapu Island. The real estate website depicted a one-acre rural paradise with potential rooftop sea views for the paltry asking price of $46,500. "It'll be a homecoming," I told Warren.

Warren didn't need a homecoming, he said. Australia was home now. But when I pointed out that we could both work remotely in our jobs, negotiate part-time hours, and return to Melbourne whenever we wanted, he seemed to warm to the idea. He even suggested marriage once we'd settled in to the place.

I should have recognised a fickle city-lover when I kissed one.

CHAPTER FIVE

NOW. **Ruatapu Island**

I touched the wire onto the two I had already crossed. One turn. Two. Three. The engine roared into life. I gave the accelerator two depressions, shifted into gear, released the handbrake, and edged out of the garage. In the house, a whisper of movement. Yet, when I looked in the window, nothing.

I eased the HR onto the gravel road and was immediately thrown into the temptation to put the car through its paces. Yes, I had shouted a promise to look after it, but a little gentle reaming surely couldn't hurt.

It took three corners before I calibrated to the heavy steering, then I changed down and opened up the gas. It handled surprisingly well on the metal road, but it required all of my concentration. I had to feather the accelerator to avoid over-steering, and I quickly learned that it was easy to overcorrect once I opened up the throttle after decelerating. After driving a few klicks towards Port Keulemans, I eased off the accelerator. I had plenty of time to reach Warren, and I needed to work out what I was going to say to him. I'd begin with his name, then I'd pull the best punch in my heavily depleted arsenal: "If you love me, you wouldn't do this." It wasn't a sure shot. His actions weren't particularly indicative of feelings of abiding love, but I could always revert to spine extraction. It was then, as I'd released his coccyx with a satisfying pop for the second time, that the accelerator suddenly offered no resistance.

"No, come on. Don't do this to me," I pleaded to the dash.

The HR wheezed. Then it backfired. Then it died. The steering wheel became slick beneath my palms as I coasted to the side of the road. I disconnected and reconnected the wires a dozen times before I gave up and gave in to despair. With each, "No!" I drummed the heels of my hands against the steering wheel. Then I attempted to shake it free from the steering column. "Fuuuuuuuuuuuuuck!"

I ungritted my teeth, swept my hair from my face, and looked at my watch. I had a little over two and a half hours to run, I guessed, about fourteen kilometres, a task that might have been straightforward if it weren't for the numerous valleys between me and the port. Slamming the door shut, I turned to begin my long slog, and was immediately thrown back against the door and onto the ground. I unleashed one of my bird silencing screams and stood to free my skirt from the door.

AN HOUR AND A HALF, one Italian cycle tourist, and two hundred sheep later, I rounded a bend and heard a vehicle approaching behind me. I stood in the middle of the road, and with my arms out, made myself as big an obstacle as I could.

A cheap-to-hire campervan, the kind favoured by young backpackers, emerged around the corner. The driver changed down, but the van's speed didn't alter. It began to toot as it got within ten metres of me. Moving aside, I dropped my arms into a gesture of supplication.

As the van passed me, the driver's window wound down, and a young man with a top knot and undercut said in a thick Slavic accent, "Sorry, we must –" He flapped his hand forwards in a shooing gesture. "– go for ferry," and continued driving.

"I must go for ferry, too. Wait! You fuckers!"

The van's graffiti-like decal on the back door read *You looked better from behind.* One final up-yours. Clearly, despite my ability to present The Distressed Look with a decent level of authenticity, and the fact

I was a woman alone in the middle of nowhere, I wasn't needy enough to interrupt their itinerary. "If I get to the wharf in time, I'm keying the shit out of your misogynistic arse," I shouted at the disappearing bumper.

I looked at my watch. Twenty-three minutes until the ferry departed. I needed to run faster. The problem was not my ability. With round, muscular calves I had the strength to keep up a solid run. The problem was their length. I had a mere sixty-nine centimetres of them, which allowed me the luxury of three strides to the average person's one.

I looked down to take stock before I launched into an aggressive final assault on the Port Keulemans Road. A fine layer of road dust covered my clothes and lightened the dark tan of my skin. Sweat tracked down my arms in dark runnels from where it had gathered in my armpits and the crooks of my elbows. My shoes, designed for the smooth pavement of the city and the gentle pace of café hopping, were frayed at the toes, the stitching on the embroidered violets unravelling in a slow denuding of their petals. I took a deep breath. I had to make the best of what I had, and a pair of hobbit-proportioned legs was all there was. I thought about the reckoning I would bring to the back of the campervan and placed one flowered foot in front of the other in rapid succession.

BY THE TIME I reached the top of a steep, windy and, I prayed, final ascent, my pace had slowed considerably. My sure-footed, rhythmic run had degenerated into a toe-dragging stagger. My mouth was gummed with thickened saliva, and I sucked in air in loud, ragged gasps. As I slowly crested the hill, the foliage thinned to reveal the nearly empty car park of Port Keulemans below and an idling ferry. I could still make it.

With renewed energy, I set off down the hill, skidding on the smooth soles of my ruined shoes at each of the road's tight corners. When I got to the bottom of the hill and the gradient decreased, I lost control of my speed and fell sprawling into the gravel. It was then, as my brain registered the sharp bite of pieces of rock in my palms, that the ferry sounded its horn. I pushed myself to my feet, and in a surge of adrenalin, sprinted towards the wharf. There were two hundred metres between me and the ferry. I knew I could cover that distance in thirty seconds.

I had almost cleared the carpark when the ferry started to edge away from the wharf. "No! Wait. Stop the ferry. Someone stop the ferry!" Between the deserted wharf and the loud thrumming of the ferry's engines that would prevent any passengers or crew from actually hearing my request, it was anybody's guess who that someone might be.

I reached the wharf proper and pounded across its concrete surface towards the now closed loading ramp. When I ran out of concrete and was forced to a halt by the wooden edging, the ferry was already a full boat-length from the wharf.

"Hey!" I waved my arms frantically, jumping up and down. "Heeeeey!"

I screamed out another "Stop!", but the "p" was lost in the high-pitched crack of my voice. When the ferry got to two boat-lengths, I collapsed onto all fours, my attempt to drag air into my oxygen-depleted lungs hampered by the sobs beginning to roll up from my stomach.

Footsteps clumped on the concrete behind me and came to a stop on my left. Through the sweat-glued strands of my hair I made out the figure of a man in an orange vis-vest looking down at me, his eyes narrowed against the afternoon sun.

"Em Stewart?"

I attempted an answer, but my choking gasps allowed no room for verbal manoeuvring. I nodded.

He held out a set of keys. The Toyota symbol flashed as it spun below his fingers. "These, I believe, are yours."

PART 2

CHAPTER SIX

PORT KEULEMANS RECEDED as I crested the hill in the reclaimed ute. Warren's ferry was now a small dot in the blue distance, and I swivelled the rear vision mirror so I couldn't see it anymore.

Beside me, the ball of paper on the passenger seat kept demanding my attention. "Em" it had started. Just "Em". No "Dear", no "Darling", no "My love". My name sat there, lonely and unadorned, and it was all I needed to understand the tenor of the letter. I didn't need to read the rest to know that it was a formalisation of Warren's desertion. It would say things like, *I realised it's not what I wanted* and then *That made me wonder if I wanted a future with you.* It would inevitably finish with *I need space to think.*

Of course, I read it anyway. I wasn't too far off the mark, except Warren didn't need space to think. The crumbling state of our future house had apparently served as a metaphor for our dying relationship. The list was short and, of course, exonerated him: I had asked him to sacrifice too much, I had changed and wasn't the person he fell in love with, I was passionless.

My eyes remained dry, but my lips formed a tight seal, blocking the invective poised on my tongue.

I changed down and rounded a bend in the road, the sturdy four-wheel drive not so much as kicking up a handful of gravel. I sighed, imagining I could slam my foot down as I approached the next corner, ease the handbrake on just enough to get the rear of the ute sliding out in a shower of stones, before accelerating out of the corner with a roar of the engine and a wild fish tail. It would never happen in this vehicle. Or this life. I sighed again. Maybe Warren had packed a sledgehammer. Surely, I could find something fit for demolition in my lovely new house.

Along a straight section of the road, a figure jogged towards me. A man. He was Māori. And shirtless. His abs flexed as his torso twisted from side to side, and sweat shone on his chest, accentuating the slight groove between his pectorals. He raised a hand as I passed, and I moved my eyes to the rear vision mirror, watching the muscles in his back shift under his skin. A t-shirt dangled from where it was tucked into the back of his shorts.

I forced my eyes back onto the road.

The next bend was not where it should have been – a safe twenty metres in front of me – it was five metres and closing, and I was going too fast. I had no choice but to brake hard as I turned the wheel to round it, knowing the outcome wouldn't be pretty. The truck skidded sideways, and I got my wished-for tail slide. Only the locked rear wheels gained momentum as they hit the slippery grass on the verge, and I was spun one-eighty degrees. I closed my eyes and hunched my shoulders in preparation for impact. With a sharp graunch of metal, the ute came to a halt up against the paddock fencing.

I opened my eyes and sat still, my knuckles white on the steering wheel. The wing mirror swung lazily from its socket. "Great," I said into the ceiling of the cab. "This is just fan-fucking-tastic. I have to do penance for sneaking a perve? What else have you got for me? I haven't had a dose of pestilence yet. You going to throw that in for fun?"

A face appeared at the window. The runner.

I jumped. My feet slipped from the pedals and the ute bunny hopped forward as it stalled. My head slammed into the back rest, and a string of saliva slapped itself wetly across my cheek. I wiped it away with the hem of my t-shirt.

"Sorry," the face said through the glass. "You OK?"

I crawled across the front seats, opened the passenger door, and stalked around to the front of the ute without answering. I climbed between the fence wires and pulled the top one out from underneath the broken wing mirror. The panel above the wheel arch was crumpled against a fence post, but the wheel itself looked intact, and more importantly, straight on its axle.

"The corners around here can be quite tight. You've got to brake before you hit them, or you'll skid."

"I know," I said flatly.

"They're a bit of a trap for inexperienced tourists."

I climbed back through the fence.

He stood, hands on hips, beside the passenger door.

"Can you get out of my way, please?"

The runner's gaze dropped to my knees. "Jesus. Are you sure you're OK?"

I looked down, pulling back the hem of my skirt. A brown line of dried blood ran the length of both shins, and my knees were black with embedded gravel. "Huh." I picked the largest piece out of my right knee and threw it into the paddock as hard as I could. I watched the place where it landed, panting slightly from the exertion.

Turning to the runner, I held up a finger. "One moment." I walked to the back of the vehicle and opened the canopy door. First to hand was Warren's holdall with his winter clothes. His two other large bags were gone.

I dragged it out by its handles and hefted it over

the fence into the paddock. Next was a half-empty shoe bag. It was light enough that I could swing it around me like a hammer thrower and, with a grunt Maria Sharapova would have been proud of, sling it several metres. It disappeared behind a hummock in the grass.

The runner stepped between me and the fence, his jaw loose with disbelief. "What are you doing?"

I peered over the tailgate and was gratified to see Warren had forgotten his toilet bag. I pulled it out and drew my arm back just as the runner stepped forward to halt my momentum.

"OK, please stop. Whatever your raruraru is, it's really disrespectful to the island, let alone whoever's stuff this is."

"My what?"

"Raruraru." He turned and vaulted over the fence. "Whatever your beef is with this person."

I threw the toilet bag anyway, narrowly missing the runner's bum as he bent to retrieve the holdall. He shook his head and picked up the other bags, slinging the holdall and shoe bag over one shoulder and holding the toilet bag in one hand. He managed to climb the fence with the same grace with which he jumped it the first time. As he passed me to put the bags back in the ute, he said, "Don't ever do that again."

"I won't need to. I feel better now." I closed the door of the canopy and turned to him. "Hey, you want any clothes and stuff? I don't need them anymore."

It took him a moment to respond. "No."

I shrugged my shoulders and walked around him. "OK."

He followed me and placed a hand on the passenger door before I could close it. "Look, I don't think you are OK. Are you...booked into accommodation tonight? You're not going to be on your own, are you?"

I looked at him properly for the first time. He appeared to be in his thirties, and his dark eyes were rimmed with thick lashes. Beneath them, rounded cheekbones offset a wide nose. He was almost handsome. How could someone be so genuinely concerned for a stranger who was not only rude, but behaved like they were a straitjacket away from crazy? I wanted to ask *Are you for real?* But what I said was, "I don't suppose you could help me tow a car? It broke down up the road."

ONCE INSIDE THE UTE, the runner replaced his t-shirt. I tried not to notice his obliques as he leaned forward to pull the shirt over his head, but I'd never seen any this close up before. The top of the V looked like it could flatten my finger should I place one in its groove. I turned my head away as he swivelled his towards mine.

"Where are you from?"

"I moved from Melbourne."

The car groaned as I backed up from the fence post.

"You *moved* here?"

"Today." I U-turned and swung the steering wheel from side to side, feeling for any wheel imbalance. The ute was steady.

"Wow, that's, ah, some commitment."

"You have no idea."

"I do, actually – I moved here a couple of years ago. I know exactly what's involved in making that decision." He gripped the seat as we approached a corner, and after I'd safely navigated around it, he said, "You don't sound Australian."

I said nothing.

The next bend revealed the HR sitting snug against the inside bank of the road.

"That's Ted's car. That's odd."

"Ted? Well, I need to get it back to him. Are you OK to steer it once I hitch it to the ute?"

"It was Ted's car that broke down?" His voice carried a note of incredulity.

"Yeah. I borrowed it and it decided to die here."

"You borrowed it?" The incredulity changed to dubiousness.

"If hot wiring it and driving off without the ex-press agreement of the owner is the same as borrowing." I shrugged my shoulders and executed a three-point turn to position the ute in front of the HR.

The runner undid his seatbelt, turned to face me squarely, and said slowly, "You know how to hot wire a car?"

I cut the engine and mirrored his movement, looking him in the eyes. I delivered a "Yes" that I hoped brooked no further questioning.

It worked – at least for the moment. He blinked and said, "Right."

I moved to open the door and was fired another question.

"You have a towing cable?"

As I swung down from the cab, I said over my shoulder, "I always carry one in my purse. Never know when you're gonna need one." It sounded witty in my head but came out sarcastic. The runner's silence forced me into a better answer. "I borrowed it from that dude at the wharf – Macca."

"Sounds like you've had an interesting first day."

I opened the rear passenger door to retrieve the cable from the footwell. "I've had worse."

WHEN WE PULLED into Ted's driveway, the easels were gone and the house looked no less fortified.

"He's pretty elusive, this Ted," I said when we stepped from our vehicles to push the HR back into the garage.

"He's a recluse. You probably scared the shit out of him." The runner turned towards the house and called, "Hey Ted, just returning your car. The lady says she's sorry." He turned back to me and raised his eyebrows.

I raised my eyebrows back, then stifled a sigh and shouted at the closed back door. "Yep, sorry, Ted. I'll make it up to you." I looked at the runner. "I probably need to make it up to you, too."

"Nah, us islanders look out for one another. There's no owing anything when we help out." He unhooked the cable from the front of the HR. "I'll push, you steer."

Once the HR was tucked up in the garage, I offered my hand to the runner. He took it and gently shook it with a look of mild bemusement.

"Look, I'm sorry for being a bit of a dick. You've been really nice even though I haven't deserved it." I looked down at my bloodied knees. "The reason I'm in this state is that my partner deserted me when we turned up at the house." I jerked my head in the direction of the roof-line next door. "Drove back to the ferry and left me standing in the road." I added, "He's from Auckland," as if that explained everything.

"Shit."

"Yeah."

He scuffed a foot. "Do you know anybody here?"

"Not a soul. Well, Macca, but he might want to steer clear of me after today's drama."

The runner jammed his hands in his short pockets and pursed his lips as if contemplating something difficult. "You're welcome to come over for a kai tonight, if you need some company."

"Dinner? No, I think I'd like to be on my own. Thanks, though."

"OK, well, let's swap numbers. For if you need anything. Phone reception's patchy, but I move around a lot, so I usually get my messages at some point in the day." He removed a mobile phone from his pocket, and I recited my number.

"What's your name?"

"Em."

"As in the letter?"

"As in two letters. E and M."

"Short for Emily?"

I didn't answer. Instead, I asked, "What's yours?"

"Anaru."

"What?"

"Anaru."

"OK, I'm never going to remember that."

"It's easy. 'Ah' as in 'up' – ah-nah – and 'ooh' as in 'moo'. A-na-ru. Can you roll your Rs?"

"Probably."

"Give it a go."

I didn't want to. I'd butcher it and make a bigger

fool of myself than I already had. "What does it mean?"

He shrugged. "It's a transliteration of Andrew."

"Can I just call you Andrew?"

"That's not my name."

"Nobody calls me by my proper name – I don't mind."

He laughed. It was more a sharp expulsion of air than an indication he thought I was funny. "The answer's still no."

My phone pinged with a text. It was an emoji of an exotic-looking bird. I pocketed my phone without creating a contact. I didn't want to embarrass myself further by asking him how to spell his name. "Do you need a lift anywhere?"

"Nah, I'll just run home. It's not too far." He swivelled to face the road, then turned back to me. "See you around, Em."

"Yep. See you around."

THE HOUSE HADN'T STAGED a Cinderella transformation in my few hours' absence; hadn't, as I'd desperately willed, been subject to the whirlwind of a house-pimping TV show. The rich network of moss still looked like it was the only thing keeping the walls on the shadowed side of the house erect. The roof still had an alarming curve to it in one corner where there should only have been straight lines. And the gaps in the weatherboards looked like black fingers paused in the act of stroking the soft green.

As I edged up the driveway to view the state of the back of the house, I squinted against the coming disappointment, as if seeing the decay through the blur of my lashes would render it less real, less confronting. Like looking at Keith Richards in soft focus.

But it wasn't the house that arrested my attention.

The vegetation, while dense and unruly on either side of the house, had clearly been cultivated at the rear of the property for one spectacular reason. Low trees and shrubs framed a wide horizon, encouraging the eye to trace the land as it gradually fell away towards the sea.

I gasped. I had thought the "sea vista" photo on the real estate website was one of those misleading drone shots, where they showcase what you'll see once you go to the expense of adding a second storey, but the photo didn't do the view justice. "Sweeping" was the adjective they should have used, or "expansive". "Breathtaking" was exactly the effect it was having on me.

With concentration, I inhaled and muttered a "Holy shit" on my exhale. I climbed out of the cab and walked to the edge of the scraggly lawn.

Far below, a wide bay welcomed waves rolling in from the Pacific Ocean. The deep blue of the water beyond the forested headlands on either side of the bay gradually gave way to turquoise as the seabed rose towards the shore. As if that wasn't Fantasy Island enough, the sand had the good grace to be almost white. This time, "Are you for real?" slipped all the way out to my tongue.

I closed my eyes and breathed in deeply. When I opened them, the view was still there. If this was what I would wake to every morning, enjoy every evening as I sipped my Pinot Noir from the deck, there was nothing the house could throw at me that I couldn't ignore. I slowly turned to face it.

I was wrong.

CHAPTER SEVEN

THE HOUSE'S shell had obviously undergone several stages of repair over the years, and the patchy paint jobs used to seal each bit of new work were garish. A different colour had been used for every mend as if the previous owners had borrowed dregs from paint tins the island over.

My retinas protested, jabbing the back of my eye sockets with merciless savagery. I closed my eyes against it and patted the top of my head for my sunglasses. Sliding them into place, I willed myself not to look at the carnival on the back wall and stalked around the side of the house to the front door.

The key slotted home easily, and I turned it with the same determination as I had just walked down the driveway. However, when the latch unsnibbed, my confidence evaporated. A montage of disastrous scenes flickered through my head: Caved in ceilings, tilting floors, cracks in walls, fungi in damp corners. I swallowed twice and edged open the door.

The interior was dark. I removed my sunglasses and felt on the inside wall for a light switch. Three pats and I located it – an old-fashioned model with a thin, protruding switch. I flipped it down.

With a brief flare of light and a ping, the bulb blew. The key shot out of my hand and into the darkness as an involuntary "Fuck!" escaped. I stood still, waiting for the frantic drum of my pulse to quieten.

Over the course of eighty slowing heartbeats, my eyes adjusted to the gloom. Five doorways opened off a hallway that ended abruptly with a closed door. Towards the far end of the hall, a second and empty light socket dangled from the perfectly intact ceiling.

Light bulbs. Strangely enough, neither Warren nor I had thought to pack any. I made a mental note to slot a couple in alongside the towing cable in my handbag for the next time I was abandoned by the most important man in my life.

I clucked my tongue at the dark ceiling and turned to inspect the room on my right. A double bedroom. The opposite doorway revealed another one, even larger.

A third small bedroom, the perfect size for an office, sat adjacent to the master bedroom, and the two doors across the hall from it revealed a toilet and a small bathroom.

I pushed against the bathroom door. It swung open with a whine, and in the dim light, the spectre of a woman stared back at me, pale and wide-eyed. "Jesus!" she mouthed as I leapt back into the hallway.

I groaned and forced the door open to its full width, stepping back into the room at the same time as the ghost. We raised our hands in greeting, and I looked around me. While the poky space found room to house a large built-in bath, no shower had been installed above it.

"Great." I smiled at my mirror-self. "Welcome to the 1950s. Where women vacuum in high heels, and never get dirty." I crossed the short space to the basin. "Who has time to run a bath, let alone actually have one?" I grumbled into the plug hole. The taps turned with more effort than I would have liked, but I was gratified that the water not only ran clean, it had a reasonable amount of pressure behind it.

I peered at the wild woman in the mirror and grimaced at her mascara-smudged eyes. Wetting my fingers, I set to work wiping away the black smears. Her matted hair would have to wait until I'd unpacked my hairbrush.

It was then that I noticed the mirror was not fixed to the wall. For whatever reason, it had been left – perhaps forgotten – by the previous owners. I pulled it away from the wall and examined the back. The glass was attached to the backing by tiny clips. Satisfied, I settled the mirror in place and turned to go and open the door to the lounge.

I knew what was coming. I had a reasonable idea of the layout of the house from the photos, but it still hit me like that wall of humidity when you step off the plane on your tropical island holiday.

Through the French doors, the last rays of the day's sun sparkled off tiny watery peaks down in the bay. Above them, the bush on the headlands glowed with a golden light, and in the space in between, birds wheeled and circled and dived. The backyard vegetation obscured the beach, but it was nothing a good trim wouldn't fix.

A wave of elation surged through me, rising from the pit of my stomach and swelling up through the roots of my hair. My body vibrated in its wake. It felt like falling in love. Or so I imagined. It was so long ago since I'd been incapacitated by that emotion, I couldn't be sure.

That, of course, made me think of Warren.

Before I could fall into the rabbit hole of "why"s and "how could he"s and "if only"s, I pivoted to take in what the room had to offer.

Someone in the house's seventy-year lifespan had the good sense to remove the wall between the kitchen and the living room, though the 1980s pink and grey kitchen cabinetry would have to be re-homed. As I repressed a shudder, a dark stain beneath one of the kitchen windows caught my eye. I walked over to inspect it more closely. It didn't look healthy.

I pushed my pointer finger against it, and the wall disintegrated around my hand. With an "Oh my God," I quickly withdrew it and bent to look at the damage. Across the driveway, leaves stirred gently in the breeze, their lazy wave perfectly framed by the new hole in the wall. The rot I'd punched through was obviously the result of being exposed to the elements, courtesy of one of the gaps in the weatherboards.

It took a beat to collect myself, and when I did, my reaction surprised me. I closed my mouth, stood upright, and said, "Fuck it. Extra ventilation."

I turned my back on it and went to unpack the car knowing there would be worse surprises to come. A hole in the wall was nothing a ball of newspaper couldn't fix. Plus, I had other, messier problems to deal with. Ones I hadn't even started to address.

I SET up the blow-up bed in the largest bedroom, not only because of the room's size, but because it would get the most sun. When done, I closed the heavy curtains and walked back into the bathroom. I stood over the bath, willing a shower to appear. Then, with a sigh, I put the plug in and ran the taps.

The bath was hot and deep. I gingerly eased my scraped legs under the water, hissing at the sting and watching small clouds of dried blood and dirt drift away from my knees. When I acclimatised and relaxed into the water, a wave of exhaustion hit me. I didn't fight it. I closed my eyes and let it take over.

I woke when I started to shiver, unsurprised but still disappointed to find it wasn't all a bad dream.

The room was dark. Evening had descended while I slept.

I quickly dried myself and sought out my warmest pyjamas. The blue flannelette ones with the sloths on them. Then I went into the living area and sat heavily in one of the two camping chairs we had brought and waited for my intermittent trembling to subside.

On the folding table beside me, the two hundred and fifty-dollar bottle of Dom Perignon we'd bought to celebrate with still sweated from having been removed from the chilly bin an hour before. Right now, a very expensive liquid dinner seemed like an excellent idea.

I tilted the bottle and expertly popped the cork into my hand. Years of Warren and our friends finding any reason to celebrate with a bottle of bubbly – or three – had given me the skill to strip and uncork a sparkling wine in less than five seconds. No one had ever beaten my record, at least not without taking an eye out.

That particular prowess gave me no comfort now. I poured the champagne into my enamel mug, raised it to the empty chair on the other side of the camping table, and said, "Here's to you Warren. Thanks a fucking lot."

I took a sip and rested the drink in my lap between my hands. I gazed down into it, watching the bubbles rise to the surface and listening to their gentle fizz.

When I eventually looked up to remind myself of the view, all I saw was the reflection of a child in pyjamas. She looked lost.

I got up and turned off one of the handful of working lights in the house. There wasn't much to see. The first stars had begun to appear, winking above the dark shapes of the shrubs and trees. I followed the contours of the land in my mind as if I were a bird soaring down over the dark hills towards the inky water.

Warren would never see it. He'd made his choice and never given it a chance. Anger bloomed in my gut, and for the first time since he'd left me coughing in the ute's dust, I allowed myself to contemplate the enormity of the day's events.

The naked truth paraded itself in front of me, bold and unapologetic: Warren was no longer part of my life. He'd opted out of the relationship in such an appalling way it was staggering.

A barrage of questions that I couldn't answer voiced themselves: If he felt the relationship was failing, why didn't he talk to me about it? Why did he agree to make the move here? Why did he leave it until past the last reasonable opportunity to back out?

And then, with sudden clarity, my anger gave way – not to heartbreak, not to a desperate keening for the man I had spent my entire adult life with, but to something much worse.

A coldness unfurled in the pit of my stomach and tracked its way with every quickening beat of my heart out to my limbs. I hugged myself as another shiver seized me.

I was alone. I was on my own on a tiny island in the middle of the ocean and I didn't have a single friend.

I'd taken a huge risk swapping out a life in the city for one on an isolated island – an island I'd never been to before. It was a desperate measure. And I'd forced Warren's hand. I'd given him little choice but to try to want what I wanted. And it had been a big mistake.

There was nothing I could do about it for at least another week. I couldn't flee back to the familiarity of Melbourne – throwing myself on the mercy of the friends I'd withdrawn from over the last few months. Not until the next ferry arrived.

I was trapped.

I stood abruptly and began pacing in front of the French doors.

Who was I kidding? When the week was out, I knew I wouldn't leave. My pride, my determination, my stubbornness wouldn't let me. It wasn't a ferry timetable that trapped me.

My new life stretched ahead of me – a dark and murky and very long path. There was nobody else on it.

The iciness in my stomach gave way to a heat that prickled on my brow and down my back. What did I really know about this place? About these people? The heat flared under my ribs. What would my life be like if I never fit in?

A knock on the front door stopped me in my tracks.

I blocked my mouth with my fist and peered in the direction of the knock as if I could see who it was through the walls.

Another knock. Louder.

I gulped at the air, trying to steady my breathing, then I tucked my still-damp hair behind my ears and opened the lounge door.

When I got to the end of the hall, I turned the light on in my bedroom so I could see whoever it was, and unsnibbed the lock.

A man with a saucepan. The runner from today. Andrew.

Behind him, the faintest tinge of day clung to the hem of the gathering night.

"Hey," he said.

I sucked in a shuddering breath and croaked out something that hopefully sounded like, "Hi."

His eyes ran down my choice of bedroom attire, but he didn't say anything.

I offered, "I like sloths," anyway.

He smiled. "You sure do." He waited for me to say something more, and when I didn't, he said, "I know you wanted to be alone, but I thought I could at least drop off a decent meal." He held up the pot. "You eaten yet?"

I shook my head.

"Good." He pushed the pot into my hands. "It's a curry – lentil. I didn't know if you ate meat, so..."

The back of my eyeballs prickled. I hoped my reddening nose and bloodshot eyes weren't visible in the dim light. "Are all islanders as nice as you?"

"We're a pretty good bunch. Community this small and isolated has to look out for each other. I guess we're kinda like whānau."

"Kinda like what?"

"Family."

"Good. I think I'm gonna need that."

A nod and a smile. "There's no reason to be lonely here." He fiddled with the zip fastener on his fleece. "In fact, I should probably warn you. This is going to sound insensitive after what happened to-day, but you're likely to attract a lot of interest. You know, being new to the place and...single."

I laughed humourlessly. "Fresh meat?"

After a pause, he grinned back at me, his teeth very white. "Yeah. You could put it like that."

"Huh, OK. Thanks for the warning. And thanks for the food." I bounced the pot in my hands, feeling its weight. "There's a lot in there."

"Should do you a couple of meals."

My throat started to constrict, and before I let myself cry in front of a stranger, I muttered another thank you and pushed the door to close it.

But before I snibbed it shut, I hesitated, thinking of the long night ahead of me.

I pulled it open again, swallowing the lump in my throat. "Um," I said to his disappearing back. He turned. "You want to join me? Company might be nice, actually."

"Sure."

I led him down the hallway and turned the lights back on in the lounge. The chairs and table looked very small in the middle of the bare room.

"Drinking in the dark?"

"Yup. It's been one of those days."

"I bet."

I gestured for him to take a seat then went into the kitchen to spoon the curry into the only two bowls I had. "You want a glass of champagne? It's the real deal."

"Whoa, what does a bottle of the real deal cost?"

"Stupid money." I added a facetious, "The deposit for this house."

He rubbed his hands together. "Awesome. I've never had thirty-dollar plonk before."

"Ha ha. It's not that bad."

"Have you seen the back wall?"

"Yes. It looks like a rainbow vomited on it."

Andrew tipped his head back and laughed. "That is exactly what it looks like."

I didn't laugh. Through a grimace I said, "I hope I've done the right thing."

"Hey," he said softly, "at least the electrics work."

I handed him his bowl and sat in the other chair. "Thank goodness we thought to organise that before we came. Forgot about Wi-Fi, though. I need it for my job."

Andrew paused with his spoon halfway to his mouth and said, "Ah," in that way that I imagined Mr Rochester might have done when asked why the rats in the attic were so loud.

"Oh God, please tell me there's internet here."

"Yeah, but not on this side of the island. Infrastructure's pretty limited. Too few people to bother, I guess."

"But..." I couldn't finish the sentence. The enormity of what this meant had scenes of career kamikaze ping ponging around my brain. There was no space left for connecting my scattered thoughts to my tongue.

"They've got a computer at the store that the tourists use," he said brightly. "Dollar a minute."

"*A dollar a minute?* I have to work four *hours* a day."

"Have a chat to them. See what you can negoti-ate. It's run by a couple called Don and Trace. Or you could hot spot off your phone."

I sat lower in my chair. "Not on the amount of data I'm going to need."

Andrew didn't say anything else. He'd run out of suggestions, and even his deliberate good cheer couldn't put a shine on the fact I didn't do my home-work. When he did speak again, it was so out of left field my jaw and spoon-hand didn't coordinate and a lump of aubergine fell out of my mouth and back into the bowl.

"You have really amazing hair. The colour, I mean."

I wiped my chin.

"It's naturally red, right?"

"Yep, one hundred percent homegrown." I prof-fered my standard comment: "My father was a gypsy."

"For real?"

I paused and gave the contents of my bowl a stir. "Who knows. Whenever I asked my mother about him, she'd shrug her shoulders and say, 'He was a wanderer'. Gypsy sounds way cooler – less of a cop-out. At least it did when I was ten." I snorted and shook my head. "Wanderer! He had a wandering *penis*."

Andrew choked on his mouthful of curry.

I sprang up to offer a helpful slap on the back, but he waved me away.

There was nothing for me to do but sit back down and watch in awkward fascination while he tried to control the spasms in his diaphragm.

When he finally cleared his airway and wiped away his tears with the heels of his palms, he looked at me without embarrassment and said thoughtfully, "You could be a gypsy."

"Nah, gypsies are willowy. I'm too stumpy."

Andrew chuckled into his mug. His laugh sounded a long way away.

The truth of it was that I had no idea what I was. The most accurate my colouring could be described was a vague "exotic". It was certainly unusual. I had olive skin with a liberal sprinkling of dark freckles across my nose and cheeks, which while cute when I was a child, looked curiously out of place on an adult. My green eyes would not have been striking in themselves were it not for my dark red hair – an auburn that streaked ginger in the summer. The combination of dark skin, green eyes, freckles and red hair invited a lot of comment. There wasn't much I could truthfully say about it. My mother was a fair-skinned, bottle-orange.

Before my thoughts settled fully on the woman who gave birth to me, Andrew changed tack again. "So, how you doing – after today?"

I took a deep breath in and searched for where I

stood on the dumpee continuum. It wasn't hard to locate. "You know, I'm pretty bloody angry. I keep waiting for the heartbreak to kick in, but all I want to do when I think of Warren is beat the crap out of him." I fiddled with my spoon. "Mostly I'm scared. I'm here on my own now."

"Nobody's ever on their own in a place like this, unless you choose to be, like Ted. You'll find your groove, make friends. People are pretty welcoming here."

I can't have looked convinced, because he said, "Hey. You've already made one friend."

He looked completely sincere. I didn't doubt it. He'd been patient and understanding and giving to someone he'd just met, where many wouldn't.

I stood outside myself and tried to see what he seemed to – a person that invited friendship, that was worth the effort of reaching out to.

An unusual-looking woman in children's pyjamas sat in a canvas chair. She had "needy" written all over her. Clearly, Andrew had a very generous spirit. "Thanks," I said. "It was remarkably easy given how I acted."

Through a mouthful he replied, "It's not hard to look past someone being a dick when they've just been through what you have."

If Andrew was the measuring stick for island hospitality, I wouldn't have much of a problem fitting in. But I couldn't quite allow myself to believe people could be as generous as him. Nobody here had any need to make a new friend. I would have to be the one to make the effort. It would be my priority. After I'd found some Wi-Fi.

When Andrew had finished chewing, he asked me why I had taken the radical step of relocating to a remote island.

I told him. I stripped out any emotion and gave him the short, factual version.

"Good decision," he said with a nod, then turned his attention to the invisible landscape on the other side of the glass doors. "This is a healing place. Many people find their strength here."

I swirled the contents of my cup and said, "Well, that's what I'm hoping for," before draining it. "Why'd *you* come to the island?"

"Work. I'm a ranger for the Department of Conservation, and I took a promotion to oversee the management of several breeding programmes. I specialise in kiwi."

I sat up straighter, leaning slightly towards him. "There's kiwi here?" I shook my head and sat back. "No, I did know that." I gave him a small smile. "How rubbish would I be if I didn't research my new home? Things have been falling out of my brain today."

"Understandable."

"There's a recovery programme, right?"

"Yeah. It's doing well. We've got a pretty healthy

population of three different species. You might hear the odd call tonight."

"What does it sound like?"

"It's not beautiful. The male is shrill, the female more guttural." He demonstrated the first – a high-pitched call rising sharply at the end. "The female, depending on the species, can be a bit unnerving sometimes. Sounds like a human screaming. If it repeats about twenty times, it's not your neighbour being murdered."

"I'm not convinced I have a neighbour."

"Ted'll make himself known when he feels comfortable." Andrew delivered the next sentence with what looked like a smirk. "Hopefully *you'll* feel comfortable when he does." Before I could ask what he meant, he said, "I can take you kiwi spotting one night if you like."

"I'd love that. I've never seen one before."

When Andrew had answered all my questions about the breeding programme and our bowls were empty, he insisted on washing the dishes. I acquiesced, on the condition that I dried.

We moved through to the kitchen, and when he attempted to twist the old-fashioned hot tap, it refused to move. He looked at me. "Did you do this? You're stronger than you look."

I shook my head. "Haven't touched it."

His knuckles paled as he tightened his grip, and with a pop, the entire tap came away from the wall, the mechanism still connected to the copper pipework.

Andrew's mouth gaped in mortification.

Given the day's events, there were only two reactions I could possibly give him – F-bomb-laced rage or laughter. Offering a resigned shrug, I chose the latter. "Don't worry. I did this earlier." I pointed to the hole beneath the window. "If you go outside, I can shake your hand from inside the house." I waved my hands in a spirit fingers flourish. "Magic."

He pushed the pipe back into the wall and settled the tap into place. It listed to the right. "Wow. You got yourself a winner with this place."

"Yeah, but I traded in my spineless boyfriend for a million-dollar view. I reckon I'm ahead." I handed him the dish mop. "Just be gentle with the other tap. I need that one."

THE COOL NIGHT air rushed in when I opened the front door to let Andrew out. I glanced at my makeshift bed and thought of the fabulous view I would wake to, a view that with some garden maintenance would only get better. "I don't suppose I can borrow some gardening stuff? Like hedge trimmers? In fact, anything you can spare would be good."

"Sure. I'll drop them off tomorrow."

"Thanks."

He stood still, looking at me.

I pulled at the bottom of my pyjama top, willing my eyeballs to drag themselves away from his. Was his warning about the attention I would soon receive a hint? Was he really desperate enough to have already formed an interest, and callous enough to act on it less than twelve hours since I was roundly dropped by my boyfriend from a dizzying height? My other hand played with the door snib, turning the nob from side to side with a soft *chink*.

His eyes narrowed, and he asked, "How do you know how to hot wire a car?"

I dropped my hands to my side.

"Misspent youth," I answered, not completely untruthfully.

Andrew's eyes stayed narrowed, but his lips turned up in a slow smile. Then he pivoted and stepped out of reach of the light.

"Pō mārie, Em."

I guessed at his meaning. "Night," I replied into the darkness.

BEFORE I WENT TO SLEEP, I slipped the photo I had kept buried in my Melbourne sweater drawer into the back of the bathroom mirror. The bottom left clip kept it neatly in place.

CHAPTER EIGHT

I WOKE to early morning light slipping around the edges of the curtains and a heaviness sitting on my chest. It had the weight and shape of Warren. So I told him to take a holiday in the outer reaches of the solar system. But much less politely.

As I rolled over to claim his side of the bed and seek the anaesthetic of more sleep, the mattress farted in rubbery friction with my body, and I rolled back again, trying to replicate the noise. I snow angel-ed my limbs, testing the stiffness of my legs from yesterday's exertions, and the resulting series of squeaks and burps lightened the gloom of the room. I giggled. "See how much fun I'm already having without you, Warren?" I said to the ceiling.

I eased myself into a sitting position on the edge of the bed, the fresh scabs on my knees making it difficult to bend them. I felt for the windowsill underneath the heavy curtains and wheezed as I pushed myself upright using the small ledge for support.

The wall gave under my pressure, the bottom of it yawning open and spilling light into the room where the skirting board should have been.

I paused in a half crouch, my sore muscles screaming against the strain of the pose, then tried my weight against the wall again. It swung outwards, tethered at either end where it met the adjoining walls, and the line of light widened into a foot-deep down-turned mouth.

I collapsed back onto the bed, willing myself to see the funny side. I squeezed my eyes shut and screwed up my face, but no laughter burbled in my chest. I let the breath I had been holding go and groaned. There was only one thing that might provide sufficient medicine. The view that floored me yesterday. I stalked out of the bedroom and into the lounge.

A neat pile of gardening tools lay outside the French doors.

THE PORT KEULEMANS STORE, a converted Edwardian villa, stood in a small enclave of houses on the crest of a hill, several hundred metres down the road from the port proper. Below the hamlet, fingers of bush-clad headlands stretched and curled into the deep green water of Keulemans Harbour. At the far edge of the houses sat the pub. With its large multi-panelled windows, the pub looked like it might have had a prior life, a century or so back, as a classroom.

A young man in his early twenties, with an angry-looking shaving rash on his neck, stepped out of the store, a can of Red Bull and meat pie in hand. He looked me up and down, then glanced at his food and said with a smile and a wink, "Breakfast of champions."

Ordinarily I might have replied with, "Breakfast of pre-diabetics," especially given the cock-sure way I had been addressed by someone barely out of puberty, but I needed to get off on the right foot with every person I met.

So instead, I offered a "Sure is," and left it up to him to determine whether I was being ironic or not. Then I stepped past him and stopped two feet into the coolness of the interior as a woman in a Department of Conservation uniform brushed past on her way out with an "Excuse me."

The three heads at the counter and the two amongst the rows of goods swivelled towards me, and the gentle patter of discourse immediately ceased. Of the pair standing behind the counter, it was the woman who spoke. "Ah, now, you poor love. You must be in complete shock. Come and have a coffee on us." Her words were flung at me in a rapid assault, and I flinched at the force of them.

She turned towards the coffee machine stationed behind her and fired over her shoulder, "I've just put the cream in the Black Forest cake. Slice of that'll make everything feel better."

I didn't move. Had Andrew already broadcast my arrival and newly acquired relationship status? I doubted it. The port proper was two bends in the road away. It wouldn't have taken Macca long to find willing ears with which to unburden his tongue.

I took a step forward, accepting that this was what life would be like now. Everyone would know my business, and probably, whether I wanted to or not, I would know theirs. No wonder Ted did an excellent job of pretending to be invisible.

I thought back to my resolution to make as much effort as I could to connect with people here and put one foot in front of the other towards the sound of the coffee grinder.

Disembodied by the short shelves of groceries, the eyes of the two customers on the shop floor glided ahead on either side of me, their gaze never leaving my face.

I stepped free of the rows to find myself facing a tight semi-circle. Two women flanked me, a man in t-shirt, jeans and work boots leaned on the counter at ten o'clock, and the proprietors took up twelve and one o'clock positions. I took a step backwards.

"Here you are love." The proprietress pushed a steaming cup of black liquid towards me. "Nice and strong. I can heat milk if you'd like some."

"Um," I replied.

The man at her elbow gave me a soft smile, and without taking his eyes off me, said, "Give the lady some space, you lot. You're sucking up her oxygen."

The two female customers obligingly shuffled backwards. I remained where I was.

"Black's fine, thanks." I pulled my lips into an upward curve and directed it at each of them in turn.

Five polite smiles mirrored mine. Nobody said anything.

The proprietress picked up the cup and walked around the counter. "You don't want to drink it with us all gawking at you." She led me to an annex that ran the length of the shop and housed three cloth-covered tables. Putting the coffee down on one of them, she said, "I'll bring you some cake. On the house."

As she disappeared, the quiet conversation between the man and the proprietor began again, and the two female heads drifted back into the shelves.

I pivoted in my chair, studying my surroundings. Behind me, waist-height windows looked out onto manicured lawn and at the far end of the annex, a cubed monolith of a computer monitor sat on a small desk, its white plastic having long turned a grubby cream. Above the computer and stuck to the wall, a curling handmade poster declared the exorbitant rate for use in a faded serif font. I groaned inwardly. If I was really lucky, the connection would be dial up. I took out my phone, thumbed open the Wi-Fi connections tab and lay it on the table while I waited to see if any networks appeared. Then I continued my scrutiny of the shop.

From where I sat, I was just able to view the counter past the end of the shelves of goods, and in front of me, either in a clever bid to move customers on quickly in order to free up tables, or in complete oversight, lay the sanitaries aisle. "Café" goers sitting on the inside of the tables were rewarded with a view of tampons, sanitary napkins and incontinence pads. I stifled a laugh and turned at the sound of a rhythmic tapping behind me. It was a very small, very ugly dog. A backwards sloping face with milky eyes protruded from long, ratty fur.

It clip-clipped past my table, hobbling directly for the shelf of condoms.

"Ah..." I looked up to see if anyone was troubled by the trajectory of the blind dog. No one paid it any attention.

I watched in morbid fascination as the dog used its head as a brake against the bottom shelf. A packet of "New Tingle Edition" lube fell onto the floor with a soft *thunk*.

The dog backed up, did an about-face, and headed straight for the leg of my chair, so I put a hand down to prevent it from head-butting the metal. It gave me a brief sniff, wagged its hairy stump of a tail, and sat at my feet. With a wheeze, it shuffled its paws forward and lay its head in the space in between.

I gave its head a half-hearted pat and sat upright at the squeak of the proprietress' shoes.

"Here you are, love," she said, as she deposited the cake in front of me and perched on the edge of the table. The cake was almost black in its richness, the berry-infused cream oozing between the layers.

"Thank you," I answered wetly, the saliva already edging its way out of the corners of my mouth. I sucked it back in.

"Pleasure." Without pausing for breath, she blasted on. "Now, Em, we all know who *you* are, but I expect you don't know many people on the island."

I shook my head, unable to stop eyeballing the cake.

"Well, you're in the right place to meet people. Bit of a hub, our shop. Most islanders come through every other day, if not to buy something, then to do a bit of tongue wagging. I'm Trace." She nodded over her shoulder. "Don's my other half. And that's Wolf."

I glanced down at the dog.

The man at the counter raised his hand. "Tēnā koe."

"Mr Tamihana, to most of the kids." She lowered her voice. "A bit in awe of him I think, but he's just our Wolf to us. And those two lovely ladies are Cath and Jules."

Cath and Jules each chorused a cheery "Hi," then Trace introduced me to Kevin. The dog. "Doesn't see too well."

"Kevin?" I queried.

Don nodded at his wife. "Has a bit of a thing for Mr Bacon."

"Ah," I said, utterly perplexed as to why anyone would choose to name a hairy, smelly and aesthetically challenged pet after a Hollywood crush.

"So," Trace said as I raised the first mouthful of cake towards my lips. "You bought the Langdale place, didn't you?"

I closed my mouth and reluctantly put the fork down. "I don't know who owned it before me."

"Moss-covered place with holes in it?" Don's words were a drawl compared with his wife's rapid staccato.

"Yeah," I said in a defeated tone.

"Langdale's," Trace said with a nod.

I shovelled the forkful of cake into my mouth before I could be asked another question. The cherry and dark chocolate battled each other in a flavour explosion, and my eyes rolled back into my head.

"Makes a good cake, that one." Don smiled at his wife then shifted his eyes back to me. "Met your neighbour yet?"

I washed the chocolate from the roof of my

mouth with a slug of coffee. "No. I, ah, understand he's not very sociable."

The corners of Don's mouth twitched. "Well, he's a busy man, our Ted. He might introduce himself when he's got nothing on."

The toilet paper to the left of the tampons tittered.

"Don! Don't scare her." Trace admonished.

I couldn't for the life of me work out what was frightening about what he'd just said, but I didn't seek clarification. My attention was back on the cake. I loaded as much as my fork could take and deposited it with unseemly haste onto my tongue. Cream oozed out between my lips.

"I' weawy goh," I said up at Trace.

"See? Told you it'll make you feel better."

I nodded.

"Now, have you got everything you need over there? Milk? Bread? Lav paper?"

With effort I swallowed my large mouthful, my fork already balancing the next one.

"Light bulbs."

"That we can do." She turned and rattled out, "Don love, can you get Em some light bulbs?"

He moved out from behind the counter. "How many?"

"How many?" Trace repeated in case the noise of my vigorous masticating blocked out all other sound.

I held up two fingers. Then quickly added another one. A spare was probably sensible.

"Three," Trace shot above the shelves.

"What are they for? You want dim or bright?"

"Dim or bright?"

"Fuh hawway," I answered. A small brown glob shot out of my mouth and landed beside Trace's hand.

"Hallway lights," Trace interpreted.

"Somewhere in the middle then," Don decided for me. "Bayonet or screw?"

"Bayonet or screw?"

I looked wildly between her and the top of Don's head on the far side of the shop. I hadn't thought to check.

"Get both, Don." Trace smiled down at me. "You can return what you don't need next time you're in."

"Fanks."

"Is there anything else we can get you, love?"

I swallowed and looked at my phone. The only network available was called KevinBarkon. "Yeah, actually there is. How would you feel if I contributed to your monthly Wi-Fi bill in exchange for four hours access on weekdays?"

Trace wasn't sure and needed to check with Don.

Don was happy if Trace was.

Trace asked what Wolf thought.

Wolf thought it would be fine as long as it didn't

set a precedent. "Don't want your café turned into an office."

I assured Trace, Don, Wolf (and Cath and Jules for good measure) that it would be temporary until I found a better solution. "And I'll need caffeine and sugar. That's two streams of income every day from one customer." I stretched my lips into my very best smile and hoped my teeth weren't blackened with cake innards.

"Aw, what the heck," Trace decided. "You've had a rough start to your new life here. Least we can do is try and make it a bit easier for you."

"Thank you."

"Can't run a business over the net on your side of the island. Everybody out east makes money by producing. Did you know there's a big nut farm?"

I shook my head.

"Hazelnuts, mostly. They don't have to worry about a ferry schedule to get fresh produce to the mainland before it spoils. There's a berry farm near you, too. Makes gourmet jams. Delicious if you can afford it, though we're not really their clientele. Rich city people will pay anything if something's boutique and organic."

I acknowledged this with an "Oh," Trace brushed an invisible crumb from her pants leg, and Don said, "Would you look at that? Kevin obviously thinks you're alright. He doesn't claim ownership of every customer."

I looked down at the dog at my feet. His ears didn't so much as flinch at the mention of his name. "Is he deaf as well?"

"Selective hearing," Trace answered, then added in a stage whisper, "Learnt from the master of half-arsed listening." She nodded her head in the direction of her husband.

Don walked over, put a hand on his wife's hair, and tousled it. "I didn't hear that," he said, looking at me and smiling. "Now, are you sure light bulbs are all you need?"

I mentally went through the short inventory of stuff I'd brought with me, and an image of the swinging wall flitted across my mind. "Are there any builders on the island?"

Don shook his head. "Not anymore. Every man fancies himself as handy, though, so I'm sure you'll have plenty of volunteers."

Trace snorted. "You lot posing in your tool belts? I think Langdale's might be a bit beyond your skills, my love."

Wolf uncrossed his ankles, shifted two inches to the right, and crossed them again. "We can't call it Langdale's anymore, Trace."

"No, I guess we can't." She smiled down at me. "Thumb on the button, as always, our Wolf."

Don put a knuckle to his pursed lips, then said, "You could always ask up at the station. They're a pretty self-sufficient lot up there – do their own building work. Isn't that right, Wolf?"

Wolf gave a non-committal shrug.

"Can't say as much for the DoCos. Just drift around looking official most of the time," said Don.

"There is an awful lot of them, isn't there?" asked Trace.

I shifted in my seat. "Maybe I could get a woofer," I said, thinking of my large, very empty, very lonely house.

"What's that?" Trace asked.

"Someone who you feed and house in exchange for work. Just a few hours a day."

Trace's eyebrows attempted to hide in her hairline. "Em, love, you need a builder. Someone who's qualified, or at least really knows what they're doing. I don't think you'll find someone like that on a casual basis."

I was willing to bet on it. I already had my internet browser open on my phone. "What's your Wi-fi password, Trace?"

WHEN I GOT HOME, I placed the bottle of Syrah I'd bought at the store by Ted's cat flap with a note that promised to get the HR going again. Then I hand-washed yesterday's underpants and t-shirt and tried not to think about the previous day's events. Regardless of the amount of teeth-gritting and knuckle-rubbing, the paint on my t-shirt from the rescued canvas refused to flake off.

After ten minutes of imagining it was Warren's face I was kneading and pummelling, I gave up. In another week when all my stuff arrived, I would have a whole wardrobe at my disposal, and the t-shirt could be relegated to house renovation attire.

I hung the garments on the washing line in the backyard and sorted through Andrew's tools, selecting an old but oiled and sharpened pair of hedge trimmers.

WHEN THE VIEW-OBSCURING bushes had been pruned into view-framing shrubbery, I pivoted to return to the house and stopped mid-step. The washing line had been partially denuded. Only a single pair of lace-frilled briefs adorned the outside line, and beside them, two empty yellow pegs swung lazily on the wire.

Between the snipping and effort-induced grunting, I hadn't heard a thing.

CHAPTER NINE

I AM IN THE UTE. Andrew sits beside me.

As he pivots towards me, his obliques shift and the V deepens.

I reach out and put my finger in between the ridges of flesh. He is warm and firm, and the muscles soften as he gasps.

I track the line of muscle to where it disappears into his shorts, and as I hook my finger under his waistband, his hand encloses mine.

I am guided further beneath to where there is more warm, hard flesh.

We are in the middle of a downpour, and the world outside the ute is rendered in watery, muted tones.

The world inside the ute is cocooned by the

thrumming of the rain on the roof, our heavy breaths the only other sound.

A raindrop lands on my cheek.

Warren looks at me wide-eyed and waxen from the driver's seat, then starts the engine.

Another drop lands in the same place as the first, and I think it must be the tears I haven't yet shed.

"Who are you, Em?" he asks. "I don't know you anymore."

I think very hard how to answer, but my mind is filled with the beating of the rain on the tin roof and the wetness on my cheek. It's cold. Not hot like the spill of any grief would be.

"I..." I can't finish the sentence. I don't know how it ends.

I WOKE as the next drip found its mark on my left cheek and a gust of wind machine-gunned rain at the window.

I blinked, my brain struggling to keep pace with the transition from dream to real. As the tightness in my chest and the warmth in my groin receded, another droplet hit my face and I understood.

I threw back the covers and leapt out of bed, my body moving quicker than my brain. I turned on the light and using my hand to shield my eyes from the worst of its glare, peered at the ceiling above my bed.

A large stain spread from a crack in the plaster.

In that moment, my unfinished answer to Warren's question surged into the front of my brain from my already half-forgotten dream. Another drip landed on my pillow, and I knew that even in wakefulness, I still couldn't answer the question. With a clenching of fists and grinding of teeth, I was overcome with a surge of fury that wasn't entirely directed at Warren or the state of the house.

I was disappointed in me.

Thirty-two years old and both feet seemed to have stumbled off the path to self-discovery.

I turned my attention to the ceiling and railed at it, "You have to be fucking kidding me. Can't I have eight fucking hours of crappy-house-ignorance? Is that too much to ask?"

I gesticulated to the imaginary audience at the foot of the bed with outspread hands. "Apparently it is. Apparently I can't even get a decent night's sleep without being reminded I bought a SHIT BOX." The last word was a roar – all the anger from the last two days, coupled with this new self-directed rage, distilled down to two explosive syllables.

It shocked me into silence.

Before the ceiling could think it had got off lightly with one shouted word, I jabbed a finger at it. "You *suck*. You couldn't even choose Warren's bloody side of the bed to piss on."

I grabbed one corner of the bed and dragged it over to the other side of the room, well away from any danger of collapsing ceilings. Then I stalked towards the hall and, forgetting I hadn't got around to replacing the light bulbs, turned on the switch. "Good one, Em," I said into the dimness. Thankfully my bedroom cast enough light that I could make out the doorway at the end of the hall. "How many dumpees does it take to change a lightbulb? One, you'd think," I grumbled as I marched towards the kitchen. "Great place this is turning out to be. Neighbours stealing my clothes, everyone knowing my fucking business, nice bloody helpful DoC rangers..."

I stopped with my hand hovering over the living room doorknob. On that last word my mind was sucked back into the beginning of the dream. Heat unfurled in my chest and oozed through me from organs to pores. It took me two attempts to land a hand on the door handle. I groaned. "Shit, I don't need this."

I stepped through into the lounge and turned the light on. Looking up at the perfectly unmarked ceiling, I asked, "Are you listening? My life is complicated enough as it is." The lights dimmed as a flash of light illuminated the wild night outside the French doors, and a deep boom enveloped the bay.

I jumped, my startled "Fuck!" lost in the bass of the receding thunderclap. It took a beat to collect myself, and when my heart rate had slowed, I addressed the ceiling again. "It was meant to be rhetorical. No need for theatrics."

I collected one of my dinner bowls and returned to the bedroom, placing it under the drip, then settled back into bed.

The first drip hit the bowl with an aggressive splatter. Half a minute later, the second drip attempted to outdo the first in its watery explosion. The third drip *splosh*-ed and the fourth drip *ba-doing*-ed.

I sighed and threw back the covers again. Using my phone light, I picked up the dirty pair of underpants I'd discarded on the floor at bedtime and cushioned the bottom of the bowl.

"Right, everything shut the fuck up so I can get back to sleep." I curled into my customary fetal sleeping position and offered a last complaint. "Not even anything to show for being left in a wet patch."

My grumble was lost amid the drumbeats of a sudden squall.

A TEXT ALERT woke me at 7.34am. I pulled myself out of the fog of sleep and willed myself to roll over and check the phone.

027 993 412: Wow, you were awake early this morning

The text didn't make any sense to me. I allowed my thoughts to sharpen into wakefulness and read it again. Perhaps someone saw my light on in the wee hours while I dealt with the aftermath of the bed wetting. I decided to play it cool.

Me: Hmmm that's a slightly concerning message to get from an unknown number. Are you the dude with the binoculars or the one with his face pressed to my bedroom window?

027 993 412: LOL it's Anaru. Sorry Em sent text to wrong person. I assure you I have neither binoculars nor my face pressed to your window

Me: Just as well. You'd be disappointed. Had night from hell. Imagine I look like creature from hell

027 993 412: Eye bags and demon breath?

Me: Crazy hair and dribble crusts

027 993 412: You're right. I don't want to see that

Me: Wild night, huh?

027 993 412: Are you talking about the weather?

I was. But his playful comment made me think about the masterful way his dream-self had encouraged me to discover the secret parts of him. I couldn't think of anything to text back.

027 993 412: Add me to your contacts. So rude

Me: I know. Poor start to our relationship

Me: *friendship*

Oh God.

Me: That was unnecessary wasn't it?

027 993 412: Yes :) Have a lovely day Em

I groaned and dropped the phone. Shoot me now.

It took me ten minutes to find the will to move past my embarrassment and start the day. I opened the curtains, and the light of a cloudless sky flooded into the room, the greens of the neighbouring trees made more intense in the post-rain sun.

Maybe I'd explore the beach today.

My bladder strained against my abdomen and I turned to head towards the toilet.

In the middle of the floor, my undies floated at the top of the bowl like a frilly garnish to an exotic soup.

THE WATER in the bay was surprisingly clear and calm for having been tossed by a storm only a few hours before. After parking my car, I stood at the top of the beach where the sedge met the sand and scanned the length of the crescent-moon bay. Not another soul.

I hitched up my bikini briefs for the fourth time since putting them on and clucked my tongue. I had lost so much weight over the last few months that my once rounded body looked hollowed out. My bikini top sagged against the skin that used to house breasts, and not wanting anybody to see my new scrawny physique, I had added a layer of kaftan to my swimming outfit.

With no one around to watch me, I whooped and skipped down the sand dune, breaking into a run as the gradient levelled out. I charged into the glimmering water, and when I could no longer clear the surface and my stride faltered, I dived headlong, one hand clamped to my briefs through the fabric of the kaftan.

Surfacing at the end of my hastily gathered breath, I turned over and spread my limbs out in a star, closing my eyes and listening to the calls of the seabirds and the *shissss* of the water gently lapping the sand. The tension in my body unfurled, dissipating in a handful of slow breaths. I floated, my body lolling with the push and suck of the water, and thought of nothing.

"Do you have a permit to park your vehicle on the dunes?"

Startled, I uprighted myself, finding the sandy bottom only a foot beneath me. I sat in the water and squinted up at the owner of the question.

A woman with short black hair and Asian features stared down at me, legs astride, hands on hips. She wore a Department of Conservation uniform. Her cargo pants were tucked into the top of high-topped black boots like army fatigues, and holstered to her hip like a gun was a walkie talkie.

"Um. No?"

"You didn't see the sign that said, 'No parking beyond this point'?"

"I...yes, I saw the sign. But –" I hesitated. I didn't have any excuse for ignoring the sign except for a desperation to get in the water as quickly as possible.

"There was no one else around, and I didn't think it mattered."

"It didn't occur to you that said sign is in place for conservation purposes?"

The fact that the sign had a big Department of Conservation logo on it was, on reflection, a bit of a clue. "It does now."

Her face was expressionless. "I take it you're not from around here."

"As of two days ago, I'm a full-time resident."

She shifted her weight slightly and rocked once, twice, on the balls of her feet before turning and saying, "Please accompany me to your vehicle."

I looked about me as if seeking an explanation from fellow swimmers. Then I squinted at her marching backside for several seconds before deciding it might be a good idea to comply.

I stood up, leaving my bikini bottoms floating around my knees. The pale and now wet kaftan did nothing to protect my privacy.

With a "Hoh," I sat back down again.

The ranger turned and said, "I beg your pardon?"

"No. I mean, nothing. I'm –" I yanked the briefs to crotch level and stood back up again, one hand placed firmly on either side of the briefs, the arse of them sagging with a sudden weight. "– all ready for accompanying." I smiled at her.

She narrowed her eyes then pivoted to continue striding towards the dunes where I'd parked my ute.

I followed, scooping sand out from the back of my pants and checking the beach to make sure I hadn't provided indecent entertainment to any newcomers.

When I arrived at the car, she had a notepad open and was writing in it. "What's your full name, please?" she asked without looking up.

"Look," I said, "I'll just move the car. No biggie." I jingled my keys.

"I'd appreciate it if you answered the question."

"I don't believe I have to," I said slowly.

She looked up and eye-balled me. "I am an officer for the Department of Conservation –"

"You're a *ranger*."

She started her sentence again without changing her tone. "I am an officer for the Department of Conservation. I am here in an official capacity to maintain the protection of the delicate ecology of the foreshore of this bay, which is on Department of Conservation land. I'll ask you one last time. What's your full name please?"

I tried very hard not to roll my eyes. "Em Stewart," I said after a beat.

"I said full name, Ms Stewart. M for...?"

"It's E-M. Not the letter."

"Can I see some ID?"

"I didn't bring any with me. Officer."

"You do realise it is an offense to drive a vehicle in this country without being in possession of your driver's license?"

"Yes," I said.

"You look like a law-abiding citizen, Ms Stewart. Please locate your license for me."

I stared at her. It had been a long time since I'd been forced to bullshit my way out of a situation with a person of judicial authority. I was rusty. She stared harder.

I exhaled sharply out my nose, drawing my lips into a thin line and turning to find my driver's license in the glove box. I handed it to her.

She peered at it, not a single muscle in her face betraying her thoughts. "I see, so not an 'Em' after all. It would help you in this situation if you were fully compliant, Ms Stewart." She handed the card back to me and returned to writing on her notepad.

"Don't..." I looked around to see if anyone was in hearing distance. "That's confidential, right?" I asked, pointing at her pad.

"This information has been obtained in the line of duty. It is a professional requirement that I record it in our database of offences against the Conservation Act 1987. It will not be shared with any other government agency or anyone who does not have access to our system."

I thought of Andrew and quickly dismissed it. Surely, he'd have no reason to check the offences database.

She continued to write for another minute, then looked up, tucking the pen and pad into a breast pocket. "Well, Ms Stewart. If you are to become a responsible resident of this island, you will learn to heed official signage and educate yourself on the various issues pertaining to native species' population and habitat sensitivity. I'll let you off with a warning this time, but any further transgression will be regarded as a breach of the aforementioned act and will be treated as such. Do I make myself clear?"

My fingers twitched to salute her, but I figured the decision to warn could be reversed at any point. I settled for a "Yes, ma'am," its tone deliberately ambiguous.

She nodded at me and said, "Have a good day," before turning and walking towards her DoC branded ute, which was positioned in a perfect execution of the space-saving diagonal park in the official car parking area.

"WHO'S the officious DoC ranger? The woman who does an excellent Robocop impersonation?" I asked when I walked into the Port Keulemans Store that afternoon.

Wolf leaned on the counter in the exact position I remembered him in when I'd left the previous day. Trace stood behind the counter, and Don stacked items in aisle two.

"Beats me," said Trace. "All the DoCos look the same to me."

I headed for the chair with the view of the non-applicator tampons and placed my laptop on the table with a *clack*. "She read my pedigree over some parking infringement."

"You know," said Trace, "I wish they'd all go back to where they came from. I feel like they're taking over."

"Give it time, my love," said Don as a ranger walked into the store. "They're just different, that's all," he whispered. "They'll assimilate eventually."

Wolf crossed his arms and frowned. "It's only been what, Trace? Twenty, thirty years since the sanctuary was set up?"

"I'm just saying," said Trace, lowering her voice, "why does there have to be so many of them? I don't trust them."

"They're alright," said Wolf.

"Well, you have more to do with them than me," said Trace, giving the counter a vigorous wipe.

Wolf sniffed, and Kevin tapped his way towards the table as I started up my laptop. I lowered my hand to pat him before he could walk into anything solid.

My computer farted into life, and Kevin wheezed into repose.

"You don't want to change your bet before it's too late?" Wolf called from the counter.

"No way. I have nothing to lose and too much to gain."

"Except for the money you'll be handing over. I'd call that a loss."

Ignoring him, I asked, "Right, gentleman, shall we?"

Trace nodded. "I'm ready," she said as she walked out from behind the counter. Don appeared from the shelves. They gathered behind me, leaning over the back of my chair towards the screen.

I opened my inbox.

Two emails from marketing sites, one from a human rights organisation, one from my subscription to a classic arts magazine.

And one from NZWWOOF.

I looked up at each of their faces.

Don said, "Let's do this."

I clicked on the email link and read, *Ruben Schreiber, a 22-year-old qualified carpenter from Germany would like to offer his services.* My hands shot skywards, narrowly missing chins and noses. "Yessss. Double cake portions for a week!"

Don said, "I think we can absorb the loss of capital."

Trace said, "I'm happy to lose this bet, love." She patted my shoulder. "Well done."

I emailed Ruben, sending him information about the ferry and warning him that if he came on the next one, his first job would be helping me to unload a furniture removal truck.

Trace delivered a coffee and my two slices of cake, and I signed into the remote access site for my work. I wasn't due back for a few days, but I wanted to catch up on emails.

The majority of them were all-staff or team-specific updates on policy changes, new initiatives and best practice – nothing I needed to respond to. The last one was a recruitment announcement from Human Resources entitled "New appointment announcement".

It read: **As you are aware, Tineke Hannah, our long-serving General Manager of our private equity arm has left us for the warmer climes of Brisbane and a wonderful employment opportunity in the banking sector. As we are committed to providing career pathways for our staff, we made the decision to recruit internally. The position has now been filled.**

We are pleased to announce that Warren Barton is the new General Manager of Chron PE.

I stood up from the table, slopping coffee into the saucer and startling Kevin into a *yip*. I stared at the screen, willing a new name in the place where Warren's appeared.

As of Monday, Warren would be my boss.

CHAPTER TEN

"EM, darling, are you alright? You look like you've had a shock." Trace squeaked across the floor and laid a hand on my shoulder.

I sank back into my chair and stared at the screen for a few more seconds. Then I closed my mouth and deleted the email.

"What is it, love?"

"It's fine. I'm fine. Nothing I can't deal with." I smiled up at her and took a sip of my coffee to show everything was as it should be.

She raised an eyebrow but retreated to the counter.

Who was I kidding? It was going to take two bottles of Pinot Gris and four reruns of *Dirty Dancing* to deal with this clusterfuck. The bastard waited all of twenty-four hours, after making an irrevocable life-changing decision that left me in a steaming turd pile, to brown nose the CEO so that he could assume a position of power over me. Talk about kicking me to the curb and reversing over me for good measure.

I got out my phone and opened up my Messenger app. The conversation I was about to initiate was best left off the professional record.

I jabbed out a message that took three attempts to correctly type.

Em Stewart: You didn't waste any time. It might have been nice to learn about it in person rather than an all-staff email

A message *ting*-ed on my phone twenty seconds later.

Warren Barton: Hi Em. I'm sorry about that. I haven't known how to reconcile my terrible behaviour towards you and so I've been very head-in-sand the last couple of days

Em Stewart: You're a GM now. You have to be able to communicate with your staff no matter how difficult. You can't run away from everything

Warren Barton: You're right. Not a good start

Em Stewart: You're not very good at finishing things either

Warren Barton: No. And I'm sorry I haven't been in touch

Em Stewart: You've been too busy moving onwards and upwards it would appear

Warren Barton: Em, I really want to make amends

for being a coward. Please help me do that

Em Stewart: Because you have to work with me or because you admit you've been a complete wanker and feel awful about hurting me

Warren Barton: Well both to be honest

I looked down at the dog. Since I'd startled him, he'd resettled himself between my feet.

"What do you think, Kevin? Should I give the fucker the benefit of the doubt?"

He grunted, which might have been indigestion, but was good enough for me.

Em Stewart: You know what Warren? You need to figure this out on your own. I'm not doing any of the work for you. I'll talk to you on Monday when I return from my leave

I closed the app.

The doorbell chimed and an elderly gentleman dressed in a tweed jacket, ill-fitting grubby jeans and gumboots stepped into the shop. He nodded at Wolf and looked over at me with a smile. Tugging the bottom of his jacket, he took a step in my direction.

"Rob, love, now's not a good time," Trace said, pointing at me with her chin.

"Or ever," added Wolf. "Punching a bit above your weight there, mate."

"Can't blame an old dog for trying, aye, Rob?" Don said with a chuckle from aisle three.

I stood up before Rob could continue on his course to my table and said, "I need to go for a walk. Nobody better eat my cake or – God help me – I'll eat them." I pushed past Rob with a "Sorry," and stepped into the sunshine.

THE ONLY WAY I could possibly deal with this shit storm was to keep busy. By the time I got home that afternoon, I'd organised:

1. Andrew to help me assess materials so that the woofer would have work to do when he got here (if I ordered them to come on the next ferry).
2. Wolf to round up a furniture moving team so that the truck turnaround was quick and they were back in Port Keulemans well in time for the return ferry.
3. I downloaded instructions on the most efficient way to convert lawn to garden without ready-made compost. I had the land and I had work-free afternoons. It was time to learn to be more self-sufficient.

I set off for home with a pair of Port Keulemans Store-bought gardening gloves.

ON THE WASHING LINE, exactly where I'd left it yesterday, hung my t-shirt. A dark shape covered its centre.

I sidled up to it and pulled the corners of the t-shirt taut so I could see the shape clearly.

It was a bird. It was the bird I'd seen sketched on the canvas I had shielded with my body when I knocked the easel over. And it was an incredibly beautiful one.

A sleek head with an extraordinarily long beak swept down to a lean body of blue-black feathers. Yellow-orange wattles adorned its face just behind its beak and its long tail feathers were tipped in white.

I'd seen this bird before, but only in pictures.

The portrait was stunning. Even on such a difficult canvas, Ted had managed to apply enough texture to lend the bird a three-dimensional quality. He'd obviously studied fine art in his life previous to the island. It reminded me of an artist, only I couldn't recall who.

I carefully unpegged the t-shirt and carried it inside, laying it on top of the breakfast bar. I looked at it for another few minutes, feeling the dabs of paint with my fingertips, reading its depths like braille.

Then I changed into shorts and headed for the backyard.

I decided on an area that bordered my boundary with Ted's and set to work with the spade, scooping out lawn in small chunks to make a rough rectangle.

As I neared the boundary, the grass became more difficult to slice through. Ivy and jasmine were thickly entangled through the hedging, and they had started to encroach on the lawn.

I gave up on the spade in favour of a trowel, deciding I needed to follow the vines to their roots and dig them out.

It was slow going, and the haphazard way they'd chosen to grow made the root-seeking challenging. As I cleared the first patch and neared the boundary, I discovered the mother root of the jasmine. It thickened the deeper I followed it into the soil, and I systematically detached its feathery rootlings from the earth. I couldn't find where the root ended though. I dug up more and more soil, tracing its lifeline back to its dark beginnings.

Eventually the root began to thin again, and I knew I had exposed enough to, if not kill it, seriously damage its health.

I pulled on it. It didn't budge.

I placed my feet either side of it and heaved. Not a millimetre of movement.

"Come on you fucker," I growled through clenched teeth and gave one almighty tug.

The root snapped and I hurtled backwards into something solid.

It *oomph*-ed.

I scrabbled a foot away from it and turned, looking up into a set of sagging and grey-fringed male genitalia.

CHAPTER ELEVEN

"BEST WAY TO get rid of that stuff is to poison it," an English-accented voice said from above me.

"Erkh," I replied involuntarily as I shuffled further backwards, unable to drag my eyes away from his crotch.

"Leave any pieces in the soil, and it'll grow more rampant than ever, gradually taking more and more control. Like Chester Hendrickson."

"Um," I said, pulling my eyes away from his bits to his face. Piercing blue eyes looked down at me from beneath wild eyebrows. The rest of his face was framed by thick, wiry hair. There was a slight groomed quality to the arrangement – the hair with a hint of a parting, the beard longer than the average man's, but uniform in length, as if it innately knew to grow in such a way as to keep up the appearance of the good breeding his well-rounded vowels suggested.

Andrew's and Don's odd comments about my neighbour shed their cryptic veil and stood as obvious and naked as the man himself.

Ted was a naturist.

"Horrible little shit," he continued. "Beautiful boy, though. Face of an angel, heart as black as midnight." He took a sip from a glass of red wine. "I approve of your taste in wine. I like a strong tipple of dry, aged fruit."

My eyes slipped back to his genitals. "Look, can you just..." I looked around me then reached across to the hedging, snapped a small branch off, and handed it to him. "Hold it –" I positioned his hand so that the foliage obscured his privates. "– there."

"Ah! Like Adam when the weight of the world's future sins fell on his shoulders."

"OK." I stood up. "Now I can concentrate."

"Have you come here seeking absolution, too?"

"No." My answer sounded quick and defensive to my ears. "I mean, I don't think so." I grabbed my spade and leaned on it. It wasn't absolution I wanted or needed. It was a few more kilograms, more beach days, and not to be made a fool of by my treacherous boyfriend. Ex-boyfriend.

And something else. Something much bigger I had only just begun to put my finger on.

Before I could revisit the reason for my irrational

fury the night before, Ted asked, "Did you like the t-shirt?"

"Yes! I love it," I gushed. "You're a very talented painter, Ted. Do you sell your work?"

His eyes narrowed and his head jerked to the left. It was almost like he had flinched. "No." The word was sharp and final.

I changed tack and asked, "Why'd you paint my t-shirt?"

"Seemed a waste of a beginning. The first brush stroke is the most important. Everything that comes after must be applied very delicately. It's like the foundation for a house of cards."

I think I understood what he meant. One false stroke and the artistic effect is ruined – the house comes tumbling down. "Is it a huia?"

He nodded. "Saw one in the garden one day."

It took me a moment to respond. "Haven't they been extinct for about a hundred years?"

"Someone's been wrong a mighty long time, then."

I scratched my ear. I wasn't sure how I should respond to the ludicrousness of his belief.

"It didn't do much. Just sort of hopped about a bit, but I recorded its likeness in my image vault." He tapped his head.

"Right. Well you, ah, rendered it beautifully."

"Thank you very much. Your name's Em?"

"Yes."

"Like in the James Bond stories?"

"No." I hoped he wouldn't attempt to seek clarification. I needn't have worried.

"Hmmm?" Ted cocked his head towards his house and listened. A faint mewling drifted through the leaves.

"I'm right here, Fenwick."

The mewling grew into a yowl.

"Alright, my love, I'm coming."

He dropped the branch, giving me a last glimpse of his dried, aged fruit and turned to disappear through the hedge, the loose skin of his bottom jiggling with each step.

"Nice to meet you," I called after him. "And sorry again about the car."

I didn't receive a reply.

"YOU COULD HAVE WARNED ME," I threw at Don on Monday, my first day back at work.

"I did," he said when he had finished laughing at my tale of meeting Ted's "sugar stick" (Wolf's contribution).

"No, you said something vague about him being busy and introducing himself when he had nothing on. Highly amusing."

"I thought so," said Wolf. He still leant against the counter, one foot crossed over the other. I wondered if when he finally found the motivation to get on with a life outside of the store, he'd leave behind a Wolf-shaped groove in the wood, like those monasteries with hollowed out stone steps from hundreds of years of monks walking on them.

"I don't get it," I said. "Why would someone who's so afraid of people hide from them one day and reveal themselves in their full naked glory the next?"

Don said, "He's a bit touched in the head."

Trace said, "He's lovely, but –"

Wolf finished, "Completely pōrangi." He twirled a finger by his right ear.

I had to agree with them. The whole business with seeing a bird that had official Dodo status was decidedly barmy.

"Does he ever get out?"

"Hasn't left his property in years that I know of. We drop off his groceries once a week, have a cup of tea, make sure he's still ticking along OK," said Trace.

"And the knitting club meets at his house on Thursdays," said Don.

"You're kidding! Knitting?"

Don shook his head. "I'm serious. The widows Velda and Patty. And Ted."

Wolf said, "Not much in the way of geriatric poles round here. Remind themselves what one looks like."

"Wolf!" Trace admonished. "It's lovely they don't

mind his lifestyle choice. I have a lot of respect for those women."

"What on earth does Ted knit?" I asked.

"They make tiny vests and booties for premature babies in – where was it, Don?"

"Somewhere beginning with K," he answered slowly, then frowned in thought over the top of the tinned peas.

The shop went very quiet.

Trace pursed her lips and tapped them with a finger.

Wolf said, "Kuwait."

Trace snorted.

"Kyrgyzstan?" I ventured.

Trace gasped and pointed at me like I'd said the winning answer on *Who Wants to Be a Millionaire?*

"Bangladesh," Don said with a nod and continued stacking the shelf.

I opened my laptop with a sigh that might have been a groan and said to Trace, "Triple shot today, please. Got any bourbon?"

"Not if you're thinking of adding it to your coffee, I don't."

Kevin was already nestled at my feet. I looked down at him and said, "Today's the day, pal. Have to face my new turd-flecked reality."

Kevin's ability to reassure reached as far as letting me know he was still alive. After several alarming seconds of inertia, his ribcage expanded in a deep, shuddering breath and creaked to stillness again.

"Thank you, Kevin. Very comforting."

My work inbox housed two emails from the new General Manager. One designed to buoy the team and reassure everyone that a change of leadership wouldn't also mean Change. The kind that had you reworking hundred-page documents to align with new policy or shuffling desks with sideways restructuring. It was business as usual. I'm sure everybody else could see as clearly as I could the invisible "for now" at the end of that sentence.

The second email was written just to me. It was a welcome back email. Two sentences – an email that a boss might write to any of his employees after they'd returned from holiday. Warm and impersonal.

I couldn't be upset about it. Warren and I had to maintain a front of complete professionalism at work and leave our messy private life outside the virtual world of our digital workplace. However, there'd better be a great big grovelling email in my Gmail account. Or I'd reach down the fibre optic cabling and garrotte him with his new senior-management-tier silk tie.

I ATE my two pieces of cake, had a second cup of coffee (only double shot this time), took two pee stops, and made an effort to smile at and say "Hello" to a half dozen locals who paused in their purchasing to ogle the newcomer. Before they had time to draw breath to say anything to me, Trace would "Shush" their mouths closed and inform them I was unavailable for chit-chat until 1pm. Between the crowd control and the coffee delivery, she made an excellent P.A.

By the time I'd completed my allotted four hours, neither Kevin nor Wolf had moved from the positions they had been settled into on my arrival.

I raised an eyebrow at Wolf.

"April Fool's Day 2009," he said.

I had no idea what he was talking about, so I asked him to clarify.

"Don laced the front counter with super glue."

"Yeah, what a mistake that was," said Don. "I've had to put up with his ugly mug all day every day for over a decade. Didn't think that one through very well."

"Oh, go on, you two," Trace said through an indulgent smile as she stacked cups on top of the coffee machine.

"Don't you ever have to go to the toilet, Wolf?" I asked.

"Yep," he said with a smile that told me to work it out myself.

I chose to humour him by rolling my eyes and stood up to stretch before I changed gears from work brain to personal admin brain.

As I lowered my arms, a man entered the shop. There were two notable things about him: He had a bunch of wildflowers in his right hand, the kind you might find growing on road verges and in amongst hedges, and he was extraordinarily tall. So tall in fact, that he had stooped when he walked through the door. My eye line was somewhere around his belly button.

He stopped short when he saw me, emitted an "Oh," and dropped his flower-adorned hand. Turning on his heel, he pushed the bouquet into Don's hands and exited the shop.

Don beamed at his unexpected gift, and Wolf laughed.

"Oh, Em," said Trace. "Sorry love. That's our Dave-o. Not the best with people."

I held up my hands. "No, fair call. We'd have to shout at each other to be heard across the distance." I offered an "I'm really not offended" smile and sat down to open my Gmail account. Sure enough, Warren Barton had sent me a message. It wasn't long and was to the point. He admitted what a prize arse he'd been and felt the least he could do was give me the house in reparation. We'd split everything else.

So, he hadn't changed his mind about splitting from me, then.

It was a nice gesture, but then he didn't lose a lot of money by gifting me his half of the house's value.

He'd also gone to the trouble of listing all the

stuff he wanted me to send back to him. He'd systematically gone through a mental stocktake of all we owned and divvied it up in a way that was "fair and equitable". I could keep the rosewood dining table, he said, but he wanted the crocodile leather couch.

My reply was also of a succinct length and pertinent nature. "Warren," I wrote, "where did you imagine I might find a new couch on an under-populated and geographically isolated island? I'll have more chance of spotting a winged unicorn." Or Ted's huia.

I told him I would buy him out of the stuff I needed and send his personal items back. Take it or leave it.

Just as I was readying to close my laptop, my Skype app stirred to life, the call tone bouncing and blipping loudly in the quiet shop.

Warren.

I carried the computer outside, almost colliding with a young woman in Department of Conservation khakis. She was the third ranger I'd seen in the shop that day.

I found some shade and answered the call.

Warren's expression was one that affected concern tinged with sadness. Or was it perhaps regret? "Hi, Em," he said.

"Nice tie," I answered. "Mulberry or Tasar Silk?"

"Look," he said, ignoring my question, "now that

you're off the clock, I thought we could talk about, you know...stuff."

I wasn't interested in us holding each other's hand while we explored the troughs and peaks of our emotional landscapes. I was still far too angry. "Let's keep it to the practicalities, Warren. I think we both agree what a shit you've been, and now I just want to get on with my life. So –" I casually brushed cake crumbs from the laptop's keyboard. "– how can I help you?"

Warren looked like I'd flicked his ear and took a second to regroup. "Well, you're right, about keeping things you need for the house. I'm happy to research what they're worth and you can approve the amounts before you buy me out."

"I'm only paying you for half of everything."

"Right. That's right."

"OK. What else?"

"We'll need to get in touch with our lawyer about you now having sole ownership of the house."

"Yes."

"Okay," he said slowly, nodding. "I'll do that."

"Good."

"And we need to close our joint bank account and divvy up the funds."

"I'll send you my new account details."

"I guess I'll organise that, too."

"Great. That's all you wanted to discuss?"

He frowned.

"What?" I asked.

"What's that on your t-shirt?"

I'd forgotten I'd decided to be a living canvas today. "A huia."

"A huia? I've never seen you wear it before."

"That's because I haven't. It's new."

Warren raised his eyebrows. "You can buy clothes on the island?"

"No. My neighbour painted it on one of my old t-shirts."

"That's good, Em. You're making friends already."

"I'm not sure what kind of a friend he'll be. He's a bit strange. Reckons the huia in question visited him in his garden."

"Really?" Warren looked off to the left of the camera, his eyes focusing on something in the distance. After a couple of seconds, he brought his attention back to me. "You're right, that is decidedly strange."

"Anything else?" I asked shortly.

Warren tipped his head slightly to one side and appeared to consider me, or steel himself for something. "Yeah. There's actually one really important thing I wanted to say in this conversation. I know it's going to muddy the waters, and I'm sorry about that. But you've been very clear about how you feel, and I want to communicate where I'm at."

"So, shoot."

"I'm –" He fiddled with something to the right of the frame. "– very confused about everything."

I didn't say anything. I didn't like where this was going.

He shifted his eyes from his hand and back to me. "I do know that I still love you, Em."

There it was, the punchline I hoped he wouldn't deliver. "Jesus. What the fuck does that mean?"

"I don't know."

A fierce heat coiled itself tightly in the pit of my stomach. "How dare you, after what you pulled?"

Warren opened his mouth to say something, and I stopped him with a "No." Pointing my finger at him, I continued, "You don't have the right to even attempt to backtrack. You knew the score when you made your decision to drive off." I left my father's past actions unsaid, but Warren knew exactly the meaning and weight of my words.

"I know. I did a stupid, stupid thing. It was a mistake."

The ball of fire in my belly started to unwind, spreading its heat into my limbs. I said very quietly and clearly, "Fuck you, Warren."

Closing the lid of the laptop with a *thunk*, I looked up and into a group of boys' faces at a nearby picnic table. They turned away from me, sudden and synchronous, like the movement was choreographed. In the middle of the table sat a large bottle of orange fizzy drink, and one boy ate a strawberry from a bag, throwing the stem onto the grass behind him. As I walked past, they all froze. Only their eyes followed me.

I stopped at the end of the table. "Shouldn't you be at school?"

One of them shrugged.

One said, "Nah, miss."

One said, "School holidays."

The kid nearest to me, one of two white boys, might have been twelve where the others ranged between fourteen and seventeen judging from the amount of down, or lack of, on their upper lips. He said, "Did Anaru do that?" and pointed to my caved-in wheel arch.

"No, a fence post did that. He had...very little to do with it, actually."

"My cousin said Anaru stopped you from driving over a bank by jumping in front of the car and his thigh did that."

The other boys jostled him, one saying, "Don't be stupid."

"Nah, he's like Iron Man. Have you seen his muscles?"

As one of the older boys said, "A human can't stop a car, you dick," I decided to leave them to debate the physics of man versus car and collect the rest of my things from the store. Before I left, I asked Don what the deal was with the boys outside.

"Ferry's not due for a couple of days."

"And?"

"There's not many girls on the island and those they aren't related to they've known their whole lives. The arrival of the ferry and the odd young female tourist is a weekly treat for boys with raging hormones."

"And I'm a make-do until the next ferry?"

"Most likely."

"Fantastic." I edged my head around the door. They were still there, but they were occupied.

Roboranger stood at the head of their table in her customary fighting stance – legs astride for optimum balance and readiness for flight, one hand loose and palm open, the other resting lightly on her walkie talkie holster. "You boys realise you're in violation of the Litter Act 1979? Apart from this method of rubbish disposal being the actions of an irresponsible citizen, it attracts vermin and encourages the growth of our pest populations. I'm sure you don't want that to happen."

I crept behind her towards my car.

A quiet chorus of, "No, miss," answered her.

"I don't want to have this conversation with you again. Have I made myself clear?"

Easing my door open, I climbed in and pulled it closed without locking it.

"Yes, miss."

"Right, good lads."

I hunched down in my seat and tried to start my car as quietly as possible, but I must have absentmindedly engaged the alarm system when I parked that morning, as I was suddenly enveloped in an eye-wateringly loud electronic wail.

All five heads swivelled in my direction.

"Shit," I said, frantically punching buttons on my remote.

Roboranger nodded at me. Her mouth made the shape of "Ms Stewart", but her voice was lost in the din. Behind her, the boys hid their relief at having been rescued behind laughter. They had the courtesy to be polite about it, chuckling into their hands and keeping their eyes averted.

A wave of heat washed over me. I couldn't turn the bloody thing off. It was just my luck if the battery in the remote chose this moment to execute its death throes.

I threw a glance at the table and issued another "Shit." Roboranger had disengaged herself from the group and was striding towards me.

"Are you in need of assistance?" she shouted.

Just as she reached out a hand towards the driver's door, the alarm stopped.

I wasted no time relaxing into relief. I started the car and gave the accelerator a push, revving the engine.

Roboranger stepped up to the ute, rapped the top of it twice and saluted me as I drove away.

It gave me a ridiculous amount of childish pleasure to be given a mandate to salute her back.

I'D NEVER SEEN Andrew in uniform before. Like the colleagues of his I'd noticed in the last couple of days, he wore a Department of Conservation emblazoned shirt, standard issue shorts, heavy boots and thick woollen socks. The outfit had a tendency to make the wearer look drab – the pale fabric sucking colour from skin, and the starched material masking shape. The uniform did not have the same effect on Andrew.

It didn't matter. I wasn't paying attention. I didn't pay any heed to how his shirt, tucked into his belted shorts, accentuated his wide shoulders. And I certainly didn't give the tapering of his torso into a lean waistline a second glance.

I took a deep breath and climbed down from the ute.

"What?" he asked when I failed to greet him.

"Nothing."

"You look like a man in uniform terrifies you."

"No, I don't," I said a bit too quickly, then made it worse by saying, "Because you don't."

I hadn't managed to convince him. "Flashback to your misspent youth?"

"Something like that. Right," I said, "where should we begin?"

He crossed his arms and looked up at the house. "I don't know. There are just *so* many options." He met my eye. "You ever thought about bowling it and starting again?"

"Yes. But I'm going to prove to Warren that this house is worth the sacrifice we made and make him cry when he sees what he's missed out on."

"Fair enough. Outside first, then." He raised his tape measure, pulled a length out, then with a boyish grin and a flick of upraised eyebrows, reeled it back in with a snap.

His playfulness wasn't at all cute, but I decided to humour him anyway. "Whoa, cowboy. That is one powerful weapon you got there. You better holster that thing before you take an eye out."

Andrew looked at me like I'd handed his next line on a golden platter.

"Don't say it," I begged.

His features rearranged themselves into an expression of mock sincerity, and as he fought his way through a shrub to the wall beneath my bedroom window, he said, "I would never refer to my penis in a way that might suggest I was well endowed."

I blushed. I hadn't blushed since Quinton Ellis asked me if the long toes of all the sloths on my underpants were tickly. I was seven and didn't know too much about "tickling" then, but I knew enough to turn a bright shade of red. This current blush made up for lost time. The blood drained from the soles of my feet in its rush to reach my face. Thankfully, Andrew's back was to me, and his busyness gave my body time to restore its equilibrium.

"No," I muttered, "you can safely leave that to me."

Andrew chuckled and called out a measurement to record on my phone. He straightened up and looked down to where the weatherboards ended and the baseboards began. "This wall isn't connected to the floor, you say?"

"Nope. You'd think the floor was a good place to start for something that supports the roof."

"Ah, but not this house. This one is out of the box."

"And upside down."

He stepped towards the wall. "I better measure the height as well. Might need complete reframing."

When the second measurement was taken, Andrew pushed his way back through the foliage and stood in front of me, hands on hips. "Where to next?"

I peered up at him. He had several inches on Warren, who favoured Italian shoes as much for the heels as the leather. "Holes," I answered.

"Holes?"

I led him to the front of the house and pointed to the missing sections in the cladding. "Holes."

"You don't like them?"

"This house is a giant sieve. I don't want to live in a giant sieve."

"Sounds reasonable." He bent over and parted the

bushes to get a look at a particularly impressive missing section of weatherboard.

I turned away from him before my brain had time to process the degree of tautness of the fabric across his buttocks. "How come there's so many DoC staff here?" I asked the hedge.

I turned back as Andrew stood upright and pushed against a weatherboard with his finger. The wood splintered slightly, moisture oozing out from between the cracks. "Well, it's a pretty big facility. And we've got several breeding programmes running across a few different species. You've never gone north and seen the fenced-off area? Goes from one side of the island to the other." He moved off to assess another section of wall.

I followed a few steps behind him. "This is an island. What do you need fencing off from?"

"Rats, feral and domestic cats, straying dogs, one or two humans. Pretty hard to escape them when you can't fly."

"Can't you just ban pets?"

"We could," he said, craning his neck to look at the boards beneath the soffit, "but that's a pretty extreme measure. I can't imagine it would go down very well. But we've recently implemented a new requirement which should help things a bit. All cats on the island now have to be micro-chipped and de-sexed." He turned. "You have a ladder?"

I shook my head. "What about the wild ones?"

"We trap them." Andrew moved farther along the wall.

"And re-home them?"

Andrew's reply was very matter-of-fact. "We don't use live traps."

"Oh."

"Actually, we could do with a few more staff. Our operation's large, we're by far the biggest wildlife sanctuary in the country. We have just enough resources to keep things ticking along but not really progressing well."

"Why's that?"

"Government's cut our budget." Andrew shrugged. "Lean times – something's got to give, and I guess a conservative government doesn't make restoring our nation's biodiversity a priority." He slapped the side of the house. "Thirty metres of board should be a good start. Your builder can order more when he's done a proper assessment."

I recorded the amount in my phone. "That's tough. The job must have its benefits, though. How many times have you had women hit on you by saying they're an endangered bird?"

Andrew laughed. "The old 'Ranger, I need rescuing' routine?" He stopped prodding a soft spot and looked at me, still chuckling. "None. Where exactly did you imagine a DoC uniform on the fireman-policeman continuum?"

This time Andrew was not facing away from me when I blushed.

"Goddammit!" I marched away from him and up the driveway. "I am *not* a frigging blusher." I stopped and turned to face him again.

He made no attempt to conceal his amusement.

I pointed my finger at him. "Stop doing whatever it is you're doing. My life is –" I made the noise of a bomb going off and mimed a mushroom cloud. "I need to get it back under control. This –" I rapidly gestured from his feet to his head and back again. "– is not part of the plan."

"OK." Andrew's smirk deepened slightly. "What would you like me to do about it?"

I couldn't very well tell him to go away. Apart from it being rude and unreasonable, I needed to order the materials as soon as I could to make sure they made it on to the ferry.

"*I'm* going to go inside and make a list of things that need attention, then I'm going to have a bath. Your thank-you beer is in the chilly bin. Please close the door when you're done." I turned and headed for the back door.

I put the jug on, sat down to write the list, and made myself a strong, milky tea when I had finished.

"Here," I shouted through the hole I'd punched in the kitchen wall and pushed the list through, waving it to get Andrew's attention. It was taken from my fingers and a mouth appeared, blocking out the light.

"Any chance of a cuppa?"

I picked up my cup and forced it through the hole, the surface of the tea collecting a sprinkling of wall fragments.

Andrew's voice drifted in through the hole. "Awesome. Like a cinnamon cappuccino, only more asbestos-y."

"Don't be dramatic. A little asbestos never hurt anyone." I thrust two ginger nut biscuits through the hole. They were gently taken from the palm of my hand.

"Are you sure you want to get rid of this one? Seems quite handy."

I poured water into another cup.

Andrew's voice was muffled by biscuit. "This list is quite long. The woofer only needs enough stuff for a week. I definitely won't need to look at the inside."

Silence.

"You still there?" he asked.

"Yes. I'm very busy drinking my tea."

A chuckle.

"You know, this wall thing is working well," I said. "I can't see any part of you."

Andrew was quiet for a moment. "Did you know that one of the reasons why the uniform's this colour is that it's a general match to most seabird and bat guano, so when you're crawling around burrows and caves counting heads and measuring chicks, you don't come out looking like a sewer?"

"It's shit-coloured?"

"Just think about that next time you come over all faint when you see one of us."

"What do you do about the smell?"

"Lynx Africa prophylactic. That stuff is the Teflon of the odour world."

"Yep, works like Teflon for me."

"I can buy some if you want. Just in case looking like a giant tūtae isn't enough."

"I think I'd prefer the guano."

"Big call, but OK."

I took my tea to the bathroom, ran a deep bath, and added a liberal dash of some exorbitantly-priced bubble bath I had found at the store.

I eased myself in, the cooling bubbles bursting under my chin in soft snaps, and closed my eyes.

Andrew's and Ted's voices drifted in snatches through the open window. I couldn't hear what they were saying, but judging by the amount of laughter coming from Andrew, Ted was either much more of an entertainer than I would give him credit for, or Andrew was just as generous with humouring others as he was with everything else.

I reached towards the hand basin to grab the soap and stopped mid-reach. The bath had seemed to list as I shifted my weight.

I sat back carefully and eyed the end of the bath against the bottom of the window. Sure enough, it was no longer level. The right-hand edge of the bath tilted downwards.

It occurred to me that it might be a good idea to remove myself from the water should the situation worsen.

Before I could lever myself out, my bottom vibrated with the shuddering of wood under too much strain. Then with a series of high-pitched cracks, the boards beneath the bath splintered, and I disappeared beneath the floor.

CHAPTER TWELVE

THE BATH REVERBERATED with a *TWANG* as it hit the dirt.

When the dust settled, and I had cleared my lungs in a series of wracking coughs, I enjoyed a calm moment appraising the new and rather spectacular view of the floorboards, which were now at chin height.

The bath had remained intact apart from the plughole, which stood in its original position at floor level, the plumbing having punched through the drainage hole as the bath dropped. In a rather pathetic denouement to the dramatic intensity of the previous minute, the water sluggishly wheezed and sucked its way out the gap, leaving me coated in cooling, brown-flecked bubble-bath froth.

A distant "Em?" floated in through the window, and I wondered if I should make an effort to move. Neither my brain nor my limbs could find the ability to speak to one another, so I stayed where I was.

Footsteps thudded across the living room and up the hall. It was only a matter of moments before Andrew burst in on me, and I couldn't find it within me to care.

A succession of rapid knocks echoed around the bathroom. "Em, you OK?"

I was pretty sure I was, but *erm* was the only sound my mouth was capable of producing.

The door creaked open.

"Ah..." said the voice at the door.

"Ah indeed," I responded, finding my tongue. "You know, I always fancied a sunken bath."

A second pair of footsteps beat their way to the bathroom door.

"Ooh, that's a trick," said a plummy voice. "It's lucky you weren't sitting at the other end, my girl. You would have been impaled arse to eyeballs."

I looked over my shoulder at the doorway, realising that between the foam and the level of the bath, my nakedness was more or less obscured.

Andrew's eyes were large, his nostrils flaring in a stifled laugh. Ted stood behind him, peering over his shoulder while a cat wound itself around his ankles.

"You going to invite the whole neighbourhood?" I

raised my eyes to meet Andrew's and held them for a moment before Andrew cracked, opening his mouth in a full-throated laugh and holding the sides of his belly as if it might split from the effort of it.

I might have been justified in expecting a little more concern about my well-being, but his reaction allowed me to see I had a choice in my own – give in to the shock of it and cry, channel my anger (yet again) and shout, or join him in seeing the farce of the situation.

Clinging to the side of the bath, I permitted myself to choose the latter. I let go of all the crap that had gravitated around me since arriving on the island – Warren's desertion, the subsequent and humiliating pursuit, the grim reality of buying a house unseen, my rather challenging employment situation. "This house is a shithole," I wheezed through my chortling. "I couldn't have done worse if I'd built it myself."

When I ran out of laugh, I felt a lot better.

I declined Andrew's offer to hose me down, choosing to enjoy the rest of the evening from the back porch. Just me and my new-found weightlessness.

And a bottle of wine.

Lord knows what I was going to do to keep myself clean, but after the first glass, I found I really didn't care that much.

ON TUESDAY MORNING I received a text.

Anaru: Have you got over yourself yet?

I presumed he was talking about my inability to see him in uniform without radiating heat from the neck up.

Me: Maybe. Why?

Anaru: I'm going to be checking a trap line today and thought you might like to learn a little about why we do what we do here

Me: Will you be wearing your uniform?

Anaru: If I say no will you come?

Me: Sigh. I suppose

Anaru: Good. Pick you up in half an hour. Wear sturdy shoes

ANDREW WAS, of course, wearing his uniform. It looked no worse on him than the other day.

"Liar," I greeted his open window as I approached his Department of Conservation utility vehicle. I'd heard the toot as I placed my water bottle in my backpack, and I made great efforts to walk purposefully but calmly down the driveway. I didn't want him to think I would do anything like rushing for him.

"No, I misled you."

"Misleader."

A child sat in the front seat. Its eyes peered over the top of the dash and followed me as I made my way around to the back door.

Great. I wasn't good with children, and I knew I probably wasn't going to do myself any favours in front of Andrew. I had no idea how to interact with them. The only thing I knew for sure was that they were completely unpredictable.

I climbed in and positioned myself directly behind Andrew, so that I could see as little of him as possible.

The child, who I now saw was a girl, had turned when I stepped up into the ute and rested her head against her hands on the back of the seat, watching me, eyes unblinking.

I pressed myself into my seat, placing my bag on my lap.

"Em, this is Iwa."

We eyed each other, and I remembered that, as the adult, I should be the one to make the first move. I shifted my bag onto the seat beside me and sat up straighter. "Hi, Iwa." The lightness I tried to shoehorn into my voice caused it to career upwards to a falsetto.

Iwa continued to stare at me, eyes unblinking.

Andrew gave her a little nudge. "Say, kia ora."

Iwa's mouth moved, but no sounds issued from it.

"Iwa's from the station. You know, the massive iwi-run farm behind the fence? She's learning how to be a pest control badass, aye Iwa?"

She nodded, her chin stationary against the seat, the top of her head bobbing up and down.

"Oh," I said, helpfully oiling the conversation. Then, "You don't live on the station?"

"No. All the DoC accommodation's off-site. The only people living behind the fence are the station families and workers. Like Wolf."

"Wolf lives there?"

"Yeah, he mostly does shearing, which is why he's got time on his hands at the moment. Winter shearing's a good couple of months' away."

"Is he local?"

Anaru shook his head. "Comes from Southland."

I grunted. "Odd name for a shearer. Awarded through reputation or self-anointed?"

"Hopefully not reputation." Andrew nudged Iwa again. "Sit in your seat properly."

As she turned, she said, "She has cool hair."

Andrew laughed and reversed down the driveway. "Yep. Just don't ask her where she got it from." He looked at me in his rear vision mirror and said, "The kids on the island learn from a very young age how to be the best kaitiaki – guardians – of this place that they can. The station kids get it from two directions – the school and their home environment, so it's part of the culture here, at least for the younger generations."

"That's good," I said, and peered at the back of his head, willing my brain to come up with something fascinating to say. After several long seconds of silence, I finally thought of a way to engage Iwa.

"How old are you, Iwa?"

"I'm eight," she said, and looked out the window, slamming the door on my brilliant conversation opener.

I opened my mouth again but couldn't think of another question, so I turned to look out the window, too.

After a few minutes, Andrew turned off the main road onto a narrow track fit only for four-wheel drive vehicles. The forest thickened and the canopy umbrella-ed over the road, throwing the ute into halflight. "Where are we going?" I asked.

"Why don't you tell her, Iwa?" Andrew said.

She shook her head and continued to watch out her window.

Andrew reached over and tickled her. "You got the shy cooties?" His eyes met mine in the rear vision mirror again, and he said, "She's a motormouth at home. Can't keep her tongue still enough for anyone to answer her hundred and one questions. She's got a big mind to feed." He poked her gently in the belly. "It's hungrier than your puku."

Iwa squirmed and giggled.

Andrew continued, "We're going up Maukohu, the smaller of the island's two mountains, to check the traps on one of the shorter lines. It gets done twice a week because of a concentrated population of little spotted kiwi there. Mostly we get nothing, which is great, but we still have to check regularly because the traps aren't self-setting. Once it's sprung, it's ineffectual until we reset it."

"That sounds pretty labour intensive. No wonder there's so many of you."

"Nah, most of our trapping technology is less hands-on. There's just a few critical areas we like to keep a close eye on."

"How long's the walk?"

"Not long. A couple of hours. It's pretty short as the crow flies, but we have to keep stopping and checking traps."

The road ended in a small parking area. Andrew pulled up next to a sign with a Department of Conservation logo marking the start of a walking track.

The first trap was stationed below the sign, and once we had feet on the ground and backpacks on, Andrew signalled for us to sit down so he could demonstrate how the trap worked.

He rummaged around in his bag, bringing out a set of tools.

"Chocolate brownie?" he asked, handing me a small brown square from a container.

"Yum, yes please." The square felt dry and looked slightly fuzzy. I glanced up at Andrew. His deadpan expression prompted me to hold it up to my nose and sniff it.

A rank mustiness unfurled itself in my nostrils. "Eurgh, what is it?" I looked at it again. "Is that...fur?"

A chuckle. "Dehydrated rabbit. High-end candy

in the rodent and feline world. You wanna try? It's just like biltong. I hear."

"Only hairier." I peered at the square more closely. "Is that a bit of bone?"

Andrew shrugged. "Waste not."

Iwa watched our exchange with wide eyes and an open-mouthed grin. "I bet you won't," she said to me.

"Won't what?"

"Eat some."

"I reckon you're right."

Her little face closed down, and she turned her head outwards from our people-triangle and faced the bush.

I clucked my tongue. "Alright, then."

Her head whipped around, grin reinstated.

I slowly brought the piece up to my open mouth, keeping eye contact with her. At the last moment before it entered my mouth, I darted my tongue out, licking the point of one corner.

Iwa squealed with delight and clapped her hands, and I knew I had won her over.

"Mmmm," I said. "Game-y with subtle notes of clover and dandelion." I held the dried meat out to her. "Go on, it's delicious."

She shuffled backwards, shaking her head and giggling.

I offered it to Andrew.

"God no, I'm no sucker for dares."

"Coward."

He gave a single nod. "I'm comfortable with my decision."

I tossed the square back to him, and he caught it one-handed. "Right, where's my water?" I asked into the depths of my bag. "That was gross."

Andrew studied me. "I can't decide whether you've gone up or down in my estimation."

"I'm comfortable with that," I said, taking a slug of water. "What does that do?" I pointed at a metal contraption with a hinged leg.

"This is my trap setting tool. It's pretty important, but not the most critical. This" – he held up a pair of barbecue tongs – "is the holy grail of trap clearing equipment." He held up his other hand and wiggled his fingers. "Saves these from having to go anywhere near a hand-crushing trap or a rotting animal carcass. Pays to wash the tongs first before you put them back in the kitchen drawer."

"I bet you never make that mistake twice," I said, wrinkling my nose.

Andrew grimaced and whispered to Iwa, "Don't tell my flatmate."

Iwa laughed and said, "You don't have a flatmate."

"Here." He passed her the container of rabbit meat. "You hang onto that. You can be in charge of luring the enemy."

· · ·

IWA and I took turns at setting and rebaiting the next few traps while Iwa ran a monologue of eight-year-old concerns, like whether it was OK to prefer the written adventures of Hiccup the dragon tamer over princesses with secret identities and an unlimited power to vanquish their friends' most pressing pony problems. The answer was fairly obvious, but Iwa didn't pause to hear any opinion about it.

When she appeared to collapse a lung from the dual task of walking and talking, she turned to questions.

She wanted to know what it was like living in a desert. I said I couldn't tell her because I'd lived in a city in a fairly green part of Australia. Yes, I'd seen kangaroos. No, I didn't know what one tasted like. She also determined that I'd never had snake bite, spider bite or shark bite. Iwa stopped asking me questions about Australia after that.

As we approached trap eleven, we were met by the nose hair-curling stench of decaying meat. Iwa, having taken the lead for the entire trek, stopped in her tracks and backed up a few paces.

"Oh my God, that smells awful," I said needlessly.

Andrew crouched down and peered through the grill of the trap. "Looks like we have a winner." He sat back on his haunches, wrinkling his nose. "If it's that decomposed, we must have missed this trap last check." He looked up at me. "Care to do the honours?"

"Fuck off," I said, then slapped my hand over my mouth and glanced at Iwa who had the end of her shirt sleeve pressed to her nose. "I mean 'no'. Thank you."

"I bet you, you won't," Andrew said with a grin.

I flicked my eyes back to Iwa.

She looked from me to Andrew and winked. *Winked.*

I clucked my tongue. "Fine. Being the sucker for dares that I am. Bring it on."

I took a deep breath and, crouching down beside Andrew, held my hand out like a surgeon about to perform an operation. "Screwdriver," I said, trying to waste as little as possible of the precious air in my lungs. The tool was slapped onto my palm.

I undid the screw and turned my head to take a new breath. When I turned back, Andrew had swung the lid of the box open.

Inside, flattened by the steel jaws of the trap, was a heaving grey sack with a tail. The now fur-less skin writhed with new life, the feeding frenzy unhindered by the press of metal bars. Maggots spilled from the rat's mouth, white and wriggling and fat, and the area of the rat's body not caught in the trap was tight and bloated.

"Man," said Andrew, "just goes to show what a few days in high heat can do. That's one of the best I've seen." In the hushed tones of the awestruck, he added, "I think it's liquefied."

I gave him a withering look and held out my hand again. "Trap releasing tool."

The metal contraption slid between my fingers.

I took another breath over my shoulder and eased the jaws open, securing them in place with a pin that would prevent them accidentally closing on me.

"Tongs?"

"Tongs," Andrew said, placing them in my hand.

I eased the two points around the body and squeezed them together to make sure I had good purchase. The rat squelched.

"Chuck it into the bush. As far as you can."

I pulled the small body free, raining maggots over the metal pressure pad and the wooden wall of the box, and prepared to heave it between the surrounding tree trunks.

With a *shlop*, the rat's putrefied innards emptied themselves out its anus and over the toe of my three-hundred-dollar shoe.

I dropped the rat and turned to retch into the leaf litter.

"That's a new one," said Andrew mildly. "Never had a puker on their maiden run."

"Awesome," said Iwa.

My stomach spasmed again, the trail of bile and saliva that connected my mouth to the ground twisted and thickened.

I staggered to my feet, ripping my soiled shoe off, and throwing it at Andrew. "You can fuck off."

I hobbled a few metres up the track and gasped at the stench-free air. Then I sank to the ground and star-fished across the track. Closing my eyes, I listened to Andrew finishing the trap-setting procedure and Iwa giggling into her sleeve.

I had one luxurious minute of birdsong before the crunching of leaves announced Andrew and Iwa's arrival.

"You OK?" Andrew asked.

I nodded and brushed at the tickling feet of an insect on my cheek.

"Have some of this."

I opened one eye. Andrew stood above me, a water bottle on offer in his left hand.

I sat up and took it from him, drinking without touching the neck to my bile-tainted lips.

"I washed your shoe," Iwa said, with more cheer than the task deserved. "I had to use all my water, and it still smells a bit, but it's OK, I guess. You have to wear it anyway or you'll stub your toe or something."

"Thanks, Iwa. That was very nice of you. You can have some of my water when you get thirsty."

"Nah, I'll just fill my bottle at the next stream." She turned and started walking up the track. Then turned back again when we didn't follow. "Come on!" She slapped her hand against her thigh as if calling a dog. "I want to see what's in the next one."

I groaned and pulled on my shoe, being careful not to touch any of the wet fabric.

Andrew held out his hand and, clasping mine, levered me to my feet. He gave my hand a small squeeze before dropping it. "Back on the horse, Puka-hontas. Let's go."

HALF AN HOUR LATER, the trees thinned and opened out to reveal an expansive view of the west side of the island and the large stretch of ocean between it and the mainland.

"Stop here for some kai?" Andrew asked.

Iwa and I dropped our bags without answering and sat on the ground facing the view. Andrew eased himself down so that Iwa sat between us, her small feet waggling from side to side.

I fetched two bananas from my bag and handed one to Iwa.

Andrew pulled a block of chocolate out of his, looked at our bananas, and said, "You guys won't want any of this, aye?"

Iwa dropped her banana and held out her hand.

"Only the best rewards for the best helpers," Andrew said, placing a couple of pieces in her palm.

She put it in her mouth, and I asked her if she'd checked for fur and bones. She paused in her chewing and eyed me for a brief moment before smiling and continuing her sucking.

When the chocolate was offered to me, I took a

whole row, deciding that as a rotten rat casualty I deserved it. I stuffed four pieces in my mouth, and before I could make room for the remaining two, they were snatched from my hand. I looked down into Iwa's grin, and she palmed them into her mouth before I could get a word out.

I nudged her with my elbow, and she leaned slightly into me.

We sat still, contemplating the wideness of the view, the muted crunch of chocolate and the rich birdsong the only sounds.

"Look, there's Hikurangi," Iwa said thickly through her mouthful.

I leaned over and looked down her arm, following the direction of her pointed finger. A large lump in the dark line of land on the horizon suggested it was a mountain she was talking about.

"You can see snow on it in winter," said Andrew.

"Really? I didn't think it snowed this far north."

Andrew nodded. "At altitude." He slipped a piece of chocolate into his mouth and, pocketing it in his cheek, asked, "Know the legend of this place? Why it's called Ruatapu?"

I shook my head. Iwa stared at me like I'd been living on the moon my whole life.

"You don't know?" she asked. "Everyone knows that story. My koro tells it best."

"Would you like to tell me?" I asked.

"OK." Iwa smacked her lips and took a deep breath. "Well, in Hawaiki – you know, like our homeland before we came here –"

"To Aotearoa," interrupted Andrew.

"Ah, to New Zealand," I added, to show that my moon-dwelling was more of the stopover variety.

"– there was this important chief called Uenuku who had lots of sons, like a hundred or something, and he had this huge waka built for them –"

"A canoe?" I asked.

Iwa nodded her head once and continued, "– and it was really beautiful. He had his best carvers work on it. Then he called all his sons together and began to do their hair into topknots so they would look all nice for when they sailed out on it. But when it was Ruatapu's turn, Uenuku wouldn't do his hair. He said, 'Why Dad?' and Uenuku said," – Iwa dropped her chin and affected a deep voice – "'Because you are the son of a slave woman and your hair is not tapu.'"

"Sacred," Andrew explained.

"Yeah," Iwa agreed, "sacred. 'And this comb is only for tapu hair.' And Ruatapu was really shamed out, so at night he went and put a big hole in the waka and filled it with leaves and stuff so no one would notice, and the next day when all the sons sailed the waka, they went waaaay out to sea, and then the waka filled with water, and Ruatapu just laughed while all his brothers drowned."

"That's a really sad story."

"It's not finished. We haven't got to the best bit. One survived. He was called –" Iwa turned to me and raised her hands as if doing a big reveal. "– Paikea."

I didn't know of any Paikea.

"The whale rider?" she prompted.

I grimaced.

"There's a movie. You haven't seen the movie?"

"I haven't seen the movie."

"Well, anyway, Paikea calls a whale to help him because Tangaroa was like his great-great-grandfather or something –"

"God of the sea," Andrew said.

"– and he takes off and Ruatapu knows magic and he sends big waves after Paikea, but the whale dives under the waves and the waves just bounce back off the land and waste Ruatapu. So he drowns, too. And Paikea's whale takes him all the way to New Zealand. It's an island over there." Iwa pointed up to the coast of the mainland.

"And...we're sitting on Ruatapu's drowned and bloated body?"

"Yep. Cool story, aye?"

"Cool story," I confirmed. "What's 'koro'?" I carefully tried the word out, my attempt at rolling the "r" momentarily gluing my tongue to the roof of my mouth so that it sounded like "kodo".

"Grandad," Iwa answered, giving me the moon look again. "You should know words like that. You need to come to our kura pō. We run night classes for people like you."

"Like me?"

"People who don't know their arse from their elbow."

Andrew's shoulders shuddered in a silent chuckle.

"Well, that's what my koro says. He says there's no excuse for ignance these days. So we teach them some reo and tikanga."

"Teach what?"

"How to speak Māori," Andrew answered.

"And about our culture," added Iwa, in a tone that suggested he'd forgotten the most important bit.

"I don't..." I faltered. "I'm not really –"

"You look scared," Iwa interrupted. "Don't worry, I'll be there. I'm a good teacher. We do stuff with coloured sticks. You learn with the sticks."

"Those rods you probably learned maths with at school," said Andrew.

"You can teach language with those?"

Iwa nodded. "It's really fun. Like playing with Lego."

"And," said Andrew, "you can learn how to say my name."

I didn't respond. Better to stay silent than accept or deny.

"Don't think I haven't noticed you never call me

by my name. You still think of me as Andrew, don't you?"

"No," I lied. "Look, it's right here in my phone." I booted it to life and showed him the contact entry for him.

He raised an eyebrow and said, "Ok then, how do you say it?"

I snorted and looked out at the view like contemplating its vastness absorbed all of my brain power.

"Em? Give it go."

My shoulders slumped. "I'll get it wrong."

"I'd rather you gave it a go and got it wrong than never used my name at all."

"Shouldn't we be getting on with scraping some putrid animal carcass from a trap?"

"Em?"

"OK," I sighed. "Don't hate me for butchering it."

Andrew placed a hand on Iwa's shoulder, presumably to discourage her from laughing. It did nothing for my confidence. Their two faces bore such earnest expressions of expectation, that I had to push down a rising sense of stage fright.

The first two syllables were simple enough, it was that rolled "r" that left my tongue quaking between my teeth. The problem was, it didn't really know what to do.

Andrew read my anxiety perfectly. "Rrrrrrr," he said, vibrating his tongue against the roof of his mouth.

"Rrrrrrr," I said back.

"You got it, sister. Now give the whole thing a go."

He smiled at me. One of those wide, open-mouthed types that goes all the way to your eyes and makes the person on the receiving end feel like a piece of their chest is melting.

So I gave it a go. I got through the first part and tried so hard to make my tongue reverberate against my soft palate that I completely overdid it. But the sound was there.

Andrew nodded. "Not bad. You might want to go easy on the 'r', though."

"And the 'a' at the start isn't like that," said Iwa.

"You're saying it like you would 'Andrew'. It's uh as in 'up'," he said.

"Or 'uncle'," said Iwa. "*U*ncle *A*naru. Same same."

My second attempt was much better, and Iwa gave me a high five.

"Nice one, Em," Anaru said quietly. Then his smile curled into his right cheek, and he reached over and touched a finger to my temple. "I hear your thoughts, gypsy woman. If you think of me as Andrew again, I'll commission a Rangers of New Zealand calendar and hang it above your bed."

I rolled my eyes. "That was so yesterday. I'm into hazmat suits now."

. . .

I DIDN'T GET to "the office" until 1pm. No one seemed to notice I was four hours late, either here or across the ditch. It didn't matter. I could still put in my allotted hours and be home well in time for dinner.

I worked straight through without coffee, pee or exchanging-puerile-witticisms-with-Wolf breaks. I wasn't distracted at all by thoughts of lopsided smiles and hand squeezes. And I definitely didn't spend any time envisaging broad shoulders tapering into lean, belted waistlines.

I groaned.

I wondered how practical a hazmat suit would be for ranging in sub-tropical forests.

"What are the chances of nuclear fallout around here?" I asked Don.

He didn't miss a beat. "Now, I'm no expert on these matters, Em, but I'd say slim to none."

I closed the lid of my laptop with a bit more force than necessary. "Well, we'll see about that." I stood up and headed for the door. "I'm going home to troll Kim Jong-un, then we'll see who's laughing in the morning."

NORTH KOREA DID NOT DECLARE war with New Zealand in the intervening hours between my visits to the store, but a disaster of a similar magnitude attempted to turn my day upside down anyway.

The ferry was an hour late.

After fifteen minutes of it failing to appear in the harbour below, I began to pace the shop floor. After thirty, I ordered a second piece of cake and a double-shot espresso.

I was told not to worry, the ferry often got delayed at the mainland if it had a lot of freight.

Did it ever correspondingly leave late from here? I wanted to know.

Don's "No" had me pacing double-time and sweat prickling down my back and under my breasts.

When the ship's horn finally announced its arrival and echoed across Port Keulemans and up the valley to the shop, I turned to Wolf.

He lounged in customary style against the store counter and winked at me.

I now had a fairly small margin to get my household goods shifted into my home and the moving truck back on the return ferry, or I would be putting the driver up for a week and paying for his downtime.

I had one complication. I was relying on Wolf and his mates to meet the truck at mine and help offload.

"Don't you worry yourself," Wolf said, taking a sip of his coffee. "We'll get you sorted." He placed the cup back into its saucer and clasped his hands across his lean belly.

"Don't worry? Why the fuck are you still here?"

"Language, Em."

"Sorry, Trace. I'm just," I looked at Wolf and hissed, *"freaking the fuck out.* You should have been at the house forty minutes ago, and now our window's even narrower."

Wolf smiled at his shoes then looked up at me from under his eyebrows. "You get down to the port and meet your woofer, and I'll sort the rest."

"You better fucking..." I whispered with enough ferocity to encourage a rare glint of teeth in Wolf's normally closed-lipped smile. Grabbing my keys, I ran for the door, tipping my chair over and rebounding off DoC employee-of-the-day number six as I rounded the end of the sanitary aisle. Packets of nappies *thunk*ed on the floor behind me, and I shouted a "Sorry" that I hoped would cover all sweary, demand-y and barge-y transgressions.

The four boys, their bodies positioned out to the road and towards the possible but unlikely influx of young, bronzed tourists, turned in unison to watch me scramble out the door and sprint for the ute.

"Boys," I said in acknowledgment. It came out less as a greeting and more as a bark. The nearest boy flinched.

A low-slung sedan had been parked in such a manner that it was wedged haphazardly between the grass verge and my truck. There was no time to run around it. I attempted to leap, hip down and legs raised, across the bonnet, in the hope my momentum would allow me a movie-like slide.

Only I jumped too high and hit the metal hard on my descent. I didn't so much as slide as bounce, the jut of my hip bone momentarily halting my trajectory and forcing me into a sideways roll. I landed beside my driver's door as if I had planned all along to execute my manoeuvre in such an awkward way, and had the engine running before I was in the seat.

At the table, a chorus of sympathetic "Ooooohs" was answered by a guffaw. All but one of the boys had both hands clamped over their mouths, shoulders shaking. I wound down my window, shouted, "Tell the owner I'll pay for any damage," and reversed with a squeal onto the Port Keulemans road.

I MADE it to the wharf as the first car rolled off the ramp. Macca directed it towards the car park exit and turned to gesture to the large furniture truck rumbling out of the bowels of the ferry.

"Shit, shit, shit," I muttered, swinging the ute into the carpark and leaving the engine idling as I jumped out and ran towards the truck.

The driver's window rolled down, and a heavily tattooed forearm was laid across the window slot.

"Hey-ey," I sing-songed, fighting to hide the panic rising in my gut. "How you going?"

"You Mrs Stewart?" was directed politely enough out of the darkness of the cab.

"*Ms* Stewart. Em, actually." I shielded my eyes against the sun and attempted to find a face to direct my question to. "Know where you're going?"

The arm momentarily vanished and reappeared with a smart phone. "There isn't anywhere on this earth that isn't mapped by Google."

I tried a flippant laugh but only managed a nasaly "haw", like a donkey with a head cold. "Actually, the phone signal's a bit patchy where I live. Can you screenshot the map?"

"Should be able to."

"Good. There'll be a team of helpers on site when you get there with a map of where to put every-thing. I'll be along in a while. I've got a couple of things to sort here first." I gave the truck a rap and turned to check the stream of cars descending from the ferry.

A dark blue, road-beaten van veered from the line and approached me. I waved at it and forced my lips to stretch past my teeth. I hoped they moved in an upwards direction. The memory of Wolf's calm reassurance as he attempted to do absolutely nothing played itself out in my head while the truck disap-peared around the first corner on the Port Keulemans Road.

I turned my attention back to the van, and a pale-faced, dark-haired teenager looked out at me from behind the windscreen. He couldn't have been more than seventeen.

I peered behind him to where the line of vehicles had been a minute before, but the only people descending from the ferry were the foot passengers. It appeared the seventeen-year-old was indeed the person I would be sharing my new life with.

A muted "Em?" issued from the still-closed van.

I nodded, and the door swung open.

My *mouth* swung open as the driver revealed himself.

The seventeen-year-old had come in fancy dress. Pulled low on his head was a black wide-brimmed hat with a rounded crown; a black corduroy double-breasted jacket had been buttoned tightly against the late summer heat; and black flared corduroy trousers balanced the broadness of his headgear.

"I'm Ruben," said Ruben, offering a sweaty palm for me to shake.

"You're..." I wasn't sure which words I wanted to put after that one – a toddler? Just passing through to the seventies from the Renaissance?

Ruben chuckled at my hesitation and unbuttoned his jacket, revealing a black double-breasted waistcoat over a white shirt. "I'm a journeyman." He gestured to his clothes. "This is my Kluft."

"Wait. What?"

"It's a tradition after you finish your apprenticeship. We travel for three years and one day, and work in our craft. I must wear these clothes the whole time."

"The *whole* time?"

"Yes."

"But they're so..." Impractical in this heat? Comic? "You must get a lot of attention. Do you have a clothes holiday when you wash them?"

Ruben laughed again. "Clothes holiday. I like this."

I clapped him on the back and steered him towards the ferry. "Well Ruben, thank you for assuming fresh meat status with such theatrical flair. I should be able to quietly fade into the background. Come on, let's have a look at your building materials."

I HAD to negotiate space in the wharf sheds for what we couldn't fit into my ute and Ruben's van. Macca played hard to get and hummed and hawed until I sweetened the deal with the promise of first slice in Trace's next Black Forest gâteau.

Halfway home, the removal truck approached our small convoy on a slow bend, its unloading apparently already done. Despite the curve of the road and the subsequent need to steering-wheel wrestle, a double thumbs up appeared above the dash of the truck, and I promised to share tomorrow's double cake portion with Wolf. And speak with less shout and more calm to him.

However, when I pulled up at the house, the driveway was empty. I thought it strange, given the promise of chips and beer to Wolf and his moving team. When I parked the car, I understood why.

Wolf had made sure to lay out all the contents of my house according to the plan I'd given him. Only not inside.

CHAPTER THIRTEEN

"I THINK these men must have played a joke on you," said Ruben.

"No, no. I'm all for alfresco living. You know, I should have thought of this before. Would have saved the trouble of needing to find a builder." With a "Fuu-uuuuck," I sank onto the crocodile skin couch. Ruben and I had a long afternoon ahead of us. "I'm going to kill that smug son of a bitch."

As Ruben eased himself onto the other end of the couch, the friction of the ribbed fabric of his trousers against the smooth leather sounded like air escaping from a flaccid balloon.

He grimaced and said sorry, flapping his hand in the air as if to ward away a smell.

I laughed. I threw my head back and roared at the generosity of his silly joke and the subsequent easing of tension, and I roared at the boldness of Wolf's prank. It was actually pretty bloody brilliant, if exceptionally inconvenient.

After I'd wiped at the tears on my face and my diaphragm settled into its normal rhythm, I offered a beer to Ruben. "We have a lot of beer to get through, if they didn't nick off with them all."

One beer and a question-and-answer journey into Ruben's childhood later, I decided we needed to share the joke.

I took a photo of Ruben lounging on the couch, beer in hand, bowl of potato chips on his stomach, and the house contents laid out behind him.

I sent it to Anaru with the message *Turns out I don't need the house after all. Silly me.*

Twenty minutes later, a very sweaty, very topless Anaru emerged from around the side of the house, breathing heavily from his run, but still finding room in his lungs to laugh at length at my misfortune.

"Oh, thank goodness you're not wearing your uniform. This," I said, gesturing to his flexing abs, "does nothing for me."

"No?" he said, his laughter settling into a low chuckle.

"No." I turned away from him and looked at the view. "Dry as a lizard's eyeball, me."

Anaru renewed his chortling. "God, I love that cutting Aussie humour. You love your metaphors. You guys probably come out of the birth canal saying"

– he affected a broad Australian accent – "the jacuzzi was fair dinkum but the hydro slide was a bit shit."

I forced out a bray of a laugh and said, "Put your bloody t-shirt on, you barbarian."

He pulled it out of the back of his shorts and walked over to Ruben, holding out his hand. "Kia ora. Anaru."

Ruben shook it and said, "Kia ora," as confidently as if he'd been saying it his whole life. I envied him his language-assuredness, which presumably came from being able to speak at least two languages with proficiency. "Ruben."

As Anaru pulled his t-shirt on, a bead of sweat ran between his pectorals, accelerating as it neared his belly button. Not that I was looking. "Cool outfit," he said to Ruben.

"It's his Kluft," I said, grabbing a beer out of the chilly bin. I handed it to Anaru and patted the space between Ruben and me.

"Of course it is," he said, feigning solemnity. Then he frowned at the glossy scales of the couch. "I should probably...do you have a towel?"

"In the bathroom. First door on the left," I said, pointing in the direction of a large box labelled "bathroom".

Anaru retrieved a towel and laid it over the couch, sitting with a sigh and taking a long slug of his beer. "So, tell me about your Kluft."

While Ruben explained the journeyman tradition, I closed my eyes and rolled the perspiring beer bottle across my forehead. It was *so hot*, even in my sensibly-chosen loose singlet top and short shorts. I couldn't get any closer to naked.

I cracked my eyes and peered at Ruben. Of all the thick layers of clothing he'd arrived in, he'd only shed his jacket. His cheeks bore a rosy tint, but little more than what might be interpreted as a young person in good health. Apart from that, he looked perfectly comfortable.

Perhaps it had less to do with the air temperature and everything to do with the close proximity of a particular bare-armed and bare-legged DoC ranger. I grabbed a handful of chips and tried to drown out my thoughts with vigorous crunching.

"It's difficult," Ruben was saying, "because you can only take a small amount of money with you, so it can take some time to have money for tools. I'm lucky that the wan was given to me."

"The what?" I asked, before I'd given it any proper thought. "Oh, the *van*."

"Yes, van." He tapped his forehead. "I must remember."

"So, you work for money as well as woofing?" asked Anaru.

"I woof for board and a small wage. My work is specialised enough that I can ask for a bit of money, too. I'm not permitted to take business away from local carpenters, so this way is good. Not everyone wants their workers to live with them."

"You won't have any trouble saving money here. Em's house needs rebuilding from the piles up, and there's nothing to spend your money on here on the island."

"I only need enough to travel to the next place. When I return to Germany, I can only bring with me the same amount of money I had when I left."

"Well, if you ever feel the need to shed some cash, I can think of several worthy causes you can donate to."

"A new uniform fund?" I suggested.

"Or another egg incubator. Possibly just as important." Anaru nudged me, and our skin stuck for a fraction of a second longer than the brief contact should have allowed. Ordinarily I would have been mildly grossed out by being suctioned onto someone else courtesy of our mutual sweat-glue, but I found I wanted to go back for more. More touch time, more skin.

I drew my legs underneath me and swung around so that I faced the conversation in the hope that my new position would place at least one part of my body in contact with at least one part of Anaru's. However, such was the length of the couch and the shortness of my femurs that my knees barely grazed his shorts. It might have been a good thing, given the somewhat scabrous state of them.

He placed his arms behind him on the back of the couch so that his forearms rested across it. I gave it a few minutes, then briefly went to search for something I didn't need in one of the boxes. When I returned, I sat on the back of the couch next to his right arm.

It took twenty minutes for Anaru to move his arm in such a way that it brushed against the skin of my thigh. By that time, I was one more beer down, deep in conversation, and completely forgetful of the reason for being precariously perched beside him.

The contact gave me such a surge of electricity that I lost my balance, rolled over backwards and, thanks to my compact size, executed a complete somersault. I landed on my hands and feet and jumped up in a "ta-da" pose as if I'd performed it deliberately.

Ruben snorted his beer down his shirtfront, and Anaru laughed into his fist, calling me an "egg" between chortles.

When I resettled myself onto the couch, he laid a hand on my arm and said, "You are too much. I didn't realise how dull life was here until you arrived."

IT TOOK us nearly two hours to shift everything into the house, mainly because we needed a beer break after lugging the heavy whiteware, and because I got distracted cooking sausages on my new-found barbecue when I decided that four beers apiece could probably do with some soaking up.

By the time we'd finished, I had a back lawn again but no floor space inside, courtesy of the high-density cardboard box population.

"All this fit in one truck?" Anaru had three cups of tea balanced between his hands.

"It'll fit. Once I get rid of Warren's crap, I'll have heaps of room."

"Holy shit, these are hot! There's nowhere to put them down."

"Hang on," I called. "I'll make a space on the coffee table."

"Where's that? I can't see you for the towers of cardboard."

"Marco," I said, reversing the game.

"Polo." Anaru's head appeared over the top of a stack of boxes. "You really aren't very tall, are you?"

"Small but mighty," I said, taking the first cup from his hands as he edged his way between the cartons into the tiny space I'd cleared.

We stood, not quite touching. I'd only managed to free up a small triangle on the corner of the coffee table, and the available standing room was barely a foot square.

"I wouldn't want to pick a fight with you."

"I know one person who'd bet on you winning," I said, thinking of the twelve-year-old at the store picnic table.

"It would be a wasted wager. You scare the crap out of me."

I snorted. "I do not." I raised my eyes from blowing on my tea and met his. Our gaze held for one second, then two. By second number three, the shared look had edged its way into that hazy area between uncomfortable and thrilling, and before I could determine in which direction it was moving, Ruben arrived from shifting his gear into the other front bedroom and shuffled sideways into the space.

I handed him a cup of tea.

"This is cosy," Anaru said, casting a grin between us.

"You should try living in a caravan," I said, before my brain could stop my tongue.

"You lived in a caravan?" asked Anaru.

"Once. Did you bring the biscuits?" I asked, peering into my tea as if one might emerge from its depths.

Anaru's brief silence indicated a deliberation and a choice to respect the reason for my evasion. "They're in my socks." He shrugged. "No pockets."

I smiled up at him, struck again at the extent of his generous nature. I could only hope to achieve half of his goodness.

IT WAS NEARLY eleven when Anaru finally put on his trainers to jog home. I closed the back door behind him and stumbled through the narrow path between the boxes en route to throwing myself on my queen-sized bed with crusty teeth, clothes and all.

As I walked past the bathroom, Ruben's voice drifted out. "Why do you have a picture of your family behind the mirror?"

I froze. He'd been here for all of five minutes and happened to find the one thing I didn't want anyone to see? There was no point in denying it. Even though I was a girl in the photo, she bore enough of a resemblance that I couldn't pass her off as anyone else. I settled on, "It's complicated," as an answer and moved towards the bathroom door.

"You don't want anybody to see it?"

"Not really," I said, pushing past him and removing the photo.

The bath-sized hole in the floor, with help from Anaru and Ted, had been covered up by a sheet of plywood. It had taken only one day of filth for me to crack and beg help in reinstating the bath. The feet of it now rested on planks of wood straddling the ply.

He said, "You are not close," as a statement, as if wanting to conclude the matter, but not offend me by prying.

"We're...it's complicated," I said again, walking into my bedroom to find another spot with which to secretly place the photo.

"You can tell me another time."

"Not likely, mate," I murmured, unzippering a

rediscovered bed cushion and slipping the photo inside. "Goodnight," I called, putting cheer into my voice, then adding an inane, "don't let the bed bugs bite."

"Gute Nacht," came the reply.

I ambled to the light switch and, finger hovering, turned to face my bed. "Hello you beautiful thing. I've missed you."

I LEFT VERY LATE for the store. I had risen early and unpacked as many boxes as I could, so that Ruben and I had somewhat of a functional living space. It took me longer than I wanted it to, but then it also allowed me to delay my Skype meeting with Warren. It was "catch-up on how Em's work's going" day.

I had left Ruben securing a bathroom floor solid enough to hold a full metal bath. As much as weather proofing the house was a priority, I figured a second bath-disappearing act might not end as well for the occupant as the first. I promised a fridge-full of culinary choices when I returned from work, hoping that Ruben showed as much prowess in the kitchen as he did wielding a drop saw.

Wolf was not glued to the counter when I arrived.

"Keeping a low profile today, I'd say," Don said when I asked where he was.

"Can't face the music?"

Don laughed. "Running scared."

"So he bloody should be," I said to play my part, but I couldn't help wondering what it was about me that frightened the men of Ruatapu.

"That was a rotten joke," Trace said, starting up the coffee machine for my long black. "Is everything still outside, or did you find some help?"

"I got it all in, thanks."

"Oh yes, your woofter's here, isn't he?"

"*Woofer*, Trace," said Don. "A woofter's another thing entirely." He contemplated the tin he was shelving. "Could be both, I s'pose. Is he both?"

"We didn't get around to discussing his sexual preferences, Don."

"He dresses a bit odd, from what I hear. Could prefer anything."

"And that would be fine if he did." I kept my voice flat in the hope it would sound pointed.

"As long as it's human and of age," Don said cheerily, *thunk*ing a can on top of another one.

"Don!" hissed Trace. "There could be other customers in here. You can't say things like that."

"Trace," I said, over the top of Don's reply, "I'm going to take my coffee outside. I have a meeting."

"Alright, love. I'll bring it out to you."

Kevin, hearing my voice and using his head like a

battering ram, trundled to my usual table and lay down underneath it.

I went over and gave him a pat. "Sorry, Kev. I have another man I have to be with right now, but he's got nothing on you. I'll be back soon."

Kevin wagged his stumpy tail as if he understood and I opened my laptop, clicked on the Skype app, and walked outside.

"God, you look good, Em," Warren said instead of greeting me.

"This is a call in a professional capacity, Warren. It's inappropriate to speak to your staff like that."

"Yes, you're right." He shuffled in his chair. "I apologise. Of course."

I took a sip of my coffee and prepared for Warren to start "touching base" with me. In a professional capacity.

"It's just things are so hard."

"Yes, they are."

Warren looked so forlorn that I stopped myself from reminding him that he was master of all of this difficulty and asked him instead if he would like to catch up on a personal level later.

"That would be nice. Thanks." He sat up straighter and put his game face on. "So...you seem to be keeping up with your projects effectively on your reduced hours. How are your stress levels?"

"Perfectly manageable when I'm not reminded

you're now my boss. I don't find this" – I gestured at us both – "particularly relaxing, but I'm starting to manage that as well. I no longer want to reach into the computer and punch you in the face. Metaphorically speaking, of course. Because that would be unprofessional."

Warren fiddled with his tie and laughed. "Good, good. I'd prefer not to have to get HR involved because we couldn't put our personal lives aside. And you're feeling better? I'm asking as a concerned boss. Mostly."

"Yep. My scalp's decided it wants to start keeping all my hair, and I'm putting on weight. And I'm enjoying my job again."

Warren smiled. "Thank goodness. I've been worried you'd ditch us as soon as you settled in."

"I'm managing my stress, so at the moment I don't feel the need to."

"It's been a good move for you, then."

"Yes."

A silence descended. It was loaded, but I didn't feel the need to explore it, and now wasn't the right time even if I did.

Warren breathed in sharply through his nose, clearly shifting gears, and said, "Look, this huia thing. I think there might be something in that."

"You're joking," I said after a pause.

"No. I mean you have to ask yourself why they have such an enormous fence."

"I don't. It's a sanctuary. They tend to have fences."

"Em, it's so big you can see it from space."

"Bullshit."

"OK, well not from space maybe, but it's very clear on Google Earth. It's massive, nearly a third of the island – way bigger than any other fenced-off sanctuary in New Zealand. It's unprecedented."

"So? Warren, do you know how ridiculous you're sounding? The size of a fence proves nothing."

"The height of it does. Or at least raises suspicion. Have you seen it?"

"Not yet."

"It's got to be fifty feet high. No predominantly ground-dwelling bird is getting out of that thing."

"Huia flew."

"I don't think they were great at it. They didn't need to be. They had no predators until humans arrived."

I said nothing. I folded my arms and let my body language do all the talking.

Warren took a deep breath and said, "It could be nothing –"

"It *will* be nothing."

"– but can you indulge my whim and see what you can find out? Get a bit cosy with the DoC staff?"

"No."

"This is a professional request, Em."

"They won't have Jurassic Park-ed an extinct bird,

Warren. They can't even afford a new egg incubator. Why am I even...this is ludicrous."

"They're short on funds?"

"Yes. And even if they weren't, they wouldn't spend it on resurrecting huia because they can't. The science isn't there yet."

"Yes it is."

I scoffed. "What?"

"I've read about it. They extract some DNA from a stuffed bird, synthesise the genes, and stick them to cells of a close relative, like another wattle bird, then they take those cells and inject them into a chicken fetus. That chicken then mates with another chicken who's undergone the same process, and their babies are huia."

"Bullshit. It can't be that simple."

"I don't think it is, but that's the gist of it."

I crossed my arms and stared at him for a few moments. "I'm not comfortable with *indulging your whim*."

"Except that it's part of your role as an analyst of potential investment opportunities to conduct research."

"No, it's not. Otherwise my job title would be Investment Researcher."

"Actually, it *is* in your job description. I checked. But let's not get into technicalities." He leaned into the screen, his eyes shining. "Now you know they *could* re-establish the huia population, aren't you just the tiniest bit curious?"

Goddamn him. I *was* curious. Highly sceptical, but my interest had been piqued. I had no doubt Warren's request was driven by some crazy idea for a potential investment, but I couldn't see why. It didn't matter. There were no huia on Ruatapu Island.

Before I went home, I sent Warren an email to his Gmail account asking how he was getting on with settling our assets.

I ARRIVED at the house to find Ruben preparing to go out on a date. The baby-faced bugger had been here for all of two seconds and was already in the game. Perhaps the women of Ruatapu were more aggressive in their approach than the men.

He still wore his Kluft, and I wondered how, after wearing it day after day and while working in the heat, he didn't smell like a horse. Maybe he had several sets and this one was his Sunday best.

"Who's your date with?"

"A woman named Mel. You know her?"

I shook my head.

"Will you be home tonight?" My query came out a little more needy than I wanted it to.

Ruben smiled and said, "Who knows."

"OK, then," I said, putting cheer into my voice. "I

won't wait up. I'll just be here. Sorting through boxes."

"This is a good idea. I think they are having babies."

His observation, though factually inaccurate, was a fair metaphor. The paths I'd cleared this morning so that we could access helpful pieces of furniture, like the washing machine, had become twisted and meandering. Boxes that *were* neatly stacked, were now strewn like debris from receding floodwaters.

It might have had something to do with me not being able to find the outfit I wanted to wear after tidying up in my pyjamas. Or I was just a glutton for punishment.

After Ruben left, I made a dinner sandwich (a normal sandwich but with twice the amount of everything) and drove to the beach for a picnic and a swim.

I carefully obeyed all parking signage, made sure there was no sandwich-eating or kaftan-wearing by-laws, and settled into enjoying my evening. Alone.

I was halfway through one of the beers we hadn't managed to drink the previous night, when my phone pinged with a message.

Anaru: Kiwi spotting? 9pm?

Perhaps I was about to join Ruben in the ranks of the date-worthy.

Me: Heck yes

Anaru: Ask Ruben

Or not.

Me: He's out cavorting with a mysterious woman
Anaru: Already?
Me: It's all that corduroy. He's lovely to stroke. Like a dog
Anaru: Are you going to write it or am I?
Me: What? Ribbed for her pleasure?
Anaru: I knew you'd come through. Pick you up at 9

I downed the rest of the beer, gathered my damp towel and sandwich wrapper, and hastened towards the ute. My urgency, I told myself, had everything to do with all the unpacking I had to do before Ruben came home and I left for the evening, and nothing to do with any kind of excitement I might have felt for spending more time with Anaru so soon after I last saw him.

Whatever the reason for my surge in energy, I managed to clear half the boxes in the lounge by the time Anaru knocked on my door.

I told him there was something I wanted to do before we left and led him over to my truck. Illuminated by the light from the kitchen window, I placed my hands on his upper arms and edged him into position.

His thigh fitted neatly into the dent in the wheel arch, though his hip would have taken much of the force of the impact. "You know, there might be something in that."

"In what?"

"According to local legend, you made this dent from stopping my car sliding over a bank."

"I did?"

"Kids think you're Iron Man." I gasped as a scenario played in my head. "That would be an awesome showdown."

"What would?"

"Iron Man versus Roboranger. How do you feel about doing mortal battle with a woman?"

"Is she particularly evil?"

I thought of my driver's license. "She's in possession of some sensitive information that could cause harm to innocent civilians."

"In that case, I'd take her down."

"Awesome." We started to walk down the driveway towards Anaru's ute.

"Roboranger did you say?"

I nodded.

Anaru laughed. "I think I know who you're talking about. Did she give you a dressing down for some misdemeanour?"

"Yeah. Man, she's one tough lady. I can't decide if I want to run screaming from her or marry her."

"She has that effect on people," Anaru said, opening his door and sliding into the driver's seat.

Once I'd climbed inside, I put on my seatbelt and looked across at him. "You could take her."

"I'm not so sure. She'd outwit me with her knowledge of parliamentary acts and council by-laws. I can't compete with that."

"You can stop a car with your thigh."

"True. I am pretty amazing."

We drove to the southern side of the mountain that Anaru, Iwa and I had checked the traps on a few days before and parked in another car park marked with DoC signage.

The headlights illuminated the bush in front of the ute. Towering podocarps, laced with epiphytes and garlands of dangling lichen disappeared into drifting banks of mist. It looked primordial, like at any moment the long neck of a Brachiosaurus might emerge from between the trunks.

"This is why the mountain is called *The Mist Gatherer* in Māori," Anaru said, handing me a head torch. "It's beautiful but kinda spooky."

"Yeah," I said, and wondered about the lifespan of the batteries. "You brought a spare power supply?"

"Got the full survival kit," he answered, patting his backpack. "Come on, let's go spot some kiwi."

We didn't get very far down the track when the first bird announced its presence with a piercing squawk.

"Fuck!" I jumped, colliding with Anaru and sending him stumbling off the path. "Sorry," I whispered. "It really is like someone screaming their last breath."

To our left, another bird answered.

"That's the male," said Anaru. "Hear how different his call is?"

"Yeah, way less Hitchcock."

"Let's wait here and see if they show themselves." Anaru squatted down on the path, and I followed. "Turn your head torch to the red setting."

"The what setting?" I turned to look at him and inadvertently shone my torch into his eyes.

He flinched and turned his head away. "Give me your torch." He held out his hand, face still averted.

He fiddled with a setting, then we were bathed in an eerie red glow. Handing it back to me, he said, "This colour is less intrusive. The birds aren't likely to be startled by it."

Anaru switched his torch over, and we settled into the quiet.

The problem was, the fright I had gotten from the bird call had forced all the excess liquid in my body to rush to my bladder. But I didn't want to ruin my chance of seeing my first kiwi by stepping out for a toilet break.

I bounced up and down on the balls of my feet, hoping the fluid would jiggle back to where it came from.

Anaru swivelled his head and watched me. "Great to see you so excited."

"I need to pee, but I don't want to miss it."

"Just go where you are. I'll shine my headlight in the other direction."

I didn't doubt him, but I wasn't keen on him hearing me expel the contents of my bladder.

The pressure ratcheted up a notch, and I knew I was in serious danger of wetting myself before I had a chance to see the national bird for the first time. I stood up, stepped off the path and found a tree with enough girth to give me privacy. Then I crouched down, the leaves of a native grass brushing against my legs and bottom.

With my small circle of illumination the colour of blood and my shallow breathing the only sound in the expansive black, I had an irrational fear that the darkness was closing in on me.

I forced my pee out to get rid of it as quickly as I could.

"You still there?" I whispered mid-stream.

"Still here."

A scream rang out somewhere to my right.

My heart jumped, flailing itself on my ribcage, and I stood up.

Fire ripped across the flesh between my legs.

I roared, bending over and peering at my vulva to see tiny seeds dangling from the smattering of stubble re-emerging after my last wax.

A red light flashed in my direction. "You OK?"

I hurriedly covered myself and stepped out from behind the tree, zipping up my fly. "What the fuck was that?" I said, all thoughts of whispering gone. "I just gave myself a Brazilian."

Anaru wheezed with laughter, rocking back on his heels, and tipping over onto his bum. "It'll be hook grass."

"It's evil."

"Look, it's got me, too." He pointed to the hair on his legs and the seeds dangling on his shins from where he had brushed up against the plants. He hadn't once uttered any word or sound of discomfort during our walk.

"You don't seem bothered by it," I said, my voice tending towards a whine.

"Used to it. Did you pull them off?"

"Fuck no. They're staying there until the hairs shed."

Anaru laughed again. "You do a good impression of a female kiwi. Curdled *my* blood." He grabbed me and held me in front of him.

"What are you doing?"

"Preparing for the stampede of horny males."

"Funny."

He let his hands drop and said, "Well, I think it's safe to say you've ruined that couple's romantic evening. We'll need to go up the track farther, see if we can find some more without freaking them out."

"What about them freaking *me* out?"

We walked in silence for a couple of minutes, our footfalls seemingly muted by the completeness of the surrounding black.

"I can't help thinking of the *Blair Witch Project*," I

whispered. "It's not helping to calm my mind. I want to be amped about this experience, and I'm failing miserably."

"You think the kiwis are conspiring to scare the shit out of you?"

"I think my imagination is."

Anaru stopped and put a hand out to halt my momentum.

"What is it?" I asked.

"Shhhh." He cocked his head. "Listen."

Up ahead of us, something crashed through the undergrowth, cracking sticks and rustling leaves.

I gasped. "It's a T-Rex."

Anaru laid a hand on my arm. "Just wait."

I did. And there, not two metres away, a kiwi stumbled out of the bush and onto the path.

"Oh my God," I whispered. "It's a real one!"

It pecked at something on the ground with its long beak, then disappeared into the foliage on the other side of the track.

I grabbed Anaru's hands and jumped up and down like an excited child. "I've seen a kiwi!" I dropped his hands and shot my pair of imaginary six-guns into the air. "All this time and I've never seen one until now."

Anaru looked at me quizzically.

I stopped dancing. "Not very stealthy, are they?"

"No, they just kind of bumble around. Make terrible ninjas." Anaru continued walking. "They can run pretty fast, though, and those back legs deliver a vicious kick when needed. They've been known to fight off some pretty nasty predators."

"That's cool to know. I thought they were a completely helpless, funny-looking ball of feathers – a predator's dream."

He turned and grinned at me. "See, there's more to us Kiwis than meets the eye."

"Oh yeah? What other talents have you got hidden away? I mean, bird-whispering and stopping cars with your thigh is already a pretty impressive résumé."

"I can solve a Rubik's Cube in under two minutes."

"Wow. That is a very admirable but very useless skill."

He laughed. "What can you do?"

"I can do a torpedo in under ten seconds."

"Is that where you pierce the bottom of a can of beer and down it in one go?"

"Yeah," I said, regretting my choice of bragging material.

"I'm piecing together a very interesting picture of your background. You're pretty cagey about it, so it's not easy. Why is that?"

"Well," I stalled. I hadn't had this conversation with myself, let alone anybody else. And I wasn't about to thrash it out with someone whom a) I barely knew, and b) if I was honest with myself, wanted to present my best side to.

"OK. I'll answer your question if you answer mine first," I said, hoping to throw him off-track. "It's a pretty crazy one."

"Sure."

"Right, prepare yourself for the stupidity of it." I paused to gain maximum dramatic effect. "Are you guys breeding huia here?"

Anaru's step faltered slightly, and it took him a moment to respond. "Ha. Why on earth would you ask that?"

"Well, you know, if any extinct bird was going to be resurrected, it would be that one. It's iconic. We've forced numerous species into extinction, but that's the loss we feel most keenly, like it was The Great Ecological Tragedy of the nation. Just the name 'huia' sends shivers down the spine of most New Zealanders. Plus, Ted reckons he's seen one in the garden."

"Does he? He probably saw a tui. I imagine they're a similar size and colour. Ted has some interesting notions."

I didn't say anything else. I waited for Anaru to fill the silence, to categorically deny the Department of Conservation had a chicken farm producing huia hatchlings. But the silence stretched on.

And my interest went from piqued to soaring. If I wasn't reading into his reaction incorrectly, and there was a huia breeding programme that he wasn't admitting to, what was the reason for the secrecy? Surely it would be something of national importance that would give the department much needed publicity, raise their profile.

I gave him another prod. "Well, you've convinced me."

He stopped and faced me. A flicker of amusement crossed his face. "How do you think we're breeding huia?"

I told him the theory Warren had told me.

"You've really thought this through." We began walking again. "That *could* work. Raises some ethical questions, though. How much do you mess with nature? Where should that line be drawn?"

Aha. An excellent reason for secrecy.

"Who knows? Maybe we'll stumble across that T-Rex, after all," Anaru said. "Maybe I've lured you out here for its feeding time."

"Well, it's in for a treat. I probably taste delicious."

"You don't look like you can run very fast. Second selection criteria after taste."

"Are you mocking the length of my legs?"

The bush to our left rustled and cracked.

"Here he comes," Anaru whispered. "Get ready to run."

BY THE TIME we returned to the car park, we had heard numerous kiwi and seen nine. Four of them, completely unconcerned by our presence, happily bumbled about their business within a metre of where we stood.

"I love this place. It's so good for the soul," I said when we pulled up outside my house.

Anaru smiled, took my face in his hands, and leaned towards me.

And kissed me on the forehead, like you would a child.

"WOLF."

"Em."

"Missed you yesterday. I *had* begun to think the super glue story was true, but I didn't see any bloodied skin hanging off the counter, so..."

"Had stuff to do."

"I bet you did." I sat down at my table and opened the lid of my laptop. "You got anything else to say for yourself?"

"Nope."

"I had a good time drinking all the beer you left behind."

"The act was reward enough."

Trace squeaked over and delivered my coffee. "Carrot cake today. Real cream cheese icing."

"I *love* carrot cake with real cream cheese icing," I said, already salivating. "Can I have your largest piece, please? And keep the coffee rolling. I had a late night last night."

"You up to no good, Em?" Don asked between *kerchunks* of the price labelling machine.

"Saw my first kiwi."

"Oooh, I bet that was a thrill," said Trace.

"Yeah, it was incredible. There were so many of them! Do you ever get to that point where you go 'Oh, it's just another kiwi'?"

"Never," said Don. "I'll never get tired of seeing them. Did you know you can see the odd one in the daytime, too? They're not always nocturnal."

"One walked right past us having breakfast on the deck yesterday," said Trace. "Not fussed by us one bit."

"Really?" I leaned toward her, wanting more but knowing the story was already over.

Don said, "That's why DoC froth at the mouth about pet dogs. Meant to have them tied up at all times. Not that Kevin would know what to do with a kiwi if it jumped in his mouth."

"I remember seeing my first kiwi," said Wolf.

"It can't be that hard, Wolf," said Trace. "They only introduced them a decade ago, you numpty."

"It is if you've been drinking depth charges all night."

"Drinking what?"

"A handle of beer with a shot of vodka dropped in it."

"Ew," I said.

"What, glass and all?" asked Don.

"Yeah," Wolf said. "So later that night, I woke up on someone's front lawn to find this ball on legs piercing the ground between mine with its needle beak. Nearly skewered my whacky sack."

"Ew," I said again.

The door chimed, and one of the older boys from the picnic table walked in, heading straight for the counter.

"Hello, Tama love. What can I get you?" asked Trace.

Tama wanted a two-dollar bag of lollies, please. As he left, digging into his bag of sweets, he aimed a sidelong glance at me.

I waved at him, and he flicked his eyebrows up in acknowledgement. I wondered if this new level of communication was the result of my inept bonnet skimming skills. That perhaps I'd earned a place in local legend alongside the infamous Iron Man, even if it was for the wrong reasons.

Before I could ask, a DoC ranger pushed past him in the doorway.

Trace nodded at the ranger as he headed for the fridges on the far wall.

One aisle back from the fridges, Don moved from where he was working and positioned himself directly behind the man, straightening boxes of crackers.

Via the security footage beside the till, Trace watched the ranger take a bottle of sports drink from the fridge. When he rounded the end of the aisle on his way to pay, she looked up and smiled at him.

The rest of the exchange was conducted with as much warmth as Trace usually showed her customers, but I wondered if he'd been a problem in the past.

"Got another parcel for you lot," said Trace, disappearing into the back room and re-emerging with a small box.

"Thanks," the ranger said when she handed it over.

As he stepped outside, Trace shook her head and said, "They get an awful lot of parcels. Not that I'm prying, but anything coming from overseas is written on the customs form." She paused and whispered, "*Overseas*. Specialty stuff."

"They do specialty work, my love," said Don.

"But pipettes? Lord knows what a scoopula is. Strange chemicals I'd never heard of. I tell you, Em, there's only one thing all that lab equipment is being used for."

"Raising chicks?" Wolf ventured.

"The coca."

"The what?" I asked.

"Blow."

No one said anything.

"Think about it. No one produces cocaine in

New Zealand. The market's wide open and they have the perfect front. *And* the perfect facility with their fence and their labs for growing the plants and turning it into angel dust. No one would suspect a thing."

"Except you," said Wolf, his mouth beginning to curve at the corners.

"I'm starting to get a very good picture of what's going on up there behind closed doors."

"Nothing escapes our Trace," said Don. I couldn't tell if he was earnest or humouring the situation.

"How can you if the doors are closed?" asked Wolf.

My Skype app buzzed over her reply and I excused myself, heading outside to take the call.

"What have you found out?" Warren asked after dispensing with pleasantries.

I pushed my new-found knowledge of the sanctuary's steady stream of overseas-sourced lab equipment aside and said, "Nothing. I asked. I got no confirmation, no denial."

"Interesting. Who did you ask?"

"Someone who would know if it was happening."

Warren tapped his bottom lip with his index finger. "Right, let's ramp this up a notch."

"Ramp what up? You have absolutely nothing to go on. It's like you're desperate to prove your worth or make waves – to let everyone know your appointment was based on worthiness and not favouritism."

Warren's expression was pained. It was hard to tell if it was genuine or contrived.

"And anyway, why would a government department be interested in partnering with a corporate investor?"

"The government's encouraging it. You know, championing neoliberal principles at a time when they're reigning in the books."

"So, they're forcing their departments into business?"

"I wouldn't call it 'forcing'. And it's the perfect opportunity for me. I mean, the company."

"Cutting budgets is an excellent way to force a department to do exactly what it doesn't want to."

Warren said nothing. Then he took a deep breath and said, "I'm sending you a drone. You can scope out the facility from the air."

"You are not sending me a drone."

"I already did. Should arrive on the next ferry."

I rolled my eyes, and Warren smiled as if my petulance was both endearing and amusing. He shuffled forward in his seat and said, "Hey, listen, I've been doing some research, and it really was a remarkable bird."

I raised an eyebrow, which was meant to convey cynicism but might have given the impression I was interested, because he continued, "It had dimorphic beaks, which is incredibly rare in the bird world. The male and the female, therefore, had different roles in food gathering which made them dependent on each other. And this is really cool – they were remarkable songbirds. They were kept as pets and trained to talk."

"Oh," I involuntary muttered. I didn't want to encourage Warren in his misguided belief that huia still existed and were living within some kilometres of where I sat, but what he was saying *was* intriguing.

"And they were highly regarded by Māori – sacred even. Unfortunately, their feathers were also highly regarded, and the birds were hunted for them, and because they weren't scared of humans they were easy to catch, which ultimately led to their extinction, because –" Warren paused to draw in a deep breath. "– their feathers were a sign of nobility, and when the visiting Duke of York had one placed in his hat in 1901, it became a sought-after accessory and incredibly valuable."

"So, they were hunted to extinction for the sake of fashion?"

"Pretty much. That and introduced predators and habitat loss. Plus, there was a large demand from naturalists for specimens because it was such a remarkable bird. So, most of the damage was done after Europeans arrived, but imagine if we could have a role in righting that wrong? Chron helping to right the sins of the past. It adds another ethical tick to the investment." He leaned towards the screen and lowered his voice. "And this next fact is a pretty strong piece of evidence for a Ruatapu habitat for them. They were mountain dwellers in the warmer months and came down into the lowland valleys in winter. They have pretty specific geographic requirements. The sanctuary offers them that – the mountain at the northern end of the enclosure and the hectares of lowland below it. It couldn't be more perfect."

I was quiet for a moment. "Your information is interesting, Warren, but my God are you desperate. What kind of pressure are they putting you under to find investment opportunities?"

He sighed. "Just do the drone thing. And don't make it obvious." He signed off without saying goodbye.

* * *

IN THE WEEK since Ruben arrived, I'd cleared all the boxes and he'd re-piled the sagging corner of the house and replaced much of the missing weatherboard. However, it was the first night in the last six that he'd decided to stay in. He'd come home after his date on the first night, and the night after that, but not the next one. I figured it was fair enough. Third date was shag date, and considering he hadn't come home again the night after that, it was fair to say Ruben was getting a thorough introduction to island life.

We sat in the lounge, beer in hand, and Ruben said, "So. Tell me about you and Anaru."

"What do you mean?"

"You have a thing?"

I snorted. "No."

"I think you do."

"He's not my type."

"Is that because he's Māori?"

I pulled a don't-be-ridiculous face but found I wasn't able to deny it. Was that the reason I had been resisting my attraction to Anaru? I was pretty sure it wasn't because of any heartbreak over Warren. The anger I'd been nursing since he left now seemed to be settling into relief. I was glad that Warren had showed his hand and forced me to realise I didn't want to live the rest of my life with a coward.

So, if I was emotionally unattached, why was I so resistant to the fact I found Anaru rather bloody nice?

Ruben watched me, no doubt reading my inner dialogue on my face.

"Look, even if I was experiencing some...relationship prejudice, if that's a thing, he's not interested in me, so it's irrelevant."

Ruben opened his mouth to speak, but I had started something, and I needed to get it out. "I mean, we spent all evening together the other night and when he drops me home and we're sitting staring at each other in his car, what does he do? He kisses me on the forehead." I leaned towards Ruben and tapped my brow. *"On my forehead."*

Ruben frowned. "It's not called foreskin?"

"Ah. No?"

"Wolf told me it is called your foreskin."

I threw back my head and laughed. "I bet he did, the little shit. I'm happy to say Anaru did not kiss my foreskin."

"What is foreskin?"

The back door rattled with a series of knocks, and a squat, middle-aged woman in a mini-skirt and jandals stepped into the room. Her enormous bosom threatened to spill over the seams of her tie-dyed tank top, and her brassy hair escaped from her ponytail in wild waves.

"Fuck me, that back wall's an eyesore, Em."

It took me a couple of seconds to calibrate my brain, and when I did, my voice escaped my constricted throat like the high-pitched whine of a pierced balloon.

"Mum!"

PART 3

CHAPTER FOURTEEN

"HOW...?" I faltered, watching her drop her handbag on the kitchen counter and sweep her eyes over the living area.

I tried again. "How did you know I was here?"

"My hair's a bloody mess." Ignoring my question, my mother attempted to smooth the wayward strands down, but as soon as her hand passed over them, they bounced back. She laughed and omitted a low, unhealthy gurgle from deep in her chest. "Stood on the ferry deck on the way over and got a whole new degree of blow wave."

A man, just as stocky and wearing a faded Slayer t-shirt, shouldered his way through the back door carrying two bags. "I reckon. She's got a hairlo," he said at me before turning to face her. "You look like Krusty the Clown, Mum."

I leapt to my feet but remained rooted to the spot, not sure what to do next with my body. "Saxon!"

"Hey, Sis." He raised his chin in greeting and dropped the bags with a thump at his feet. "Saw you'd moved back. Thought we'd visit now you're closer to home." He raised his thumbs and little fingers in a shaka sign and shook them. "And living on an island!"

"But..."

"It was the Facebook," said my mother.

"Just Facebook, Mum. There's no 'the'," Saxon said, in the voice of the long suffering.

"Well, I wasn't about to wait for an invitation," she continued. "I'd be waiting until the next millennium." She pushed me back down onto the couch and sat next to me. Then she looked between me and Ruben and said, "Are you going to introduce us?"

"Um. Sure," I said, emerging from the fog of shock. "Ruben, this is my mother, Janey, and my brother, Saxon."

"Toy boy are you?" Saxon asked Ruben as he leaned over and shook his hand.

"Grow up, Saxon. He's my woofer. He's fixing up the house."

Saxon grunted and nodded at Ruben's clothing. "What's with the gear?"

"It's the uniform of my guild," Ruben said. "Traditional carpenter dress."

"Will you excuse me?" I asked the room without looking at anyone in particular and stood up. "I just need to..." My words trailed off as I walked to the hallway door, closing it softly behind me.

I put the heels of my hands to my eyeballs and let out a "Fuuuuuuuuck" on my exhale. I hadn't even been on the island a month, hadn't had a chance to establish myself in my new home, or find a place in my new community before my family had descended on my life like a flock of gulls on a discarded fish and chips packet. I could already feel myself sinking under the weight of their presence.

I got out my phone and dialled Anaru.

"Kia ora, Em," he said after the second ring.

"Please tell me you're home."

"I'm home."

"Great. Where do you live?"

"I'M JUST POPPING OUT," I said when I re-entered the room. "Need to organise something for you to sleep on. Ruben's got the blow-up bed."

Janey said, "Can't you have a bit of a catch-up with your mum and brother before rushing off? Anyone would think you're not pleased to see us."

"I'll catch up with you when I get back." I looked at Saxon. "Are you blocking me in?"

"Yeah but –"

"Give me the keys to your car."

Saxon's naturally high-pitched voice raised a half-octave. "No way."

"Give me your keys," I said through gritted teeth.

He held up his hands in surrender. "Alright. Keep your tampon in." The keys were produced from his back pocket. They were warm and sported a Holden keyring.

"I'll be back soon," I said, casting what I hoped was an apologetic look at Ruben.

He didn't look at all fazed by my decision to flee minutes after my family walked in the door. He raised a hand in farewell, then asked the guests if they would like a beer.

I pulled the door to and walked to my brother's matt-black V8 Holden Commodore.

ANARU'S HOUSE was on the west side of the island and one of three houses on a kilometre-long road. It was small, of the prefabricated-looking cement board variety, and presumably the property of the Department of Conservation.

I rapped on the door and asked, "Do you have spare bedding?" before he had fully opened it.

Anaru surveyed me for a moment, then said, "You look a little freaked out. Everything OK?"

"Can I come in?" I asked, pushing past him without waiting for an answer. I stepped into his living room, my eyes passing over the worn furniture that had likely been passed on from one ranger resident to another, settling on the kettle in the tiny adjacent kitchen.

I strode towards it and threw a "Cup of tea?" over my shoulder. My hand shook as I reached for the tap.

"So what's going on?" Anaru asked when I opened my eyes after the first sip.

"You know how my life is out of control?"

"No. I know you feel that way, but I think you're doing a good job of dragging it back on track."

I harrumphed. "That might have been true until fifteen minutes ago."

"What happened fifteen minutes ago?"

"My family arrived. Unannounced."

"I take it that's not a good thing?"

"They're just so...larger than life. I haven't even got my breath back from the whole nervous breakdown and boyfriend desertion thing, and now I have to accommodate their" – I waved my hands in the air – "overwhelming-ness."

"How long are they staying?"

"Fuck knows."

"You know you swear an awful lot?"

I shrugged. "Wait 'til you meet my mother."

The statement was not an exaggeration, and as I said it, the full reality of the situation set in. Everything I'd been side-stepping, all the details about my past I'd not admitted to would stand out like dog's bollocks as soon as Anaru set eyes on Janey.

Anaru dunked a biscuit in his tea and sucked on

it, looking at me thoughtfully. "Well, they're here now, and there's nothing you can do about that."

I grunted.

"So all you can do is embrace the fact and turn it into an opportunity."

"For what?"

"How long since you last saw them?"

"Three years."

"*Three* years?"

"Yeah. How often do you see your family?"

"Any chance I get."

"You're lucky then."

Anaru opened his mouth to say something, then changed his mind and grinned. "I can't wait to meet yours. I think you'll make a whole lot more sense."

No shit.

I frowned at him, baring my teeth and snapping a biscuit between them.

"Look, this is a chance to get to know each other again. A lot can happen in three years. Tell yourself it's an opportunity to reconnect, and then you'll feel in control of the situation."

I didn't say anything. We both knew he was right.

I tipped my mug back, and when I placed it on the table, Anaru asked if I was done.

Smacking my lips together, I said, "Yup," and he pushed himself up from the table.

"Come on."

"Where are we going?"

"I've got spare pillows and blankets and stuff, but no mattresses. We'll have to go to the marae."

The tribe's meeting grounds, where Iwa helped her koro with the language classes. The thread that had wound itself around my lungs on my family's arrival, and that had been unspooling in Anaru's presence, started to cinch itself tight again. "Am I allowed there? I haven't been welcomed on or anything."

Anaru smiled at me. I could tell he was doing his best to make it more a don't-worry-yourself smile and less a your-ignorance-is-endearing smile. "Yes, you're allowed there. Once you've been, it won't be so scary." He put his hands on my shoulders and pushed me out the door.

WARREN HADN'T EXAGGERATED. The fence *was* formidable. Thick wire mesh stood fifteen metres high and ran in each direction from a wide gate. The bottom of the fence was lined with a metre of steel and attached to the top of the fence was a soft net – large enough for insects to get through, small enough for no bird to fly through. It stretched back from the fence and up into the tree canopy.

The road Anaru took followed the fence for a few hundred metres before forking at the enormous entrance gates. As we neared, another set of gates behind the first came into view, forming a holding pen for vehicles – presumably the outer gate had to close before the inner gate opened.

"Wow," I said. "You guys are pretty hardcore about your security."

"Yeah, we haven't had a single rodent enter this area since we eradicated them two decades ago."

"I'm claiming refuge when the zombies come," I said, watching the foliage carefully for any hint of formerly extinct birds.

"I'm not sure the zombie hoard could manage a 250-kilometre swim."

"It only takes one. Can you imagine how devastating a zombie roboranger would be?"

Anaru grimaced. "You're right. That image is terrifying."

He drove on, turning at the fork and away from the fence.

"We're not going in?"

"The marae's not there. Only the station and the breeding facility." Anaru turned onto another road and said, "Did you know the sanctuary is a partnership between DoC and the hapū, a subtribe of Ngāti Porou?"

"No."

"Ngāti Wherereitanga ō te Rā Hou. Means the birth of the sun or the new day. We're the first people to see the sun in New Zealand, or the world for that matter."

"That's a beautiful name." Then after a pause I said, "We?"

"Yeah. We're a remnant tribe. Most of us left for the mainland a couple of generations ago, and hardly any have come back. Yet. None of my whanaunga – anybody in my extended family – has any memory of this place."

"So, you're returning to your – what do you call your homeland?"

"Tūrangawaewae. My standing place."

"And you think others will, too?"

He nodded. "With more opportunities. DoC have a programme that supports anyone from the hapū who wants to work in the sanctuary, even if that means university. We want local expertise and we want a true partnership."

"And you're the first?"

He nodded. "Best thing I ever did."

We rounded a bend, and the bush opened into grassland. A few round-bellied sheep grazed the stalky pasture, and on the other side of a hillock the carved meeting house revealed itself, sheltered by a stand of trees. Beside it were a couple of other small buildings and two houses. A Victorian-era cottage and a larger, 1950s weatherboard bungalow.

An elderly man stepped onto the porch of the cottage as we pulled up.

"Taiporutu," Anaru said. "Most people call him Tai."

Tai waited until we had climbed down from the ute, then he stepped down from the verandah and walked to meet Anaru. Gripping Anaru's hand and closing his eyes, he pressed his nose against Anaru's and breathed in deeply. Then he straightened up and smiled. "Kei te aha?"

"Kei te pai," Anaru answered.

The old man looked at me, still smiling. "Ko wai ō māua manuhiri?"

"Em!"

I turned in time to catch a flying Iwa. She ran at me, arms extended, and I staggered backwards at the point of impact.

She looked up at me, arms still wrapped around my waist. "I'm staying with my koro tonight. He makes hot chocolate with marshmallow submarines. I'm not allowed sugar at home" – she changed her voice to a whisper – "so it's a secret."

I whispered back, "I promise I won't tell."

"Koro, this is Em. She's the one that got sick all over her shoe because of the yuck rat. Anaru called her a pukahontas."

Tai laughed. "Ah, yes the one with the cool hair." He reached for my hand and said, "Tēnā koe, Em." Then closing his eyes, he pressed his nose to mine, taking a slow breath in through his nostrils and finally kissing me gently on the cheek.

When he released me, my awkwardness chose to

present itself in a giggle. Feeling ridiculous, I decided to go for broke. "I prefer Pukasaurus rex."

"'To Em or pukahontas?"

I giggled again.

"You know," said Tai. "I've seen you before. At the store, working on your computer."

"You have?" I grimaced. "I'm sorry. Sometimes I get into the zone and don't know the rest of the world exists."

"Ae. Whenever I've been in there, you've been frowning at your computer. You need more sunshine, less worries."

I laughed. "I do, you're absolutely right."

Iwa tugged on my arm. "Are you staying to have hot chocolate with us? Tama says it's a little kids' drink, but he still drinks it anyway."

A movement on the porch caught my eye, and the teenager stepped out into the light and raised a hand. "Kia ora, kōrua."

"Kia ora, Tama," called Anaru. He looked at me, and I knew I had to be brave and wrap my mouth around the words. I flushed under my own pressure and said the best "Kia ora" I'd ever managed, which didn't mean much given I'd only said it half a dozen times.

Anaru placed his hand on the small of my back and removed it after a couple of seconds. I knew the gesture was one of support and reward, but the heat of it burned into me long after his hand had returned to his side.

I looked down at Iwa and said, "I would love to, but my family's just arrived and I should get back to them."

She *aww*-ed, and Anaru flashed me a grin.

"I tell you what," I said to her, "next time you're at the store and I'm working, we can have a hot chocolate together. How does that sound?"

Iwa's face split into a broad smile, and she nodded. "Can I bring my cousins?" She looked over at the other house and said, "They're not here at the moment, but they like hot chocolate, too."

"Sure. How many cousins have you got?"

She held up three fingers.

"Hot chocolate for five it is."

Tai put a hand on Iwa's shoulder and said to me, "You know you're welcome here anytime." He gestured towards the meeting house, where visitors to the marae slept. "This place is yours, too."

I thanked him, adding "Kia ora" as an afterthought and followed him to collect the mattresses.

Anaru caught my hand and squeezed it before letting it drop. I looked up at him, and he smiled. It was a grin that said, *See? No reason to worry*. And he was absolutely right. I couldn't help but grin back.

SAXON STOOD at the back door, smoke blooming around his head and a black instrument in his hand.

My step faltered, and I had to take a deep breath before I could urge my next foot forward. I reminded myself this was an opportunity to reconnect.

"Fuck it," I said, and strode towards him, determined to find a foothold that would re-establish our relationship.

"Hey, Sax. You on the vaping train?"

He rolled his eyes back into his head and smiled. "It's cherry flavoured."

I'd never known Saxon to do anything that wasn't considered a testament to his testosterone. Anything less was best left for "girls", "poofs" or "pussies". If this was a sign he was finally reaching some level of maturity, even a small one, I'd allow him to have it without any big-sisterly teasing.

His facial hair, on the other hand, was fair game.

I reached out to touch his top lip, and he leaned away from me. "What's with the 'tache?"

"They're in. It's called being fashionable, Em. Where have you been the last couple of years?"

"You look like a paedo."

"Fuck off. Aaron Smith and Sevu Reece rock one."

"Yeah, but All Blacks can get away with sporting something that makes everyone else look like a douche."

"*You're* a douche."

I reached up, placing my hand on the back of his neck and using my body weight to pull him down into a head lock.

He slapped at my arms, but his flailing only made me increase my pressure.

"Em, stop," he squealed.

I mussed his hair with my knuckles, and he put his hands on his head to protect it.

"Muuum. Mum! Em's being a dick."

Behind us, the kitchen window rattled with the percussive force of rapid knocks.

I turned my head to see Janey, face a frown, spatula in hand. She pointed a finger at me and said, "You let your brother go or I'll kick both your arses."

I released him, and Saxon looked at me like I'd delivered that eternal injustice of the bigger, stronger older sibling.

I smiled at him and gave him a loving push on the shoulder. "Nice to see you, Saxxy. Thanks for letting me borrow your car."

"It better be mint."

"Come on. Help me get the mattresses in."

AT THE STOVE, Ruben hovered at Janey's elbow, spooning mixture into a pan for her to flip. He looked up when we came in struggling with the foam mattresses and smiled a genuine I'm-happy-to-be-here smile. Apparently, my family's intrusion, our terrible behaviour towards one another, and Janey and Saxon's cultural idiosyncrasies were nothing to raise an eyebrow about. It was almost as if we were a normal family.

It gave me hope that I wouldn't be judged by the rest of the island for where I came from.

I moved Ruben into the redundant "office" so that Janey and Saxon had plenty of space in the other double bedroom. I figured they wouldn't mind sharing, given the three of us had spent a couple of years breathing each other's air in the tight confines of a caravan.

After Saxon and I had finished making the beds with only minor argie-bargie and stepped back into the living room to the aroma of fried corn, Janey turned from opening the back door, an unlit cigarette between her lips. She nodded at the plates on the counter. "Dinner's ready. Go wash your hands. And when you've done that, Saxon, go get the goon bag out of the car, will you?"

"You know, Janey," I said, "I have a nice bottle of Marlborough Sauvignon Blanc in the fridge. Wouldn't you prefer that?"

"Wine tastes better when it's less than fifty cents a glass. Save the posh stuff for yourself."

I sighed and said to Saxon I'd get the goon bag, leaving him to have the bathroom first.

I'd stashed the mattresses and bedding on the Holden's large back seat, so it was rather a surprise when I popped the boot to find five casks of medium-dry white wine neatly packed into one corner.

"Jesus. How long are you planning on staying for, Janey?" I called, grabbing one and heading back to the house.

She dragged on her cigarette and wheezed on her exhale, "As long as it takes."

Oh God. "As long as what takes?"

"Not a bad view, that," she said, pointing at the ocean with her cigarette. "Shame about the house, but you've lived in worse shitholes."

I clucked my tongue. "I take it you're keeping it as a surprise, then?"

She didn't answer.

"Wine glass or tumbler?"

"Is the pope a prick in a dress?"

"Tumbler it is."

***

ANARU GAVE me a nudge in the direction of opportunity seeking and invited the household to join him at the pub the following evening.

I couldn't pretend this didn't cause me a level of anxiety. I'd no longer have the advantage of being able to hide behind the fact that no one on the island knew me. Two days ago, I could be anyone I wanted to be. Now, I would be the girl raised on petrol fumes and AC/DC rock anthems. My only hope was that, despite it being a Friday night, the island community had little interest in unwinding with a drink after the working week.

WHEN WE ARRIVED, the small car park was full.

I fought the urge to place my head on the steering wheel and groan. I prised myself out of the driver's seat and held my breath as Saxon swung down from the ute and puffed his arms out at his side.

As he neared the door, he adopted an exaggerated swagger. Saxon, in true Saxon style, looked to make a big entrance.

So I gave him one.

Just as he put a hand out to push the double doors open, I put a foot out and ankle-tapped him. He fell through the doors and into the pub's hubbub in a running stumble.

When he recovered himself, he turned, a look of indignation on his face, his voice high and reedy. "What'd you do that for?"

"No one wants to fight you, Saxon. Stop being a dick."

The pub was reasonably well-patronised for a small community, but then again, it was Friday night and the pub was on the diminutive side, so it didn't take many people for it to feel cosy. A handful of young tourists sipped drinks in pairs, locals ate burgers or steak with an eye on the large wall-mounted television, and a group in jeans and walking boots who were clearly off-duty DoC staff clinked glasses and scattered from the bar like a disturbed flock of birds. At its centre and remaining still as he watched our entrance, stood Anaru.

My pulse surged and stuttered, and I stopped walking. Someone crashed into the back of me.

"Fuck's sake, Em," muttered Janey. "Keep going." She gave me a little push and the quickening of my heart rate was replaced by the tightening of my lungs. I felt as if, surrounded by my very small family, I had been stripped naked.

When I stepped aside to allow my mother entrance, the entire pub paused, held its breath, then carried on as if having shaken the vision out of its head.

My mother had decided to wear her medieval maiden rock chick outfit – a tight, crushed velvet dress hemmed in lace, falling to mid-thigh and with a ribbon-tied front that barely contained her breasts. She had thrown subtlety to the wind with her eye liner, and her black Doc Marten boots were bedecked with a line of plastic flowers running up the front of her laces.

I strode over to Anaru, took a swig of his beer, and when he gave me a look that said "I know you now", I about-faced and stepped up to the bar.

Wolf leaned against it in the exact same position

as he did at the store, like he'd been casually tele-ported in.

I ordered a Pinot Gris and turned to him. "You know, I don't think I've ever seen you move. Have your muscles atrophied into that position?"

"You got an entourage?" He nodded over at Anaru who now sat at a table, where Ruben was doing the job I should have been doing and intro-ducing Saxon and Janey.

"My woofer. And," I lowered my voice, "my mum and brother."

"Met your woofer before. He's been here looking pretty cosy with Mel."

I grunted. "Mel has a lot to answer for. She's robbed me of a housemate for the last week. I had thought my evenings would be filled with laughter and a shared love of crochet or something, but they've been sad and empty."

Wolf tutted.

"And now they're overflowing with sound and colour." I turned my head and watched as Anaru effort-lessly engaged the group in conversation. As one, they laughed, and I turned back to the bar. "I'd better order them a round. Pretend I'm not avoiding the situation."

"Why would you avoid the situation? Your mum looks like one pretty cool lady."

As I looked up at Wolf in amazement, my moth-er's voice rang out across the pub floor. "Maxine

Sharon! You better be ordering drinks and not avoiding us."

I flinched and hunched my shoulders.

Wolf raised an eyebrow. "Maxine?"

"Yeah," I croaked. "Mum had a big thing for Sharon O'Neill."

"The singer?"

I nodded.

"Isn't 'Maxine' a song about a prostitute?"

I curled myself over my glass and said into it, "She didn't realise. Until later."

Wolf slapped the bar and laughed long enough for me to place the drink order for the table and the barman fill it. He sniffed. "Maxine's not such a bad name."

"It's a terrible name. The whole thing is just...bad."

"Nah. Just unfortunate. If you were named Maxine – no backstory – I bet you wouldn't mind it."

I asked to borrow a tray and loaded the drinks to take to the table.

"You could be called Max. Don't chicks dig being called by a bloke's name?"

"When they're twelve," I said, picking up the tray and walking to the table.

"See you later, Max," he called after me.

As I passed out the drinks, Anaru raised his eyebrows and mouthed "Maxine?"

I gave him a wry smile and said I was sorry, I had forgotten to order him a drink.

He lowered one eyebrow and took his beer from the tray. Then he said, "Your mum was just telling me you guys aren't actually from Australia."

I took a sip of my wine to avoid grimacing and said, "I never said I was."

"So you're going to get out of misleading everyone on a technicality."

"Yep."

"You are an interesting and complex creature, Maxine Sharon."

Janey said, "Em's not very proud of where she comes from. Couldn't get out of there fast enough. Forged my signature on the passport documents and buggered off at sixteen to the land of Oz."

I slapped my glass down on the table, slopping wine. "Janey! Stop wilfully trying to embarrass me."

"I'm just saying it how it is. If it embarrasses you, you've got no mettle for the facts of life. I had you at sixteen. I could have run away from teenage mother-hood, given you up for adoption, but I didn't. I embraced my life choices and soldiered on. And not a lot of bloody thanks from you, either." She downed her Jack Daniels and coke in one hit and said, "Go and get me a soda and lime. I'll drive."

Under the table, Anaru laid a hand on my thigh and gave it a gentle squeeze. When he promptly removed it, I figured the touching was more of the sympathetic variety and less of the "you getting a serving like you're still a child is making you seem really sexy right now" sort.

"I'll go," said Saxon, giving me an I'm-glad-it's-you-and-not-me look.

"Suck up," I said to him.

"It's worth buying favours, Em. You're just out of practice."

"So," I said to Ruben, both out of genuine interest and a fairly urgent desire to take the focus off me, "is Mel here?"

"Ja. Yes."

"You've not said hello?"

"She knows I'm here. We are, how do you say it, having a casual relationship."

"It's just sex, then."

"Em, stop being nosy," said Janey.

Ignoring her, I said, "Which one is she?" I craned my neck around looking for a likely candidate. There were a couple of women in their early twenties, but both of them were partnered-up.

Anaru nudged me with his elbow and jerked his head over his right shoulder.

A black-haired woman stood in a familiar wide-legged stance at a table behind us. She wore purple cargo pants, yellow canvas combat boots and a yellow shirt, as if she'd gone home and changed into her bird-of-paradise-stake-out camos. She leaned towards the other person at the table, the exchange brief and intense, then she straightened and bounced up and down on the balls of her feet like she'd delivered a conclusion to an argument that categorically ended all further debate.

My mouth dropped open, and I turned back to Ruben. "Roboranger?"

"I beg your pardon?" he asked.

I closed my mouth and invited my brain to work before I said anything else that might make Ruben feel uncomfortable and me sound like Saxon. Like, *I hope you're delivering the goods. She could do with a good loosening.* Or wondering about the likelihood of her having dominatrix tendencies.

"Good for you, Ruben," I said, clinking glasses with him.

As I took a sip, I muttered, "Kinky," to Anaru, and he chuckled into his beer glass.

"Where's my bloody drink?" Janey asked mildly.

We turned to the bar and saw Saxon holding forth with Wolf, Saxon's legs wide and bent, his arms pumping backwards and forwards.

Wolf watched, a small smile playing on his lips.

I groaned inwardly. Any opportunity for my family to draw attention to themselves and they jumped in, steel-capped boots and all.

"What do you reckon they're talking about?" Anaru asked.

"How to be a ninja," said Ruben. "He is punching the stomach like lightning."

"Masturbation tips," I said. "They belong to a secret society. Like Fight Club, but about aggressive self-love."

"Car mechanics," said Janey in a way that diminished any doubt. "He's miming a crankshaft. I've never seen anyone more in love with engines than that boy. Always has been."

A "Hello chaps" brought our attention back to the table.

Mel stood at one end, an empty glass in hand.

"Hi Mel," I said, "nice to see you relaxing."

"It's not all about the job, Em," she said, patting her pockets and removing a bird counter, her black notebook and an opaque sample vial.

"Ah, there it is." She took out a bank card. "Next round's on me," she said, disappearing towards the bar.

I picked up the vial. "What do you reckon's in here?" I put my thumb under the lid, testing its tightness.

"I wouldn't," said Anaru. "It'll be –"

I popped the lid and sniffed. An acrid stench seared my nasal passages and my toes curled against the rung of the bar stool.

"– cat scat."

"Oh my God." I thrust the vial away from me and rubbed the back of my pointer finger across my nostrils. "I probably have toxo."

"Probably," Anaru laughed.

"Who carries cat scat in their pocket, let alone to social occasions?" I asked, replacing the lid and putting the vial back with the other items.

"People who are dedicated to their job," said Ruben, taking a sip of beer and *almost* hiding his expression of pride behind his glass.

"You're absolutely right. No one could fault her that." I said it with sincerity. It was no longer fair for me to think of Mel as an officious automaton. Not only was she connected to my new family, her colourful outfit showed a flair for the bold and hinted at a personality that had far more depth than I'd given her credit for.

When she returned to the table, she cocked one leg on a table rung and engaged Janey in a conversation about bird hierarchy in the dawn chorus.

As I listened, I fingered her notebook, absentmindedly flicking it open and closed. When the conversation reached a lull, I switched my focus from Mel's face to the book. It was full of sketches of birds surrounded by tiny, meticulous handwritten notes.

A flash of yellow on black stilled my hand.

Before I could investigate further, Mel slapped her hand on the book and pulled it towards her, sliding it into a pocket on the side of her cargo pants and buttoning the flap.

"That's official documentation there, Em. A bit of respect would be appreciated. It could disclose sensitive information. Like the full legal names of local offenders." She dipped her head, drawing her chin into her neck and peering at me as if looking over the top of spectacles.

"They already know," I said resignedly.

"Ah." Mel nodded her head in a way that might have been commiserating.

"Speaking of offending," I said loud enough for Saxon to hear, "are there any by-laws about moustaches on men under forty?"

Mel looked at Saxon, her expression as deadpan as her ranger game-face. "Only those that favour a ginger hue."

Saxon clamped a hand to his upper lip. "It's not ginger!"

"It's ginger, Sax," I said.

He puffed out his chest and smoothed the short hairs down with his thumb and pointer finger. "It's golden brown with auburn highlights," he said.

The table erupted with laughter, and Mel spat her mouthful of beer back into her glass.

"What?" Saxon said, casting his eyes around the group. "Even Wolf commented on its complexity of shades."

Wolf nodded solemnly.

Mel chuckled.

I opened my mouth to say something else and Janey raised a finger without taking her hand off the table. I shut it again.

Saxon called us a bunch of philistines and turned back to Wolf.

I glanced at Janey, who had started drawing a pattern on the table with the condensation from her glass, and decided the risk was worth it. "Is the colour of your mo' the same as your pubes?"

"No," Janey answered, without looking up.

Saxon gazed at her wide-eyed, his mouth turned down at the corners. "How would you know, Mum?"

"Yeah, how would you know, Mum?" I said.

"I'm his mother. I know everything."

"Hopefully not everything," Anaru said into his beer.

I walked over to Saxon, pulled him towards me, and kissed the side of his head.

"Gerroff," he squealed.

I released him and said, "It's a shame we don't have more siblings — share the load of the evil eye." I glanced at Janey. "She's like Sauron."

"A big flaming vagina?" Saxon said sulkily.

I lowered my voice to the dramatic tone of a movie trailer narrator. "There's no escape from the Gaze of Humiliation."

"And don't you forget it," said Janey. "If you behaved better, I wouldn't have to."

"I behave fine, thank you very much. Most of the time." I returned to the table and said to Mel, "Where are you from?" It was partly out of curiosity but mostly because I thought I should make more of an effort to get to know her better.

"Ah, New Zealand?" she said, her eyebrows knit. I wasn't sure if her expression was due to confusion or disapproval.

"Sorry," I said. "I'm just...you know what I mean."

"No."

I cleared my throat. "I mean, what's your ethnicity?"

"Right," she said, giving a single nod. "You do know that's an entirely different question? If you meant ethnicity, you should have said it. My ancestors are Chinese and European, but I'm fourth generation Kiwi. Probably just like you."

"*Third* generation on my side," Janey said, and raised her glass at me. "Good lesson there, Em." Then she clapped her hands together. "Right, who's for a game of pool?"

Mel and Ruben followed her to the pool table, and Saxon retreated to the bar, leaning against it next to Wolf and mirroring his stance.

Wolf looked across to where Anaru and I sat and raised his eyebrows and his glass. I nodded, and he ordered a round from the bartender.

Saxon ferried the drinks, continuing his conversation with Wolf over his shoulder as he delivered round after round.

My fifth drink arrived in a whiskey tumbler and

had miraculously intensified in hue. "What's this, Sax?"

"A real drink. None of that poncy piss water."

"I happen to like poncy piss water," I said, bringing the glass to my nose and inhaling. A hint of caramel and smoky wood. I closed my eyes. It had been sixteen years since I'd tasted bourbon.

Saxon winked and retreated to the bar, and as I tipped the glass towards my mouth, Anaru said, "Tell me about your life in Melbourne."

I let the first sip roll across my tongue, its spiciness hitting the back of my throat. "Why?" I took another sip.

"I'd like to know what you ran to."

"A fair question." I put the glass down on the table and swirled it. "You can see what I ran from."

Anaru didn't smile. He tilted his head, encouraging me to answer his request.

So I told him about my progress up the Chron career ladder from a stint as a secretarial temp. I told him about the plays, the exhibitions, the fusion cuisine, the gigs, the rooftop bars. I told him about my love of the city art gallery.

"You don't miss it?"

"Sure. I miss the fun, I miss the buzz, the culture. I just don't miss the pace."

Anaru said nothing for several seconds.

"You know, Em, for all your embarrassment about where you come from, who your family is, you slip right in without thinking about it. I haven't seen much evidence of a Melbourne-ite since I met you, but I've seen plenty of the blue-collar trailer-home girl." He gestured at my brother. "You're more them than you are that high-flying city woman," he said, slightly slurring the last two words.

I chose to jump on the opportunity his mispronunciation presented rather than think very hard about his message. "Did you just call me shitty?"

He smiled and said, "I think I'm a little drunk. I should probably stop the beer." He looked towards the bar. "You know what I feel like? A hot chocolate."

I nudged him with my shoulder and said, "You *look* like a hot chocolate."

Anaru turned towards me, a slow smile spreading across his face. "What did you just call me?"

"Hot chocolate. You heard correctly, ranger cowboy."

He tipped his head back and laughed. "*You* need the hot chocolate. Are you always this funny when you're drunk?"

"I'm not drunk. I've only had –" I counted on my fingers. "– four wines and one bourbon." I raised my finger and pointed at him. "Only one of them was a double."

"So, six drinks."

"Whatever. I'm high on life."

Saxon tripped over to the table, his face flush, and

planted his glass with a *thunk*. He leaned in and said conspiratorially, "I'm taking Mum *down*."

"There's no taking Mum down, Sax."

He stood back and winked at me, then turned to the pool table and placed a coin on its edge to reserve the next game. "Play you next, Mum," he said, returning to the table.

"Sax," I said, "I say this out of my undying and boundless filial love. You're an idiot."

"No," he said. "Exceptionally good at pool is what I am. I know my capabilities."

"Your capabilities would be better if you hadn't just downed half a keg."

At the pool table, Janey sank the black, ending the final best-of-three game.

Mel and Ruben, who'd been playing doubles against her, headed to the bar to refresh their drinks.

Saxon took a step towards Janey, and I laid a hand on his arm, saying, "Oh God. Please don't." I looked around me at all the other pub patrons whose attention, no doubt, would shortly be drawn to the latest Stewart Spectacle.

"It'll be sweet. Just watch."

"No," I said, swinging my feet around on my stool so that I faced the bar.

"Suit yourself," said Saxon, as Anaru wished him good luck.

"Luck's for sissies," he called over his shoulder.

I swung my feet back round again, unable to ignore the pull of watching an inevitable disaster.

When he reached the pool table, Saxon said, "You can break," his tone adding the "little lady" he didn't have the courage to say out loud.

Janey heard it anyway and set her features to grim game-on. I slumped a little lower in my chair.

She sank two balls off her first shot.

"Fluke," said Saxon. "Bet you can't sink the next one."

She did.

And the next three after that.

Gradually the pub patrons began to take interest – a middle-aged woman dressed like a medieval princess exploring her punk tendencies roundly teaching a young hothead a thing or two about the finer points of ball play.

Saxon looked like he didn't know his mother was a pool shark. He leant on his cue and watched with a smugness that couldn't be anything other than decidedly patronising.

When she sank the next one, the last of her coloured balls, he looked like he now remembered and wished he hadn't been so generous with his "ladies first" attitude.

He started pacing as she lined up her final shot, the eight ball positioned in a difficult spot behind one of his.

Janey expertly deflected the white ball off the

edge of the table so that it avoided Saxon's and knocked the black into the corner pocket.

The pub erupted.

She straightened up, took a bow to the crowd, and said, "And that son, is a bona fide down trou."

Saxon's laugh was high-pitched and forced as he walked over to Janey with his hand raised for a high-five. "Nice going, Mum."

She crossed her arms, leaving him hanging. "Well?" She nodded at his groin. "You gonna show us what you've got?"

Saxon's voice cracked on his "No!" and he reflexively placed his hands over his genitals.

A chant of "Get it out!" – initiated by Wolf – rang out around the pub.

"Oh my God, my family," I muttered, lowering my head and shielding my eyes from the pool table. "Poor Saxxy."

Ruben, his black tie askew and his shirt nearly unbuttoned to his navel, had developed a stronger German accent the more the evening wore on and the more he drunk. "I love zis kivi axent," he said. "You sink your brother iss sexy." He slapped the table and wiped at his eyes.

Saxon looked wild-eyed between Janey and me.

I gave him a "them's the rules" shrug.

He edged his way around the pool table so that it provided a barrier between him and the rest of the pub. "No fucken' way." He pointed a finger at Janey.

"I've had like twelve beers and you've had one poxy whiskey. You took advantage."

"As soon as you picked up that cue you entered into a contract."

"You can't break the pool code, Saxon," Wolf called. "Fifty years' bad luck, mate. Or your dick drops off or something."

"She's not really going to make him, is she?" asked Anaru.

I grimaced. "I reckon so. Mum's big on lesson learning."

Saxon's eyes now darted between Janey and the door. If he did a runner, Janey would never let him live it down. Even I didn't want that level of humiliation for my very annoying and very juvenile little brother, but I couldn't think of a way to rescue him.

Then something extraordinary happened.

Wolf uncrossed his legs and pushed away from the bar like you might from the side of a pool.

He strode across to Saxon's end of the pool table and laid a hand on his shoulder. Turning to Janey, he said, "I'll take one for young Saxon here. I believe, according to the code, a player can forfeit a down trou if someone volunteers as proxy."

The hubbub hushed while the victor considered the terms.

Janey gave a single nod, and Wolf undid his belt. He dropped his pants and stood with his hands on his hips, his "sugar stick" on full display.

The pub went deathly quiet.

Between Wolf's legs was no ordinary penis. He was hung like the proverbial horse.

"Holy shit, Wolf," I said despite myself. "How can you walk straight with that thing?"

Janey put her finger in the air and twirled it. Wolf obligingly rotated so that everyone could bear witness to the price of a thorough defeat.

A "Whoa!" issued from somewhere near the back of the pub.

When he returned to his original position and bent to pull up his trousers, a round of applause broke out.

"Your mum is either really awesome, or truly terrifying," said Anaru.

"It's a fine line," said Mel. "I like to walk it. Keep the punters on edge."

"I did call it," I said. "I tried to warn him."

"Zis iss ze best night off my life," said Ruben, raising his beer with a "Prost," and sliding off his barstool.

CHAPTER FIFTEEN

I AWOKE to a pounding in my head and a shuffling across my bedroom floor.

"Go away," I croaked into my pillow. "I'm trying to be hungover."

The curtains were thrown aside, and light flooded the room.

I groaned and pulled the covers over my head.

"Get up, Em," said Janey. "It's nearly eleven."

"No."

She pulled the covers down and held out a large glass of water with a fizzing orange tablet in it. "I've made some Tabasco and eggs. Best cure."

"Urnh," I said.

Placing the glass on the bedside table, she turned for the door. "The others are up. You've got two minutes before it's a bowl of water."

Groaning, I rolled across the bed and slid out of it so that I could find the floor without getting upright. I looked up at the glass and groaned again. I'd have to be some extent of vertical to drink it.

I pushed myself up into a sitting position and winced at the sudden weight of my brain. I turned my head to focus on my arm coordination, and my brain rolled to one side, knocking against my skull and ricocheting like a pinball.

I clamped my hands to my head, steadying it before attempting to reach for the drink.

Through the bottom of the glass, my mother, pinprick head and elephantine legs, filled the door frame, a bowl of cold water and ice in her hand. "Good," she said. "Your eggs are getting cold."

I handed her the empty glass and put my hands and knees to the floor, following her to the kitchen.

She stopped and turned. "Why are you crawling?"

"It's better."

"It doesn't look it."

Ruben and Saxon sat on the outdoor table, a platter of eggs and toast before them.

Squinting against the bright late morning sun, I pulled myself up onto a chair and reached for the coffee plunger. "Is it strong?"

"Enough to have to chew it," said Saxon, sporting sunglasses and a Ford cap pulled low. He was hunched over his plate, shovelling toast in with one hand.

"Sax?"

"Hmm?"

"Giz your glasses."

"Nuh." A small piece of egg fell out of his mouth and onto his plate.

"Your hat then."

He smacked his lips in a tut and slapped the cap on my head.

"Love you, Saxxy."

Ruben chuckled.

The coffee came out black and syrupy, and I poured myself a large mug, breathing in the bitterness before taking a sip. My brain relaxed, nestling into the bottom of my skull and staying still.

I was suddenly very hungry. I buttered three pieces of toast and forked on four eggs, their edges slightly red from the Tabasco sauce and butter Janey had fried them in.

"Where's Janey?"

Saxon lifted his chin to indicate behind me. "Garden."

I pivoted and watched as Janey, using Anaru's garden fork, broke up the soil I'd exposed a couple of weeks ago. Then she tipped in compost from the bags I'd bought and mixed it into the earth.

"Nice going, Janey. You didn't have to do that."

"Had to do something while I waited for you buggers to rise from the dead." She turned over a solid chunk of soil and beat it with the back of the fork until it broke up. "It's not the right time to plant anything, but best to get the soil ready now for your winter veges. Let the compost settle in."

I turned back to my breakfast, took a mouthful, and jumped as a *shling* issued from behind me. Ruben and Saxon dropped their cutlery.

Ruben stared at Janey, his mouth an O, his face waxy.

Saxon arched back in his chair, his forearms shielding his face.

"Oh God, what's she done?"

Saxon let his arms drop and shook his head, his mouth turned down in distaste.

I slowly turned.

Janey stood in the middle of the garden, fork raised, a cat dangling from its tines. "Little shit was looking for a place in my beautiful soil to do its business."

"Jesus, Janey," I said in a fierce whisper. "People own cats here." I peered over towards Ted's house but couldn't see any movement.

"This isn't a pet, Em. Look at it." She shook the fork and the cat's back legs and tail swung violently. "It's mangy as fuck."

The cat was dark like Fenwick, Ted's cat. And it had the same tabby stripes.

My insides loosened.

I pushed my chair back and ran over to the garden, my ankles rolling slightly in the newly softened earth.

"That's a whole family of kiwi you'll thank me for saving," said Janey, as she shook the fork. The cat slid off the end and hit the soil with a dull thud.

I knelt in the dirt and inspected the poor creature. It was skinny and had hair missing in small patches on its shoulders and hind legs. It wasn't Fenwick.

I sat back and let out a long breath. "Please don't ever do that again, Janey. Leave it to the professionals to catch the wild ones."

"Pass me that spade." She pointed behind me.

I handed it to her and watched as she dug a hole.

"What are you doing?"

She answered by throwing the cat in.

"You can't bury it where I'm going to grow food!"

"More compost," Janey said, filling the hole in. "You'll get a thick crop here of whatever you grow. Soil'll be nice and rich."

I turned back to the table and eyed my plate of food. I didn't feel particularly hungry anymore.

Walking past the table, I said, "I'm going back to bed. Wake me when she's a normal mother."

WHEN I WOKE, it wasn't to a pounding in my head, but to a rhythmic banging issuing from somewhere near the back of the house. It was Saturday. Ruben was not obligated to work on weekends, but perhaps he wanted to get ahead.

I sat upright and tested the movement of my brain. Everything felt steady. I placed my feet on the floor and pushed myself up into a standing position. No spinning. No gut lurching.

I picked up my phone. 2pm.

I'd just spent fourteen hours sleeping. I should feel invincible.

I walked to the back door, picked up a banana from the fruit bowl, and headed outside.

It wasn't Ruben that I'd heard hammering.

Saxon knelt by my front tyre, one hand behind the dented metal of the wheel arch and the other tapping at the front of it with a broad-nosed hammer.

I stopped in my tracks. "Sax!"

"Yuh?" he said, without stopping what he was doing.

"You are the best brother," I said, walking over to him.

"Yeah, well, I don't have my whole kit with me, so it's not going to be perfect."

I wrapped my arms around his neck and squeezed him. He stiffened.

"Thank you, Saxxy," I said against his cheek before kissing it and releasing him.

He wiped at his cheek with his shoulder. "No

worries," he mumbled, before continuing with his tapping.

I leant against the driver's door and peeled the banana. "Dare I ask this question again today, but where's Janey? Please tell me she hasn't done anything else outrageous."

"It's not outrageous for *her*. She'd tell you shock factor's all a matter of relativity."

"Except that her behaviour still shocks us, despite constant exposure."

Saxon straightened up and grinned at me. "Dare you to tell Mum to her face that her theory's bullshit."

I snorted. "Unlike you, Sax, I have a strong sense of self-preservation. What were you *thinking* last night?"

"It wasn't *me* thinking. It was the beer."

I laid a hand on his shoulder. "I can't protect you from her if you don't help yourself."

"I don't need protecting, Em. I'm not scared of who she is." He didn't add *like you are*, but he didn't need to. It hung in the air like the bile-inducing stench of putrid rat.

He turned back to the car. "She's next door."

"At Ted's?"

He shrugged. "I don't know whose place it is. Mum invited herself over when she finished the garden and got bored."

"Oh Lord," I muttered, marching towards the gap in the hedge. Just when I thought she'd hit the lowest point of Project Imposition, she was now inflicting herself on reclusive neighbours.

I KNOCKED on the open door and called, "Ted? It's Em. From next door."

"Ah, Em." His voice was nearby. "Come in, my dear. I'm just through here."

I couldn't hear any talking, so perhaps Janey hadn't imposed herself on him after all.

I stepped into the lounge and found Ted partially obscured behind a canvas on an easel.

"We're having a marvellous time. I haven't had a life drawing model in years."

We?

I turned to my left. Janey lay naked and draped across Ted's couch, her upper body propped up by the couch's arm in a pose reminiscent of Renaissance paintings. Her hair was curled around her shoulders, its orange-ness at odds with the dark triangle of her pubic hair.

"Alright, Em?" she said.

My mouth dropped open, and I shook my head. I took an involuntary step backwards.

"She's coming along nicely," said Ted. "Want to see?" He swung the canvas around so that I got to view Janey's nudity in stereo.

I drew two sharp breaths and asked, "Was this your idea or his?"

"His. I popped by to introduce myself and thought having no clothes on in this weather was sensible, so I joined him."

"And I thought your mother's curves would look gorgeous in charcoal."

I flicked my eyes between the two of them. Janey stared solemnly at Ted, her cheeks slightly flushed.

"That has to be some kind of record, Janey. It usually takes you at least fifteen minutes before you get your kit off for somebody."

"He's a raging fruit, Em. Don't be presumptuous."

Ted frowned at me over the top of his glasses. "That's a bit unkind, my girl."

"I know. I'm sorry." I rubbed my temple. "It's been a challenging day." I'd only been conscious for half an hour of it, and in that time my mother had managed to hit the lofty heights of my cringe-ometer twice.

"Pop the jug on, Em," Janey said. "I'm parched."

I headed into Ted's kitchen. It was on the opposite side of his house from mine and still walled off. I filled the kettle and turned it on, its gentle burble easing my breathing into a deeper rhythm.

By the time the water had boiled and I'd found a teapot and made tea for three, I had gained some perspective. Ted was an artist, Janey an exhibitionist. Of course it wouldn't have taken them long to find some symbiosis. All in all, I reasoned, the whole thing was fairly harmless. Since Janey's knowledge of Facebook was so primitive she put "the" in front of the word, she was unlikely to post naked pictures of herself on social media. And Ted was safely in the internet black zone.

I rolled my shoulders and brought the tea into the lounge, pouring it and handing the cups around.

"Raise your chin slightly," Ted instructed Janey as I moved to stand behind him. "Thaaat's better," he drawled. "We need to have the light bathe your features evenly." He deftly copied the sharpness of her nose and its slight hook on the end with such speed and ease that I was mesmerised. He really did have true mastery of his talent. What a waste. The world would never see it.

When Ted moved on to adding detail to her torso and breasts, I turned and crouched down at the canvases at my feet. There were two dozen or more stacked against the wall in fours and fives.

I carefully flicked through them, admiring their depth and richness. I didn't see any of the three huia he had been about to paint on my first day on the island, but I had that sense again of being reminded of an artist I'd seen in the National Gallery, of a painting I'd stood in front of and let my mind swim between the layers of colour.

And then I remembered.

It was a portrait of a young boy. He held a fish in his arms like you would a puppy. If you looked carefully enough, a young man, reflected in the scales of the fish and presumed to be the painter, stared back at you.

The artist was Edward Sloane. An English painter who was prolific in the 1960s and 70s, his work sought after by art collectors and celebrities, and who disappeared suddenly in the early 80s. By the 90s he was presumed dead.

I pivoted on the balls of my feet and slowly raised my head to look up at Ted's face. "You're Edward Sloane."

CHAPTER SIXTEEN

TED'S HAND STILLED.

Then he sniffed and continued drawing.

"Aren't you?"

He used his finger to smudge a line. "I can't remember who that person is anymore. It's only the painting that ties us now."

"I..." I fought to keep my voice level and the speed of my words under control. "Look, I know you've turned your back on the world, for whatever reason, probably a really good one and I have no interest in making your identity known, so please don't worry, but I love your work. I've only seen one in real life, but I've seen others in books – you are a true master. Way ahead of your contemporaries in terms of composition and technique and –"

"Em," said Janey, "get a hold of yourself. You're frothing."

I clapped a hand across my mouth. Then spoke through it anyway, my voice deep and the vowels distorted. "You couldn't have picked a better spot to hide in."

"I didn't hide. I sought sanctuary. And now habit has made me a recluse."

I dropped my hand. "Eccentricity goes with the territory."

Ted took a sip of tea and bent to put it on the chair beside him. "I'd rather I wasn't considered a cliché. But the truth is I'm a nudist hermit who likes to knit. One must embrace the box they are born into."

"You're no box dweller, Ted," said Janey. "Hell, we're all a little daft. I'm an Adult Swaddling Therapist and Em has imaginary middle-class parents."

"Janey," I said, in a "do you have to?" tone.

"I'm just saying it's our oddities that make us alike."

I sat down in an armchair and nursed my tea. "No one knows you're here?"

"I send my old agent the occasional card. We were lovers. So he's either completely trustworthy or a total liability. It's been over forty years and no one's come looking for me, so I figure he's proved his dependability."

I toyed with a frayed patch on the chair's arm. "What were you seeking sanctuary from?"

Ted sighed. "The pressure of being the next gifted young thing, the publicity, the sex, drugs and rock 'n' roll. I felt crushed under the weight of it."

"I understand," I said. And I did. I might not have had the notoriety or the talent, but Ted and I had both sought escape from suffocating lifestyles. And of all the places we could have sheltered in, it happened to be the same one.

"Ted," I said, "I'm happy to be your neighbour. I'll try to be a better one."

"Like not stealing his car?" said Janey, one eyebrow raised.

"Yeah," I said into my tea, "or flinching at the sight of your ball sack. I'm really sorry about that."

Ted chuckled, and I realised I didn't just need to be a better neighbour to Ted. I needed to be a better resident of the island. I needed to find a way of connecting to the people in this community. I had to find my groove and prove I was worth having a place amongst them.

I thought of the grisly incident that morning and had an idea.

"DO you have stockpiles of traps in a cupboard somewhere in The Facility?" I asked Anaru, and switched the phone to my other ear.

The late afternoon sun made long shadows of the trees on the sand, but the temperature hadn't yet dropped.

Janey lay beside me, *Gone Girl* held above her head, shielding her face from the sun. Saxon and Ruben sat talking facing the water, arms resting on tops of knees and beers nestled in clasped hands. Ruben had finally dispensed of his Kluft, revealing a sun-starved body with tanned forearms and a brown V on his chest.

It was Sunday night – school night – the last few hours of freedom and relaxation before the working week began. Saxon had requested a barbecue on the beach.

Several other families had decided to make the most of the beautiful end of the weekend too, and children jumped and bombed from one of two pontoons anchored out in the bay, their laughter and yells loud on the windless beach and their energy creating an almost festive atmosphere.

"The Facility?"

"You're all so secretive and high-security about the sanctuary. It's like Area 51."

Anaru laughed. "I can assure you we use no anal probing techniques in our breeding practices." He paused. "Though, technically we could, I guess, given a bird's anatomy."

"Ah yes, the multi-functional cloaca," I said, hoping to impress him with my knowledge of bird reproduction.

"Indeed," said Anaru, not sounding particularly awed. "So, what kind of traps?"

With the phone clamped to my ear so I could hear above the occasional shriek from the kids playing in the water, his voice was deeper than normal, and I shivered.

"Rats, I guess. Ones that anyone can use."

"Why?"

"OK. So I have this idea. Rats are attracted to human activity, right? Because we're wasteful and have cosy places for them to nest in. So what if all the residents on the island were responsible for trapping the rats on their property? It'd be a back-up to all the work you're doing."

"Yeah," he said slowly, "it would."

"People here can have a role in making this island totally predator free. I think they'd really jump on board."

"It's a great idea, Em." His voice was soft and filled with an emotion that might have been pride or admiration or wonder, and a warmth flooded into my chest and receded out through my limbs.

Out in the bay, a girl backflipped off the pontoon

and another was pushed in. Her scream echoed between our phones.

"Where are you?" we both said at the same time.

We laughed, and Anaru said, "I'm in my truck in the car park wishing I didn't have to work in this weather."

"We're on the beach. Come and watch us drink beer if you like."

"Do you mean to say you're in violation of bylaw 391.2, the prohibition of the consumption of alcohol on public reserves?"

"There's a liquor ban?" I said, unable to keep the dismay out of my voice. I watched as Janey sipped wine from a thermal travel mug, the ice clinking as she resettled it into the sand with a couple of twists. The news that we'd have to have a dry barbecue would not go down well. "I'm not telling them. You can."

I smiled despite myself at the sound of Anaru's car door closing. "I'm just pulling your leg. Bylaw 391.2 is the prohibition of any form of merriment on a Sunday, especially that which requires the exposure of skin above the knees."

"I'm safe, then. I hate the beach. And I swim in a sheet these days."

"So I just need to arrest the twenty people that *are* enjoying themselves?"

"Is 'arrest' in your job description?"

"No, thankfully. I reckon my truck could comfortably fit eight people. Fifteen uncomfortably."

The sand behind me squeaked. I didn't turn.

"Shit day," said the voice in my ear and the man who bent to sit beside me.

"Bloody awful. I'm having a miserable time."

Anaru grinned at me, the phone still clamped to his ear. "You gonna hang up?"

"You first."

"On the count of three."

Janey looked over at us and rolled her eyes but smiled into her book.

"So. This plan of yours," Anaru said, pocketing his phone.

"Yeah. We just need to find out how many residential properties there are, get that number of traps, and call a meeting. You can teach them how to set them."

Anaru nodded. "I can get a small team together to do that. We'll need to record data – the catches and their location. Digital would be best, but that's not doable for a lot of people."

I drew a spiral in the sand, thinking. It took me to the fifth circle to find the answer. "Have a record at the store. Everyone goes there. No internet necessary."

Anaru didn't say anything. He simply looked at me, a small smile on his lips and his eyes shining. I chose not to read into the latter. The direct sunlight would make the most sun-hardy eyeballs water.

The smile, however, was real. I watched his lips from safe behind the darkened lens of my sunglasses. He had a little dimple in the middle of his bottom, very full, very soft-looking lip. I fought the urge to reach out and press my finger into the dent. If he kissed me on the forehead again, I would implode into a little pile of humiliated ash.

Anaru's eyes travelled to my brow and I blurted "Foreskin" before my feverish brain could stop itself.

"Excuse me?"

I slapped my hands to my cheeks, pre-empting any rush of blood. "Um. Funny thing. Wolf told Ruben 'forehead' was 'foreskin'."

Anaru smirked. "Sounds like Wolf. Why'd you mention it? It's a bit random."

I stood up. "I'm going for a swim."

"In your sheet?"

"It's a kaftan. And yes. I'm too skinny."

"She's too bloody skinny," said Janey, without looking up from her book.

"You look alright to me."

I plucked at the fabric, pulling it away from my body. "I'm putting on weight, but I still feel...un-womanly."

Anaru undid his laces and tugged at his boots. "Women are interesting creatures."

"What does that mean?"

"He means no guy would worry enough about how they looked to bother wearing something impractical to swim in," Janey said.

Anaru placed his socks inside his boots and started unbuttoning his shirt.

My indignation drained as I watched his slender fingers release one button, then the next, revealing his smooth, dark brown skin.

"Yes, that," he said. "And not being happy with your body shape. It seems to be a female preoccupation. Makes me kinda sad."

He pulled off his shirt, his muscles flexing in sequence as he dropped it on the sand, and stood up. He unbuckled his belt, picked his towel up, and wrapped it around his waist.

I turned and faced the sea. "You have the privilege of advantage."

"Advantage?"

"Being a man in a patriarchal society. Not feeling constantly scrutinised for how you look from a very young age."

"And it doesn't stop," said Janey. "It gets bloody worse the older you get. Men can go to seed, but bring out the air horns if a woman's lipstick dares to run into her lip wrinkles."

"No, you're right." His belt rattled as his shorts hit the sand. "I don't know how that feels."

"And you have the advantage of a ridiculously perfect body."

Anaru laughed. "Ridiculously perfect?"

"I bet you never worried in your life about how you looked."

"Course I have. Try being a brown-skinned person in a white society. Not much of an advantage, that."

I didn't say anything. There was no possible counterargument.

A shadow fell across me, and I looked up into Anaru's face. "Race you. See if white privilege beats male privilege." I took off before he could think about it.

"Cheater!"

"Just claiming my handicap. Your legs are longer than mine," I called over my shoulder.

Anaru humoured me until we reached the water's edge and then he charged ahead. "Last one in marries a rat."

"Rotten egg," I shouted after him. "Marry a rat if you step on a crack."

Anaru was ten paces ahead of me and already struggling to leap over the surface of the water. He dived, surfacing a couple of metres away and turned, grinning. Then he faltered. "Ah, you might want to –"

A series of splashes to my left drew my attention, and I turned my head just as Saxon tackled me, the force of the hit throwing me sideways and under the water. Its coolness flowed freely between my buttocks, and I surfaced, keeping to a crouch.

Saxon pushed himself away from me, spluttering out a laugh.

I grabbed his arms and pulled him to me, saying in a fierce whisper, "Find my bikini bottoms, or I'll kill you."

His eyes widened, then he roared with renewed laughter.

"Saxon!" I searched the water around me, arms outstretched to provide a net. "It's not fucking funny."

"It *is* fucking funny. Here."

I looked up, and my briefs hit me in the face with a wet slap before sliding off into the water.

I grabbed them and pulled them under the surface.

"Piss off," I whispered, struggling to balance myself while I put a leg through one of the holes.

Saxon looked between me and Anaru and grinned. "Don't let me cramp your style." He pushed off back to shore, shouting, "You kids have fun."

I doggy-paddled towards Anaru, not trusting my bikini briefs enough to stand up.

He wore a sideways smile.

"What?"

"Your relationship hasn't matured much past annoying little brother, provocative older sister, has it?"

"I like to think of it as 'playful'." Then after a pause I added, "I left home when he was twelve. It never really got a chance to. Plus, he's still a little boy in a man's body a lot of the time, and I get reactive."

"Understandable." He looked out to sea and back at me. "Swim out to the pontoon?" The second pontoon was farther from shore than the one the kids were jumping off and so was perhaps too much of an effort for them to get to.

"I'm not racing you this time," I said, setting off at sedate breaststroke pace.

"That's a relief. I bet you'd kick my arse."

I smiled. "You betcha. If I didn't have unreliable tog elastic, you wouldn't see me for spray."

The water around the pontoon was dark with the depth of the water, and I was glad Anaru was with me, knowing I would never make the swim on my own.

"You ever see any sharks around here?" I asked, as I slapped my hands on the side, looking for a decent handhold.

"All the time," Anaru said, hoisting himself up the side of the pontoon. "This bay's a bronze whaler breeding ground."

He reached down a hand to help me up, but I didn't need any better motivation to get out of the water. I kicked hard and pulled myself up, twisting around so that I landed on my bottom. I had to lift a butt cheek at a time to hoist my bikini briefs an inch to their original position. "All the time?" I asked, panting from my exertion.

We sat on either side of a corner, our legs dangling over the side, our bodies facing away from each other.

"Well, from time to time, I guess. Often when I'm out in the boat."

"The boat?"

"Observation. For the marine reserve."

I *ah*-ed as if I knew the waters here were protected.

"You know, I've seen this bay from the air? There were hundreds of them, just fifty metres offshore."

I drew my legs up out of the water. "You're having me on."

He laughed. "OK, well, not hundreds."

"How far are we from the shore?"

Anaru peered towards the beach and stuck his bottom lip out in deliberation. "About fifty-three metres, I reckon."

I shoved his shoulder and stood up. "Aren't you meant to be working?"

"I am. This is community liai –" Anaru looked up at me, his face going slack for a moment, before he recovered himself and said, "You know, your sheet isn't doing a very good job of hiding you."

I looked down. The pale fabric was completely see-through and clung to every inch of the skin above my knees. The effect was marginally erotic. I pulled at it, the kaftan making a soft sucking sound as it lifted from my belly. Slowly, my body became re-obscured behind a haze of material.

I looked down at Anaru, and he quickly turned his head away.

Heat bloomed beneath my ribcage, and its energy rolled up to my face and out of the widest smile it had been forced to accommodate in a while.

I saluted the heavens and brought my arms down to my chest, my hands balled in a small fist pump.

"Are you gloating?" Anaru said, still facing the shore.

"Heck yes. I haven't had a man look at me like that in a long time. Not even Warren." I lay down on my stomach, my head nestled on my forearm.

Anaru leant back to peer at me, beads of water running down the six abs I could see at this angle. It wouldn't surprise me if he had ten – six for show and four more for good measure.

I squinted my eyes, looking at him through my lashes so that my perving wasn't as obvious as I suspected it might be.

"Your sheet's indecent."

I purred. At least my diaphragm emitted a soft whimper that I hoped was only audible to me.

"And kinda redundant." He swung his head towards a series of soft splashes that were approaching the pontoon. "We have company."

If it was Saxon again, I would knife his tyres.

The swimmer approaching us had the smooth pull of a trained freestyler and arms that were much longer than Saxon's. Ruben slowed a couple of metres out from the pontoon and swam the last few strokes with his head above the water. His hair, blackened by the water, was plastered to his skull, and his face, whitened by sunscreen, looked almost ghoulish.

"Nice stroke, brother," said Anaru. "Where'd you learn to swim like that?"

I rested my head on a closed fist and watched him climb up onto the platform.

"I belonged to a club when I was a child, but I didn't have the" – he knocked his fist on his belly – "to do well when we raced."

"You weren't competitive enough?" I asked.

"Genau. Exactly."

A hoot from the other pontoon drew our attention. The water in front of it was white and churning, and as a head surfaced a moment later, a girl leapt from the platform, forming a V and landing inches away from the swimmer. A jet of water arced high above her point of entry, and another series of hoots rang out from the kids watching.

"School goes back tomorrow. Looks like they're making the most of it," said Anaru.

"You call this 'doing a bomb'?" asked Ruben, as another boy, red with sunburn, landed one in the same style, the height of his splash a metre lower than the girl's. The spectator hoots were full of derision.

Anaru nodded. "Those ones are called 'popping a manu'."

An older boy, who might have been Tama, ran

from one side of the pontoon to the other, leaping into the air with his arms and legs splayed like he might belly flop, then he tucked his arms and upper body under his legs at the last moment. With a *badoom*, a wall of water was forced up and out several metres.

"That's your classic staple," I said to Ruben.

After a pause, he said, "The Māori kids are better."

"Superior race," said Anaru, his face deadpan.

"It's like seabirds drilling into the water for lonely fish."

Anaru nodded. "Manu means 'bird' in Māori."

"That was very poetic, Ruben," I said.

He nodded as if my comment was not unexpected. "I am a poet."

I looked up at him. "You are?" I tried to mask the incredulity in my voice, but there were so many things I hadn't yet had a chance to discover about Ruben – thanks to his dedication to nights with Mel and the arrival of my family. A poet was not one of the things I had imagined.

"Yes. I do slam poetry."

"What's that?"

"You compete against other poets at a live event. You try to make your poems short and powerful."

"Like rap?"

"Sure. I listen to a lot of hip hop. To get, you know..."

"Inspiration?" suggested Anaru.

Ruben nodded. "I struggle a bit in English. I can't...what's the word?" He snapped his fingers. "Riff, in English. I have to write it first and research the right words."

"Can you do some now?" I asked. "Slam us with your poetry skills?"

"OK. I can give you some lines from a poem I've been working on. It's about being a slam poet." He dipped his head and cleared his throat before lifting it and gazing at the horizon. "I experience the world – I distil the taste of it, the noise of it into a small ball of high pressure, like a grenade made of words. Then I make sure the world experiences me."

Anaru and I were quiet for a moment.

"Whoa," Anaru said.

"That was one hell of a slam," I said.

Ruben grinned down at us. "Thank you."

"You'll have to perform some for Janey. She'll love it," I said, knowing that she'd be enraptured by his word-skill, by the power he could pack into a couple of sentences. Janey was a stalwart for self-empowerment. "Now I think you should show us how you can slam the water with your bomb skills."

Ruben laughed. "OK. I don't think I'll be very good. I only know one style." He took two steps and jumped off the pontoon, drawing his arms and legs into his body as he hit the water.

"Cannonball!" I shouted when he surfaced.

"We'll have to teach you a better one than that before you leave," said Anaru.

"Yes," Ruben said as he hoisted himself back up. "I want to pop a manu."

Anaru and I laughed. "We can arrange that," said Anaru.

"Do you have beaches in Germany?" I asked. "For some reason I picture a landlocked country."

"We do. Our coast is in the north between Holland and Poland. Denmark is in the middle."

"I've never been to Europe," I said. "I feel so ignorant about so much of the world."

"You must visit. When I finish my Wanderjahre – being a journeyman."

"I'd love that. I can buy a wan and travel the continent."

Ruben stood over me and shook like a dog, the drops of water cold on my hot skin.

"Hey," I said in mock outrage, rolling away from him and stopping close to the edge of the pontoon.

Anaru leant over and gave me a push. I reached for his arm but only grabbed air, my momentum pulling me over and into the dead space between platform and sea. I landed face and belly first onto the water with a slap.

I swam down and under the pontoon, surfacing on the far side.

The platform had tipped slightly under the combined weight of Ruben and Anaru, their bottoms in the air as they kneeled on the pontoon's side, peering into the water.

"You just wanted to see me being indecent again."

They turned in unison, Anaru's look of concern melting into relief, then humour. "Yep."

He reached down, grabbing both my arms and hoisting me up. I raised my legs to prevent any bikini bottom accidents, and as he overcorrected his balance and staggered backwards slightly, I planted my feet, bent forward, and wrapped my arms around his waist. Then I pushed against him at a run.

We toppled over the end and into the water, his knee connecting with my ribs and my elbow spearing his forearm.

I came up coughing and laughing and rubbed at my side.

Anaru beamed at me, then frowned. He pointed at my nose. "You got the snots."

Oh God.

I turned away from him and wiped furiously at my upper lip, expecting to feel a telltale sliminess. Nothing. I pinched the area beneath my nose between my thumb and forefinger and looked at them. Still nothing.

I turned back and was met by a wide grin.

"You shit!" I said, kicking forward and pushing down on his shoulders so that he sunk beneath me.

My kaftan billowed around me, and as Anaru reached to pull me down after him, he clasped my exposed hips, the contact of his skin against mine sending an electric pulse to my gut.

We surfaced face to face, my kaftan trapped under my armpits. Anaru's arms encircled me, his hands resting on my bare back.

We grinned at each other, the air between our mouths warm with our shared breath.

And then my legs, independent from my brain, wrapped themselves around his waist, which while being about as subtle as a sledgehammer bearing the words "I'm finding this all rather hot", is a sure-fire way of helping someone to drown.

Anaru's smile faltered. From the way it flickered and died and the intensity at which his gaze met mine, it wasn't from the exertion required to keep us both above water.

This time, his eyes moved to my mouth. They stayed there for that extra beat that makes desire clear, then they slid back up my face as his hands slid back to my hips.

A *BOOM* issued from the beach and echoed around the bay, and we detached as quickly as the thought KISS had just commandeered all room in my brain.

Saxon stood in front of the kettle barbecue, flames billowing up from its rounded base. He held a yellow object in one hand. A canister of lighter fluid, presumably.

Anaru groaned. "There's a full fire ban." He

looked at me. "Goes for barbecues, too. I better put my ranger hat on." He gave me a tight-lipped smile of regret and began swimming back to shore.

I hoped the regret was less for having to deprive us of our evening meal, and more for leaving me at such a delicate moment in my state of indecency.

I was going to tie Saxon by his testicles to the rear bumper of my car and make him run home.

WHEN I ARRIVED at the store on Monday, I was greeted by a wink from Wolf.

My eyes involuntarily flicked from his face to his groin and back again, and I hastened to my table before I could register any amusement or triumph in his expression.

Kevin wheezed himself into repose at my feet, Don *kerchunk*ed pricing labels onto goods, and Trace delivered a coffee and a slice of orange and chocolate cake. My world was ordered and safe, the routines the same as any other weekday.

I opened my laptop and inhaled the calming predictability of my working day.

It was no good.

Ever since yesterday's swim, my mind had been besieged. Anaru had staged a takeover and demanded complete submission. I tried to fight him. I tried to force him from my mind, but his presence was too powerful, too entrenched. And my resolve was too weak.

I reached for my coffee and Anaru stared at me in my wet kaftan.

I typed in the characters of my password and Anaru's hands were on my back.

I retyped the password I spelled wrong and Anaru's hands slid to my hips.

I sighed and speared the cake with my fork and Anaru looked at my lips two achingly unfulfilled seconds too long.

Anaru. Anaru. Anaru.

I closed my eyes as I wrapped my legs around his waist again and pressed my groin into his pelvis.

Something warm and wet slid between the toes of my left foot and encircled the big one, before slipping back between the middle two.

I gasped and jerked my foot back, looking under the table to an expressionless Kevin. He licked his jaws and looked away from me in a daring display of nonchalance, before laying his head back down between his paws.

I groaned and put my face in my hands, rubbing my eyes with the heel of my palms as if trying to rub away the looping movie reel of Anaru.

"You OK there, Em?" asked Wolf. "You look a little distracted."

A man in a DoC uniform entered the shop and

walked down the centre aisle, his face obscured by the goods on the shelves.

My heart lurched, and my blood attempted to beat its way out of my body.

"Help you?" said Trace, her mouth a line.

"Batteries," said a deep and unfamiliar voice.

I collapsed back into my chair.

"Type?"

"Triple A, thanks. Two packs."

When the transaction was complete and the man had exited the store, Trace said in a hushed voice, "That's the fifth one today. I don't think he needed batteries at all. I think they're keeping an eye on us."

"What do you mean, Trace?" asked Don.

"All these budget cuts and" – she raised her fingers in quotation marks – "'streamlining for efficiency'. They're probably combining departments to save money."

Wolf snorted. "You're saying he's a Security Intelligence Service and Department of Conservation double agent?"

"It's just fishy, is all I'm saying. There's too many of them and they behave oddly. I mean –" She gestured at the door as another person in DoC khakis walked in, and she closed her argument with a "Case in point" before the ranger had taken three steps into the shop.

"Triple A batteries, please," said the woman. Trace turned to retrieve them with raised eyebrows.

When the woman left the shop, Trace rearranged her features into an expression of smugness.

Don peered out from between two cans. "Why on earth would they want to spy on us?"

"You tell me."

"They want to know our secret to a happy and simple life," said Wolf.

"Or the recipe for Trace's Black Forest cake," said Don.

Trace picked up a package from under the counter and walked towards me. "Whatever it is they're after, it's probably something so anchored in our islandness that we take it for granted, you know, don't even know its worth," she said, bouncing the box in her hands. "I bet it's right under our noses." She placed the box on my table. "I completely forgot to give you this on Friday. It came on last week's ferry."

"Oh," I said, remembering without enthusiasm Warren's directive for drone surveillance.

"You going to open it?"

I looked at my laptop and knew I wouldn't be able to concentrate on spreadsheets and data for more than three seconds before Anaru's wet and flexing biceps shoved aside all other thought.

"Fuck it," I said, closing my laptop and picking up the box. "It's work." And I headed out the door before Trace could ask me why I needed a drone.

I DISAPPEARED down the back of my section, away from the curiosity of the household. I needed to have a practice run with the drone before I risked being discovered spying on the sanctuary courtesy of any ineptitude.

I doubted anyone would be able to hear the whine of a flying drone over the gnashing of Ruben's drop saw. I had no control over where they looked, however. I could only hope that between my shit box house, my crumpled car and my Dan Brown novel collection, there would be ample distraction.

I opened the box and settled the machine on the grass. Its sleek black body and four propellers on the end of lightweight arms made it look roach-like. I scowled at it as if it had scuttled into my new life from under the debris of my old Warren-shared one.

I sighed and crouched beside it. "Can I ask a favour? How about we shoot some stuff that looks like it's inside the fence. Keep the boss happy and my love life still on the table? What do you say? Are you in with me on this?" I took its silence as an affirmation and reached for the instructions. After a cursory perusal, I started the engines.

The mechanics seemed simple enough – up, down, hover, left and right. I raised the drone into the air, switching my focus between it and watching what it could see on the console's small screen.

An elf-sized Em grew smaller and smaller, and I rotated the camera until I could see both houses. My backyard was empty apart from a black-flared, white-shirted Ruben, measuring wood with his earmuffs on.

Over the hedge, Ted disappeared into his garage, and I swung the drone in the direction of the ocean, testing its speed and manoeuvrability. There was no one to spot it here. It sped over acres of native bush until I worried the signal from the console wouldn't be able to reach it.

I turned it around, flying it back towards my property so I could practice hovering in close proximity to trees. I stopped its forward momentum when I could see myself in the camera, and slowly lowered it.

A thunderous *CRACK* pierced the morning air.

I flinched and watched the drone be erased from existence. One moment it hovered five metres above the tree canopy, the next it had disintegrated, little pieces of plastic and metal and glass showering the bush.

CHAPTER SEVENTEEN

"GOTCHA!" said a plummy voice.

I turned and peered through the hedge.

Ted stood, legs askance, a shotgun resting in his hands. Fenwick made a dash from the garage to the house and disappeared through the cat flap with a *fwapfwapfwap*.

"Sorry for the noise, my darling boy," Ted said to the back door, "but you never know who's watching."

I waited, a hand clamped to my racing heart. No German expletives were issued, no "What the fuck was that?" shouted. I saluted the technology gods in thanks for drop saws and earmuffs and high-fived myself (which is really just tantamount to jumping in the air and clapping above your head). Then I put the console in the box and headed to the house for a cup of tea.

"WHAT DO YOU MEAN IT BROKE?"

I nestled against my favourite Skype-meeting tree outside the shop and said, "It just...fell apart mid-flight. Must have been made cheaply."

"That thing cost over a thousand dollars!"

"You're kidding? That was a rip-off."

"Em." Warren's voice dropped to a soft growl. "What are you not telling me?"

"Nothing. Except you no longer have the ability to spy on non-existent birds from the air. Can we please call it quits on this thing now?"

"Absolutely not. We need to regroup and find another way to get proof. Or I could send you another one."

"No! Please, just no. It's demeaning and I refuse to do it."

"Well, how do you suggest we gather evidence?"

"I have no interest in suggesting anything, Warren. This is *your* project. I'm simply *humouring* you, remember?"

"I have two words for you. 'Job' and 'description'."

I rolled my eyes.

"Maybe I'll come over there myself."

I sat up straight, scraping my spine against the trunk. "Ow! Alright, alright. Tell me what to do and I'll do it."

"I'll think about it and get back to you."

"Can't wait."

"Em?"

"Yeah?"

"Miss you."

I pointed at him. "Boss." Then at me. "Minion." I waggled my finger between the two of us and said, "Inappropriate."

He smiled and said, "I know. The boss part of me is sorry, the ex-boyfriend isn't."

"Well," I sighed, "I guess while we're on personal territory, why haven't you answered my email?"

"What email?"

"The one asking you where the division of assets is at."

"Ah. Yes. I've been meaning to get back to you on that one." He scratched behind his ear and said, "The um, conveyancing lawyer has been away on holiday, apparently, and is now wading through a backlog. I'm not sure when the papers will come through for you to sign."

"OK. And the money?"

He threw his hands up in the air as a criminal caught in the act might. "You got me. No excuse. I've just been really busy. I'll sort it. I promise. I'm still working through what all our stuff is worth."

"It needs to be done, Warren. It's already been a couple of weeks." I signed off and wondered briefly what plan he'd come up with. The truth was, I had one, too. A plan that I had no intention of telling

Warren about unless I felt it pertinent to, which was unlikely. It was a plan designed to curb my own curiosity.

Tonight I had a ticket to the inside.

I walked into the store and asked Trace for batteries. "Triple A, please."

***

I WAS TAGGING along to Wolf's legendary once-a-year poker game. Not as a player. That was invitation only. But as a spectator. Saxon would be taking part. Anaru wouldn't. He wasn't on the guest list.

Smoking was allowed. Drinking wasn't. Each player had to be of sharp wit and sound mind to keep the game progressing with the same level of analysis, strategy and deception. There was no tension if the players made sloppy decisions.

The stakes were arguably low – no money changed hands. Betting was with chips. However, a year's worth of pride was on the line. The winner would be crowned Poker King for that year, a status that held a lot of prestige amongst the blue-collar community of Ruatapu. Saxon was extremely lucky, as a visitor, to be allowed entry. And he was acutely aware of the honour, talking of little else for the last couple of days, and spending an hour preening in the bathroom before leaving.

In the late afternoon, when Saxon and I pulled

up at the enormous sanctuary gates set into the enormous sanctuary fence, I marvelled all over again at the formidableness of them, the height, the expense.

Saxon wound down his window and entered a pin into a keypad I hadn't noticed on the evening Anaru and I drove past.

"You need a passcode?"

"Yeah, changes every other day, apparently. Stops randoms from coming in, I guess."

"Man, they take their biosecurity seriously. I feel like we're entering the Jurassic Park compound."

We drove through to the holding cell. The gate behind us rattled on its tracks as it inched towards closure.

"You reckon they're manufacturing dinosaurs?" Saxon asked. "You know, it wouldn't be a T-rex that gave me the shits – we could outrun them easily – it's those freaky little velociraptors."

"I know. They'd smile at you and rip out your innards before you had a chance to think about running away."

The gate clanged shut, and we both jumped. I looked at Saxon, his wide eyes mirroring mine, and we burst out laughing.

After ten seconds the gate in front of us eased open.

Saxon drummed his fingers on the steering wheel. "Man this is tense."

I opened the backpack between my feet and

pulled out the batteries, cracking the packet and placing them in my torch.

"You gonna do some kiwi spotting?" asked Saxon.

"Yeah. And I'd like to see what other rare creatures come out at night."

"You're not going to watch?" he asked as he drove out of the enclosure and onto a gravel road.

"The game will go for hours. I'll be back to watch you lose."

Saxon scoffed, and I asked if he minded if I borrowed his car.

He sighed. "No off-roading. I don't want a single scratch."

"I have nothing but respect for your car baby, Sax," I said, watching the thick bush for any flashes of white or yellow.

The further we drove into the fenced-off area, the louder the birdsong became. The sun was heading towards setting, but the birds sounded as if they were ramping up for the night. I cracked my window, and a cacophony of trills and chirrups and beeps drowned out all noise in the car, even that of the engine.

"It's deafening," shouted Saxon.

I listened a while longer then rolled the window up. "It's incredible. This is what it would have been like when the first Europeans arrived. Did you know that Captain Cook had to anchor several miles offshore because of the bird noise?"

"Then they stuffed it all up."

"By bringing stoats and ferrets to a land of birds. No predators until the bipedal monkeys arrived."

Saxon nodded. "Humans can be pretty stupid."

The road forked, and a signpost signalled the DoC facility to the left and the station to the right.

I peered down the left fork as Saxon turned away from it but couldn't see anything through the thick vegetation. We travelled for another ten minutes before the bush gradually gave way to grassland, the paddocks brown in the dryness of late summer. Sheep grazed on the stubbly grass, and birds, flying between copses of trees, still sang midflight.

In the distance, the mountain Te Upoko o Ruatapu reared over the north of the island. At nearly one thousand metres high, it was an impressive landmark, giving the island a lop-sided or top-heavy appearance from the approach by sea.

"God, it's massive – the area they've fenced off," said Saxon.

I nodded. "Yeah. Four hundred hectares, Anaru said. A third of the island."

Saxon smiled and poked me in the ribs. "Anaru."

"Yeah? And?"

"You think he's hot. I've seen you giving him the eye slide."

"The eye slide?"

"When you want to check him out but you don't want him to know you're checking him out, and you look out the corner of your eye all innocent-like and shit."

"If you hadn't gone all pyromaniac on the barbecue, I would have given him more than the eye slide."

"Good. He's a universe better than Warren. That dude was so far up his rose-smelling arsehole –"

"He wasn't *that* bad," I interrupted.

"He looked down on us, Em. And the worst thing was that he allowed you to feel it was OK to look down on us, too."

I didn't say anything.

"Does your silence mean I'm right, or that you still look down on us?"

"Saxon..." I began, not sure of the best way to tackle the rest of the sentence. I opened my mouth to attempt a reply, and a man stepped out in front of the car.

"Fuck!" I said, as Saxon hit the brakes and skidded to a stop, the bumper inches from the man's knees.

The man laughed and leaned over to slap the bonnet, then pointed to his left. "Parking's over there, brother. See you inside for the debrief."

He disappeared into a grove of trees, and as we pulled forward, Wolf's quarters came into view nestled against the northern edge of them.

I told Saxon there was no point parking and jumped into the driver's seat when he vacated it. I wished him all the best of luck before I turned the car around and headed back towards the forest we'd driven through.

With some research, I had a bit of an idea what the circadian rhythm of a huia might be. They were certainly day-dwellers, but that didn't mean they weren't active towards dusk, like a lot of birds. Ideally, I should have been inside the fence several hours earlier, but I didn't want to risk raising suspicion. The best I could do was convince Saxon to go an hour earlier to give me more bird-spotting time. "You can have lots of time to settle in, assume your poker Zen," I'd said.

Despite the deepening blue of the near-to-dusk sky, the evening chorus was still in full swing, but it might not be for long.

I parked on the edge of the forest and slung my backpack on, my torch at the ready. The light was thin beyond the tree line and I would have to stick close to the road to avoid getting lost. I stepped between the bushes, my rustling and twig-snapping doing nothing to disturb the orchestra of cascading notes, glottal stops, pips and whistles.

I settled myself against a tree in a small clearing and waited.

Within ten seconds, four fantails darted through the open area and hopped from branch to branch and foot to foot, two dog-fighting tūīs swished through, acrobatically avoiding branches at high velocity, a robin hopped onto the toe of my sandal, pecking at the strap, and a small flock of kākā crashed through the canopy, the red underside of their wings bold in the darkening green. The large parrots eyed me from a safe distance and, after several seconds, stepped carefully along their branches to get a better view.

I kept very still. I had never seen kākā before, and I hoped their curiosity would bring them close. Keeping my eyes on the parrots, I slowly opened my backpack and felt around for the muesli bar I had brought. I had no idea what the protocol was for feeding birds. It was probably a huge no-no, but I knew they were intelligent. Intelligent enough to recognise a very good food opportunity when presented to them. And so I opened the packet, broke a bit off, and held out my hand to the nearest bird. It shifted its head to one side, eyeing the offering. Then it flew down to the ground, landing a few feet away from me and edging towards me in a sideways shuffle.

A *see-seeyip* pierced the air behind my right shoulder, and I jumped, startling the kākā who flew back into the trees.

Yellow flashed in my peripheral vision, and I turned my head sharply, my pulse quickening. The bird flitted away into the undergrowth, but not before I glimpsed white and black feathers. "Oh my God," I murmured.

I pivoted so that I was facing the bush it had disappeared into and shifted my weight onto all fours. I peered into the gloom, waiting for it to reappear.

See-seeyip.

A head emerged from behind a leaf, and I held my breath.

Then the bird took off, flying to a higher tree, but not before I could see it was too small to be a huia, and the yellow I had glimpsed belonged to feathers and not wattles. A stitchbird.

I sank back against the tree and closed my eyes, opening them when my breathing returned to a normal rhythm.

The kākā had disappeared. Their raucous squawks rang down from high in the canopy.

The fantails had stopped flitting, and no robin sought a snack from my footwear.

It got very dark very quickly.

And then one by one, the birds stopped calling. Last to bed were the songbirds. The kōkakos' *took took* ceased, then the bellbirds' *swan swing,* and eventually the tūīs' symphony ended, and I was left to the owls.

I hadn't brought a red light with me, so while there was every chance of spotting a kiwi, I didn't want to upset them by blinding their over-sensitive eyes. It was time to admit defeat and call it a night.

I took the torch out of my bag and flicked it on. Nothing happened. I shook it and turned it on again. Still nothing.

I recalled slotting the batteries into its handle without checking which way they should go in and groaned. My phone, the other possible source of light, was resting in the console of the car.

I opened my eyes as wide as I could to admit as much light as was available.

There was no light. The thick canopy ensured no starlight and no moonbeams reached the forest floor. I would have to find the car by feel.

I hadn't come far, and I knew in which direction I walked in from. I felt confident I would get there without too much trouble.

If I didn't think of velociraptors. Or zombie hoards.

A kiwi screamed to my left, and I clutched at the tree I hadn't yet found the courage to leave. I'd have to prise myself off at some stage if I wanted to catch the end of the poker game, so I decided a countdown from three would give me enough encouragement.

A twig snapped behind me on "two" and I didn't need any further urging.

I peeled my hands off the bark, put them out to shield my face should I walk into something, and moved as quick as I dared toward the road, lifting my legs and taking over-sized steps so that I didn't crack my shins on anything.

I successfully fended off two tree trunks and several branches before I stepped into a dip and lost my balance. I stumbled forward, tripped over a root, and crashed head-first into a bush, getting a face full of foliage.

I spat the bitterness of the leaves from my tongue and settled on crawling. Pushing the branches aside, I felt the gravel surface of the road. It was still warm from the heat of the day.

I climbed into the car, threw my useless torch on the passenger seat, and tried to decide if I was relieved or disappointed I hadn't discovered any huia. On one hand, if there were none to be discovered, there were none to be exploited. But let's be honest — who wouldn't jump at the chance to see a previously extinct creature of legendary status? The scales tipped decidedly towards self-interest.

SIX MEN SAT around the table in the small shearer's quarters, their heads wreathed in cigarette smoke.

No one spoke. Each man was focused on the cards in their hands or the faces of their opponents with a studied lack of expression.

With deliberate unhurriedness, Wolf laid his hand of cards on the table. A collective groan went up, and Wolf collected the chips from the table's centre.

Saxon blew out a long breath between pursed lips and rocked back in his chair. Then he noticed me. "What happened to you?" he asked, looking at my hair.

I patted my head and felt a tangle of twigs and

leaves. I gave one a tug. It surrendered unwillingly and separated from my hair with several red strands dangling off it. "Ow," I said, rubbing at my scalp.

"Have a bit of a roll in the hay with *Anaru?*"

I rolled my eyes. "Saxon, you're an egg."

"Anaru is it?" said Wolf, without looking up from gathering in the cards.

"No. I don't know. Maybe," I answered decisively.

He grunted and raised his eyes. "I thought you were looking cosy at the pub."

"Haven't you got a game to be getting on with?" I asked.

"I'm in no hurry," said Saxon.

"That's because you're getting a pasting," said a man to his left.

I looked at the table. Wolf had the largest share of the chips, Saxon the least. "Poker not your game, Sax?"

"I'm just giving everyone a head start. They'll need it when the royal flush ninja decides to come out of the shadows and take everyone down."

"Who's that? Em?" asked Wolf, pushing the cards over to a man to his right.

Saxon snorted. "Em can't play poker."

"You have no idea if I can play or not, Saxon."

Saxon opened his mouth to retort, and a phone buzzed into life, its ringtone muffled.

"No phones," said Wolf. "Them's the rules."

One of the men took a phone out of his pocket

and looked at it. He grimaced. "Sorry. I have to take it. It's Erena." He tapped the screen and stood up from the table saying, "Everything OK?" in a hushed tone and stepping into the dimness of the room behind him.

Saxon looked at Wolf and raised his eyebrows.

"New baby."

Saxon nodded and turned his lips downwards in a "can't argue with that" expression, then frowned as he picked up the last of his newly dealt cards.

Wolf cast a quick glance around the group, smiling at Saxon's frowned indiscretion and saying over his shoulder, "Ready when you are, big man."

Big Man returned to the table, pocketed his phone, and placed his hands on the back of his chair. "I've gotta go. Sorry guys, next year."

The group offered a variety of mildly sympathetic noises as *Big Man* headed for the door.

Wolf shifted his eyes from the door to me and said, "You in? Can't let these hard-earned chips go to waste."

I shrugged and moved towards *Big Man's* vacated seat. He had the second-largest chip pool.

"You sure you're up to this, little girl? You're in alpha territory now. And you've got big gonads to fill," said Wolf, nodding at my booty.

"She's not up to this," said Saxon. "I give her two hands before she loses it all."

I clenched my teeth together and mentally

counted to five. Then I smiled. If Wolf was being de-liberately provocative with his gauntlet throwing, or earnest with his cocksure brand of misogyny, he had no idea who he was messing with. "You guys are prob-ably right," I said. "Tell you what, Sax, if I'm still in after two hands, you have to give me half your chips."

"I only have six left!"

"I'm just a girl, Saxon. What have you to lose?"

"Not much the way you're going, son," said Wolf, looking at the pitiful pile of plastic discs in front of Saxon.

A couple of the men chuckled.

"Fuck yas, then," he said, and turned to me. "You're on."

I picked up *Big Man's* two-card hand one card at a time. Two low cards. Nothing to get excited about. Yet.

Three players pushed chips into the middle of the table.

"Your turn, Em," said Wolf. "Blue chips are worth one, red chips are worth two, and green chips, five."

"Oh," I said, and pushed a blue chip to the centre of the table.

Saxon clucked his tongue. "It's a red-chip big blind, Em. You've got to meet it."

I replaced my chip with a red one and watched the play until it came back to the dealer to "burn and turn". He turned the top card on the pack face down and the next three face up. A three of clubs, a four of diamonds and a six of clubs.

When play got to Wolf, he placed a single blue bet.

It was my turn next. I pursed my lips and *hmm*-ed.

"Come on, Em," said Saxon, tapping his pointer finger against the back of his cards.

"Hey Sax," I said, "is it a flush or a straight that's the same suit?"

"You've got a straight?" he asked incredulously.

I pointed at my cards one at a time as if counting them. "Oh, no. My mistake."

Saxon narrowed his eyes at me, weighing up if I was being dumb or playing dumb.

I pushed a blue chip forward and, just as Saxon placed a hand on his chips to meet me, I added a red one to it. And then a green one.

Two players, including Saxon, folded.

Once again, Wolf raised the bet before the dealer revealed the second-to-last card. A three of hearts.

I pursed my lips and nodded then raised the bet enough that everyone except Wolf folded. He winked at me and raised me three greens.

I fingered the tops of my cards, flicking the corners in succession. *Fwack, fwack.*

"Quick game's a good game, Em," Wolf said, without looking up from his hand.

I sighed and pushed enough chips into the centre of the table to see him.

The dealer turned the final card over.

An ace of spades.

"Interesting," said Wolf. He looked at my pile of chips and asked how many I had. I counted them. Their total value was fifty-three.

Wolf counted out fifty-three chips and moved them forward.

To meet him, I had to go all in. I shrugged my shoulders and pushed my entire chip pile into the centre of the table.

A collective gasp rippled around the table.

Saxon squeaked and said, "Em, what are you doing? You lose, you're out."

"Too late, son," said Wolf. "The lady's made her bet. Shame to waste the hard work of our man on the first go, but case in point why we don't invite women to play." He laid his hand on the table.

It was an excellent hand – an ace of diamonds and an ace of hearts. A full house.

I whistled. "Nice hand," I said, as I laid my two cards on the table with deliberate care, revealing a three of diamonds first and then a three of spades.

Wolf abruptly sat forward in his chair as a "Shee-it" escaped from one of the other players.

A full house was one of the best hands you could have in poker. But it didn't beat my four of a kind.

CHAPTER EIGHTEEN

IT TOOK another hour for me to clean everybody out.

Wolf sank lower into his chair with every sweep of chips I took from the centre of the table and lit cigarette after cigarette off the butt of his last.

By the end of the final hand, his chin rested on his chest.

"Guess you better rename it Poker Queen," I said to him. "Or better yet, have a gender-neutral title, like Supreme Poker Being." I started stacking my chips, forming several towers that listed as I placed more on top.

Wolf sat with his arms folded and stared at the table in front of him where his pile of chips used to be.

The room went very quiet, and after thirty seconds of loaded silence, the first man stood and said, "Right. Best get home." The others followed, carefully placing their chairs under the table and exiting the room with a soft snib of the door.

Saxon elbowed me and whispered, "C'mon. Let's go."

"Let me count them all first," I said "There's *so many*."

"Don't," Saxon murmured, casting a look at Wolf. "Apparently, he hasn't lost in thirteen years."

I whistled. "That's a long time. And to a *girl*."

Wolf stood suddenly and pointed to the door. "Get out."

I smiled at Saxon, who frowned at me and pushed me towards the door.

"See you Monday, Wolf," I said. "Thanks for all the fun."

When Saxon grabbed my hand, pulling me through the doorway and leading me to the car, I started giggling.

"Get in," he said in a resigned tone.

I buckled my seatbelt and waited for Saxon to start the engine. When he hadn't after several seconds, I turned to him.

His hands were clasped on the steering wheel, and he stared out the windscreen at nothing. "What have you done?" he asked without looking at me.

"Kicked a bunch of chauvinists' arses on behalf of all womankind."

He looked at me then. "That game is a really big deal, Em."

"Then he shouldn't have invited me to play if he couldn't handle losing. You'd think he'd have learned his lesson from you."

"That was different."

"No, it wasn't. You were just as patronising towards Janey as he was towards me. Men can be so stupid sometimes."

Saxon turned the key and threw the car into reverse. "You're more like Mum than you think."

I gasped and as I gathered my retort, the similarities between the way Janey and I had chosen our method of imparting a lesson about sexist attitudes became very clear – entering into a contest in a public arena, ensuring the humiliation was a spectacle, the defeat emasculating. "Oh God, I am, aren't I?"

Saxon slipped into first and headed back towards the gates. "When dick for brains left you standing in the road, what did you do? You stole a car and hunted him down."

"I didn't *hunt* him."

"You ran most of that Godforsaken road so that you could bust his balls. Dude doesn't know how lucky he was that you missed the ferry."

I didn't bother correcting his assumption that it was revenge I was looking for when I ran after Warren. But it did make me think. "I scare Anaru." It wasn't the exact emotion I wanted to elicit in him, but, I reasoned with a cringe, at least I had his respect.

"Probably, but that hasn't put him off from what I can see."

I turned to Saxon and said, "Am I too much?"

"As in...?"

"Too in-your-face?"

"I don't think I'm much of one to judge, Em. We haven't exactly spent a lot of quality time together in the last fifteen years."

I appealed to him by raising my eyebrows and squeezing them together.

He glanced at me and sighed. "From what I can see, you just know your own mind. And you're not shy about expressing it. You're not as full on as Mum, if that's what you're worried about."

I grunted and rubbed at a smudge on the waxed dash.

"It's a good thing. You two are strong. You take no prisoners. Beats lying in the dirt and letting everyone step all over you."

I sank into silence. I didn't particularly want to be like Janey. There was nothing about her that was subtle in any way. Not her appearance, not her language, not her attitude.

But Saxon was right. It was much better to be a bulldozer than a doormat. And I got all the steel in my backbone from her.

Maybe, just maybe, it was OK for me to be like her.

ONCE WE REACHED the air lock, Saxon turned on his stereo and picked up his phone from the centre console. He tapped on it, and when the system announced his device was paired, he cued a song and turned to me and winked.

The opening riff to Motörhead's "Ace of Spades" boomed through the subwoofer speakers.

"Please don't do what I think you're going to," I pleaded.

Saxon grinned as the outer gate opened. Then he revved the engine and accelerated in a shower of gravel, the rear wheels fishtailing slightly.

"What the fuck are you doing, Sax? You're not seventeen anymore."

"Relax," he said, as he changed down to enter a corner.

I clutched the handle above the door and gripped the edge of my seat. "Saxooon!" I yelled as he hit the bend.

The car skidded around the corner at a forty-five-degree angle to the road. "Haven't you been dying to fang it on these roads since you got here?"

"No!"

"Liar. Don't pretend you haven't wished for a car that you could do this in."

"Slow the fuck down!"

"It's fine, Em. We'll see anybody coming by their lights."

"It's not fine! I have to live here. You can offend everyone and then fuck off."

"Everyone's safe. I know what I'm doing." He looked at me and said, "You know I know what I'm doing."

"Eyes on the road!" I screeched as another corner raced towards us.

Saxon spun the wheel, careful not to overcorrect, and the car drifted around it in a long slide before straightening up and speeding towards the next corner.

A horseshoe bend.

Beyond the fence on the outer side of the looming corner was nothing. The road curved above a bluff.

"Brake! Brake! Brake!" I screamed as Lemmy growled a declaration about not wanting to live forever.

Saxon pulled on the handbrake and skidded through the bend as calmly as he might remove a teabag from a mug.

"Jesus Christ, Saxon!" I hit his upper arm with the outside of my fist. "You're a munter."

He grinned. "Yep." And coasted around the next corner.

The next few kilometres passed just as fast and just as fraught.

There was no denying that Saxon was a good driver. He'd had a decent foray into the nitrous-octane-fuelled world of rally driving as a teenager courtesy of one of Janey's boyfriends. And I tried to relax and trust his level of skill, but there's something about speed and small margins of error that make it difficult not to think about crumpling metal and punctured lungs.

"Kiwi!" I yelled, pointing at a fuzzy ball bumbling its way across a dip in the road.

"Hang on," Saxon said between gritted teeth. He changed down and accelerated.

I closed my eyes and waited for the smack of bird on metal.

It didn't happen. Instead, I was momentarily lifted from my seat as the car gained air and slammed forward against my seatbelt as the Holden hit the gravel again.

"Woo!" Saxon hollered. "That's what I'm talking about, baby."

I turned around in my seat but couldn't see anything for the red glow in the dust-encrusted back window.

I placed a hand on his arm. "You bunny-hopped a kiwi."

Saxon laughed. "Nah, there was a bump in the road. The bird was just lucky."

· · ·

AS WE APPROACHED THE HOUSE, he pulled on the handbrake and skidded into the driveway, coming to a stop a few inches behind Ruben's van. He killed the motor, and the engine ticked in the otherwise silent night.

Picking up his phone, he said, "Twenty minutes to get there. Seven to get home." Then his eyes met mine, and a slow smile unfurled across his lips.

I knew I should stare him down, tell him again what an irresponsible idiot he was, but in the wake of seven minutes of pure adrenaline, all I could do was grin back. "Holy shit," I said, "that was awesome!" I drummed my hands on the dash.

"Knew you'd appreciate it. Feel better now?"

"I feel...so alive. I know that's a cliché, but –"

"Better than sex," Saxon interrupted, nodding.

I snorted. "Better than any sex *I've* had."

Saxon opened his door and stepped out, saying, "I knew Warren was a dud. Dresses like a poof."

I climbed out and closed my door. "Saxon, you're mostly a good brother, and there are times when I love you, but do you know how stupid you sound when you say stuff like that?"

He shrugged and walked towards the back door.

I followed, breaking into a jog to catch up. "Women don't find 'dumb' sexy. You know that, right?"

Another shrug.

I tried again to push him out of his stubborn apathy. "You'll never lose your virginity if your mind's smaller than your dick."

"Piss off," he said, as he pulled the door open.

"...like how you've half-rhymed 'verbal discharge' and 'therapy surcharge'," Ruben was saying, as he and Janey compared notes at the dining room table from several pieces of paper.

"Have a nice time?" Janey asked without looking up.

"Saxon bunny-hopped a kiwi in the Holden," I said.

"Em single-handedly castrated the island chief. I think we should leave on the next ferry," said Saxon.

"A normal night, then," Janey said, taking a sip of wine from her tumbler.

Saxon and I looked at each other. "Yep," we said in unison.

"Ah, that's my kids," Janey said, reclining and smiling at us. "Get yourselves a drink and tell me all about it."

I WAS LATE TO WORK. Sure, I was master of my own hours and could start any time I wanted. But I liked routine, and I wanted to be at the store when Trace cut the first slice from the cake-de-jour, and home by a respectable lunch-eating hour.

But my morning was hijacked by Janey, then

Anaru, then something that tipped my world view on its axis.

My first conversation with Janey went like this:

Janey: Why do you keep scratching your crotch? Anyone would think you have crabs.

Me: I'm itchy! There's nowhere on the island to get a wax and the hairs are growing back in.

Janey: Good. There's something wrong with a grown woman walking around with the foof of a little girl.

Me: *What* did you call it?

Janey: Foof. What's wrong with that?

Ruben (yawning): Good morning.

Me: Morning Ruben.

Janey: Would you rather I said cock holster?

Me (darting a look at Ruben): God, Janey!

Ruben: Would anyone like coffee?

Janey: Yes, please, love.

Me (whispering): Just call it a vagina like a normal person.

Janey: Normal? How very Gen X of you.

Me: Do you have any idea what you're talking about?

Janey: No. Do I have to?

Me: I'm Gen Y, mum. A millennial. *You're* Gen X. The latchkey generation, whose mothers had kids *and* a career.

Janey: My mother had God and Tom Jones. I'm lucky I wasn't called Delilah.

Me (muttering): Yeah, good thing you didn't make that mistake with me.

Janey: Oh, I've been meaning to show you. (*Pointing at her feet*) I've vajazzled my jandals.

Me: Ha ha ha. That is classic.

Janey: What?

Me: You haven't vajazzled anything. You've stuck faux diamonds to the straps of your flip flops. You've *blinged* them.

Janey: What's the difference?

Me: One involves footwear. The other (*annunciating clearly*) va-gi-nas.

Janey: Ohhhhh.

Janey: I've got some left over if you want to put a tiara on your love box. Then you and your six-year-old foof can play "princesses".

THE SECOND CONVERSATION I would rather forget. However, it is firmly etched in my mind and no amount of mental discipline or semi-naked ranger daydreaming can erase it from my memory:

Janey (distantly): Em? Where are you?

Me: On the loo.

Janey (closer): Right, well it's time to get off.

Me: I'm thirty-two, Janey. I think I know by now when it's time to finish up.

Janey (standing outside toilet door): Get out of

there, Em. You've been in there long enough to sink the whole fleet.

Me: *Sigh*. Please go away.

Janey: Not until I hear you flush.

Me (shouting): Can't a woman wipe her arse in peace?

Janey: You have a visitor.

Me: Oh God. Who is it?

Anaru: Ah, it's Anaru.

Me: *Squeak*.

Anaru: I can come back later, if you like.

Janey: No, she's had long enough in there. You go on through to the kitchen, and I'll prise her off.

Me (muttering): I hate you.

Janey (shouting from the kitchen): I heard that!

THE ONE GOOD thing about the morning was that I got to bask in Anaru. He'd come round to let me know he'd raided the trapping vaults of The Facility and had almost enough rat traps for every household on the island.

"I've booked the Port Keulemans Hall for next Monday night. We just have to let everyone know."

We sat outside at the table, trying not to be uncomfortable in the already too hot morning sun.

"Where's the hall?"

"The wharf. Doubles as the ferry passenger terminal."

I nodded and said, "I thought it looked a bit municipal hall-y." Then after a pause I said, "We could make flyers. Get Trace and Don to tell everyone who comes into the store. Is word of mouth better than Facebook here?"

"A hundred times faster," said Anaru. He sipped the coffee Janey had made him. "It'll be good PR for us, too. Some of the locals are a bit funny about the DoC workers."

"That's 'cos you outnumber islanders five to one."

Anaru pursed his lips. "Three to one *at most*."

I laughed. "Can you get more traps by the meeting?"

Anaru wrinkled his nose. "No budget."

"OK. I'll fund the rest. You order them. I'll pay for them."

Anaru gave me that smile again. The one that made me feel like I was the best and only human on the planet. My insides did a good impression of a thermonuclear power plant.

"That's very generous, Em."

I shrugged. "It's an important cause. And I can afford it."

"Well, the birds and invertebrates thank you."

I played with my coffee cup, turning it around in a circle by its handle.

"So. Seems you're a bit of a card shark."

Laughing, I said, "Man, news travels fast here."

"Told you."

"You did," I said, nodding through a smile. "I didn't like the way it was assumed I wouldn't be able to compete at their level because I lack testicles."

"And so you went for his." He nudged me with his elbow. "Bit of a chip off the old block."

I didn't pretend to be offended, and I couldn't deny it. "Yep."

"Wolf wouldn't have liked that."

"He ordered me out of his house."

Anaru whistled. "Island's in a bit of an uproar this morning."

"Because of the poker game?" I asked incredulously.

"That and the one-car rally."

"The what?" I asked, knowing exactly what he meant.

"Someone was racing on the roads last night."

"Oh yeah?" I said, picking at the wood on the table.

"People are offended. Think that kind of hooliganism has no place here. It's disrespectful."

"I can understand that."

"Good," Anaru said. "Pass the message on to your brother." He drained his coffee. "I'd better get going. Let's meet up later to discuss the details of the meeting."

"OK. I'll work on the catch record sheet for the store."

He stood up and squeezed my shoulder as he walked past. "Thank your mum for the coffee for me."

WHEN I WENT BACK INSIDE to brush my teeth and put my laptop in my backpack, I noticed a pile of dirt and detritus underneath it from the previous night. I picked the pack up and took it outside to brush it down. And that's when I saw the feather.

The tip of the shaft had gotten wedged into the weave of the backpack's bottom, presumably when I fell.

It was long. And black. And had a white tip.

There was no other bird in New Zealand that I knew of that had feathers like that. A magpie maybe, or a pukeko at a stretch. But neither species lived on the island.

It looked very much like a huia tail feather.

"Holy fuck," I breathed. The tip of the feather quivered as my hands shook.

I brought it back inside and unzippered the same bed cushion I'd put the photo of me, Saxon and Janey in, and placed it alongside.

WHEN I FINALLY GOT TO the store, Trace, Don and Kevin were there, but Wolf wasn't.

"I hear you caused a bit of an upset last night," said Don, restocking the oranges one at a time.

"Yeah. I take it Wolf's sulking?"

"Poor man, he'll be heartbroken," said Trace.

"That game is part of island culture. Wolf's kingship is legendary," said Don.

"But it's a game. Champions are meant to be challenged, and occasionally their reigns are overthrown."

"You don't mess with that stuff, Em. It's sacrosanct."

"It's just another old boys' club. If you invite a woman to take part, you have to be prepared for the consequences. That's the risk."

"Couldn't you have just played poorly?" asked Trace.

"No. Nobody else at that table felt they had to dumb down their performance. Why should I just because I'm a woman?"

"I see what you're saying," said Trace.

"But you still shouldn't have done it," said Don.

I sighed. "I think we'll have to agree to disagree and hope Wolf moves on quickly."

"Not likely, knowing him," said Trace. "He still won't speak to Macca after he bet against the All Blacks winning the last Rugby World Cup and won a couple of thousand."

I grunted at the ridiculousness of it and focused on my email inbox. Thirty-nine since yesterday. Taking a big, fortifying slurp of coffee, I focused on the first one and was instantly sucked into the digital vortex for the next four hours, twenty minutes of which was spent researching huia tail feathers.

There were plenty of photos of the sacred feathers in national museum collections, and there was no doubt my feather bore an uncanny likeness to most of them, but I needed to make sure I wasn't jumping to conclusions. The feather could, according to Google images, have come from a seabird like a black backed gull. Their wing feathers, much like the one I had inside my cushion cover, had white tips. But what would a seabird feather be doing in the middle of a forest?

When I left for the day, my curiosity level soaring and my blood humming, Don and Trace said very little to me. Presumably they felt their loyalties stretched in two directions.

I had little interest in petty local politics and wondered if it was time I found an alternative working arrangement. Then Wolf could have his counter back and feel as if he'd won a small victory because I'd retreated. I didn't like the idea of that. It made me want to dig my toes in further and stand my ground, but I also didn't want to raise tension in a place I spent four hours a day. It wasn't worth it.

WHEN I GOT HOME, the place was deserted. Ruben had packed up for the day after making good progress on reroofing, and his van was missing. Saxon's Holden was parked at the end of the driveway, but neither he nor Janey were anywhere on the property.

I heard a Janey bray from next door and squeezed myself between the gap in the hedging. Ted's garage doors were open, and the hood of the HR popped. Saxon's black-clad backside protruded from beneath it.

I walked over, my footsteps crunching on the gravel, and stood beside him.

He tensed, hunching his shoulders and moving his body deeper towards the engine block.

"Sax?"

"Oh thank fuck." Saxon stood up and blew out the rest of the breath he'd been holding. "Mum's naked. I didn't want to ask for any help."

I laughed. "You poor boy. What can I do for you?"

"Can you find me a rag?" he said, blowing on a very dirty spark plug.

I went over to the cluttered workbench and started rummaging through forty years of shed-relegated detritus.

"I've looked there. You got something at home?"

"Probably," I said, and came back two minutes later with a ragged cloth I'd found draped over Ruben's drop saw.

Saxon cleaned the plug and pulled out another one to wipe it down. "Can you try starting it?" he said, slipping the sparkplug home.

I climbed in the front seat and turned the key. The engine coughed five times before it caught.

"Give it some gas," Saxon yelled over the noise of the exposed motor.

I revved it and climbed out, the engine still running.

Saxon reached in and tweaked something, and the slight stuttering in the engine's purr smoothed out. "That should do it," he said, closing the bonnet.

A wave of fondness washed over me. "You're a good person, Sax, most of the time."

"Yeah, well, I'm going tomorrow, so today's my window."

I stood up from where I had leant on the car. "You're going? You didn't tell me!"

"You sound disappointed. I thought you'd be happy to see the back of me." He turned and rubbed at a spot on the bonnet. "I gotta go back to work, anyway."

"Mum's not going with you?"

"Nuh. Says she has things to do."

Grabbing his arm, I pulled him around to face me. "Please take her with you. This island's too small for the both of us."

He shrugged. We both knew there was nothing either of us could do if she didn't want to go.

I dropped my hand and let out a sigh. "What do you want to do on your last night?"

"Family dinner."

I smiled. "Good choice. We can have a barbie."

Saxon gripped me by my upper arms. "Please make sure Mum puts some clothes on. I never, ever want to see that again. Especially when I'm eating."

I threw my arms around him and pulled him to me. He *oof*-ed as his chest hit mine, but he didn't push me away. "I'll miss you, Sax. Thanks for turning up uninvited."

WHILE I PREPARED a salad in the kitchen, and Saxon sat outside drinking a beer and watching the ocean, Janey arrived home – fully clothed – and announced she was ready for her first slam poetry performance. Ruben, who'd turned up in time for beer o'clock, sat at the dining table, face turned up to her as she stood in the middle of the lounge and flicked open her piece of paper.

"It's called 'Woman'." She took a deep breath in, coughed, and said,

"I am wo-man

No-man

Not just the sum of my parts

A whole extra syllable

A whole other sound

I am not a derivative

I. Am. More."

Outside, Saxon raised his beer above his head and shouted, "Hear me roar!"

I stifled a laugh.

"You taking the piss, Sax?" asked Janey, hand on hip.

Without turning around, he said, "It is actually a bit derivative, Mum. Not to be anti-feminist or anything."

Janey looked down at Ruben, then at her poem, and said, "Fuck. It is, isn't it?" She let the hand holding the paper fall and slap against her thigh. "How ironic."

"No, no. This is good," said Ruben. "You're finding your voice. This poem is just practise."

"Em?" asked Janey. "Constructive criticism?"

I sliced a tomato in half, then in quarters before saying, "Well, I think you have strength in word play."

She nodded and said, "Thank you," and looked at me expectantly for the next offering.

"That's it."

Janey shrugged. "I'll take it. The only way is up."

Footsteps crunched on the driveway's gravel, and Anaru's head bobbed past the kitchen window. I'd invited him around to discuss our advertising copy for Monday's meeting and hoped he'd stay long enough to warrant a dinner invite.

WE SAT at one end of the dining room table, my computer open before us, while Janey and Ruben sat at the other end, going through her poem.

Before we could pin down any advertising details, I blurted, "Do seabirds ever hang out in forests?"

He appraised me for a couple of seconds before saying, "Not typically. Petrels do, but only in the edges of forests by the ocean. Why?"

"I um...thought I saw a gull in the bush the other day."

"A gull?" Anaru said, somewhat incredulously.

"It was a wee way away. It was probably a wood pigeon or something."

He was quiet for a few seconds. "Are you fishing again?"

I screwed up my face. "Yuck. Why would I be doing that? The only good fish is a deep fried one."

"Ha ha," he said, and took a swig of his beer. Then he pointed the bottle at me. "I've got my eye on you, lady. And I can tell you now, you need to be doing better than imaginary gulls and questionable chicken farming. Trace has got you beat hands down for conspiracy theories."

I snorted. "That she has."

I was given an elbow nudge and told to focus on the task at hand. And because Anaru had to lean into me to get a view of the computer screen without any background glare, it took my brain a few seconds to remember it had a language faculty. "We, um —" I said, pausing to inhale. He smelled of lemongrass soap. "– need as many people as possible to come, so they can persuade the no-show-ers to get involved." I drew in another breath and noted the tang of salt, like he'd dried himself in the sun after a swim. "There's nothing like some good old-fashioned peer pressure."

"I like your thinking. I'll do the word on the street bit, you can do the hard copy." Anaru turned his head away from the computer screen and towards me. His breath warmed my cheek and I swivelled to face him. Briefly flicking his eyes to my lips, he lowered his voice. "And can you get Don and Trace to tell everyone who comes in the shop?"

"I can try," I whispered, unable to break his gaze.

"Jesus, this is hard," Janey said, slapping her hand on the table.

Anaru and I jumped, sitting upright and turning our attention back to the screen.

"I need a fucking thesaurus. And a pint of wine." As she stalked towards the fridge, I said to the computer, "Don and Trace don't agree with my decision to play to the best of my poker ability. How long before Wolf gets over himself, do you think?"

"I don't know. It'll probably be a couple of days before he emerges from his man cave. He has a lot of egg on his face." Anaru placed a hand on my arm. My skin hummed under his touch. "I'd be sensitive around him for a while yet."

I faced him again, frowning. "Fuck's sake. Nobody died."

"No, but a man's mana – his authority and power – has been stripped from him. Or at least that's how he feels. It's not just a game to him."

"If it was that important, he shouldn't have blindly invited an unknown to play. You always research your opponents. And anyway, I owed him for the furniture prank."

Anaru smiled. "I'm sure he's learnt his lesson."

"Yeah, but has he got a taste for revenge?"

MONDAY'S MEETING at the Port Keulemans Hall to kick-start an island-wide backyard trapping project was, to put it plainly, an epic fail.

Thirty DoC staff showed up and five islanders, including Janey.

I looked at Anaru and said one word.

"Wolf."

ANARU and I made the most of the occasion, and five people went away armed with the motivation and equipment to put a dent in their local rodent population. But the whole thing was, naturally, incredibly disappointing.

With the sun dipping low on the horizon, Anaru said he knew just the thing to raise my spirits.

After I'd dropped Janey home to educate Ted on how to use his new rat trap and I had grabbed a bottle of wine from the fridge, Anaru climbed into my ute. Pulling the bottle out from under him, he threw me a questioning look.

"I need a drink."

He gave me a small smile and reached over to stroke my cheek. It was not the gesture of someone who was merely a new friend. It was also a gesture of sympathy. And so, I couldn't be completely sure of what it indicated.

And then he looked at my forehead.

"Don't you fucking kiss it, or I swear I'll get out of the car right now."

Anaru wrinkled his nose. "Why would I want to kiss your foreskin?"

I started the engine and pulled onto the road. After several seconds he said, "I can think of much better places to kiss."

Heat rose from the pit of my stomach, radiating out my chest and up my neck. I waited for Anaru to flinch away from it, such was its ferocity, but he stayed still, smiling at the road in front of him.

I rolled the window down and waited for the heat to subside.

"You OK?" he asked eventually.

I wasn't. I was preoccupied with imagining all

those better places, which only served to shift the heat downwards. It settled heavily in my groin.

I rolled my eyes and groaned at how easily my mind had succumbed to flights of erotic fancy. Then I cast a glance at Anaru, hoping he hadn't heard me above the noise from the road.

"What?" he said, still smiling.

Shit.

"Um," I said. "You know of anyone who has a shed or something on the Wi-Fi side of the island they'd be happy to rent out?"

Anaru laughed and said after a beat, "You thinking of moving offices?"

"I think it's time."

"I can ask around."

"Thanks."

We didn't say anything else, and I tried very hard to think of anything but Anaru placing his lips on my inner thigh. I only succeeded in thinking of two other things in the fifteen minutes it took us to reach our destination. Anaru kissing the soft skin under my ear may have been one of them.

He directed me to a lookout, high above the coves south of Port Keulemans. This side of the island was quite different from the wide-mouthed, white sand bays of the east coast. Here, bush-lined rocky shorelines descended quickly into deep, green basins and tiny islands dotted the waters of the coves.

The lookout sat at the top of a cliff and afforded a

perfect view of the sun sinking amongst pink-laced clouds over the mainland.

Anaru found a beach towel on the ute's back seat, spread it over the bonnet, and invited me to join him. And so I hoisted myself up next to him and rested my feet next to his on the bull bars.

"This is pretty special," I said, after watching the last of the sun's glow shimmer into nothingness. "Thanks for bringing me here."

"You're welcome."

I took a sip from the bottle of wine and passed it to him.

"Think Wolf'll return to haunting the shop counter now he's humiliated me back?"

"Here's hoping." Anaru read the label on the bottle then looked at me. "You know, I really admire you for sticking up for yourself. It's a shame Wolf chose to react badly, but I'm glad you didn't feel you had to apologise. You have the most spunk of anyone I know."

"Apart from my mother."

"Apart from your mother." He nudged my knee with his. "She's taught you well."

I grimaced.

"Hey. You should be proud of her. I bet she's proud of you."

"I honestly have no idea." I thought of all the times she'd seemingly set out to embarrass me to teach me a lesson or get me to reflect on my behaviour. It wasn't a method I'd employ with any child of mine.

Then I thought of the way she looked at me the other night when I returned from being crowned the new island poker champion. How she'd clinked glasses with me when I said the inherent sexism of the game had lit a fire in my belly and that I wanted more than anything to show all those men up. And so I had.

She'd said, "Way to go, Em."

It didn't seem like much at the time, but now it was clear. I'd made Janey proud.

"You know," I said, "I think you're right."

WHEN HALF THE bottle was gone and the inky blue of night had pushed out the last of the day, I lay back on the bonnet and looked at the stars.

"I'll never get tired of this. There's too much light pollution in Melbourne to see much in the way of stars, but this" – I pointed at the heavens – "is magic."

Anaru eased himself down next to me.

"I'm glad you left Melbourne behind. Not out of any concern for your health or anything noble like that." He grinned. "Out of pure selfishness. That I got to meet you. You are so different from any woman I've known."

I turned my head to look at him. "Yeah?" I said,

trying to sound casual, but not completely concealing my breathlessness.

"Yeah," he said softly.

I broke eye contact with him and peered at the night sky again. "You and I are similar, though."

"In what way?"

I rolled over, laying an arm under my head and facing him. "Were you ever teased at school for living in a caravan, having second-hand clothes, no dad?"

"No."

"Right. But you experienced discrimination, didn't you?"

Anaru mirrored my movement, rolling towards me, his face inches from mine.

"I still do. You?"

I wasn't sure. No one in Melbourne, apart from Warren, knew about my background, and the appearance of my family on the island hadn't provoked any judgement.

I shook my head.

Anaru reached across, taking my hand from where it rested on my thigh and lacing his fingers through mine. "To a certain extent you're right about us, but there's a big difference. You can hide where you come from. Move to Melbourne, make a new, more sophisticated life. I can't hide anything. Not that I'd want to."

My thumb stilled from stroking the back of his

hand. Did that mean he judged me for turning my back on the way I was brought up?

I didn't want to worry about it. I didn't want anything to ruin where I hoped this moment was going. And so I made a joke of it.

"Except it looks like I'm regressing. Look at me now. Swigging wine from a bottle on the bonnet of my car. All class."

Anaru laughed, his breath hot across my cheek. "You can take the girl out of the –"

I didn't give him time to finish his sentence. I closed the small gap between our mouths and kissed him.

CHAPTER NINETEEN

I WAS RIGHT, his lips were soft. Full and soft and embracing.

I broke the kiss, drawing my head back and finding his eyes. They were a deep brown, framed with exquisitely long lashes. He shifted his gaze to my mouth and ran a finger around the edge of my upper lip. "You have the most beautiful mouth. I've wanted to kiss it ever since that first night, when I saw you draped in sloths."

I nodded solemnly. "Sloths do it for me, too."

Anaru smiled and leaned across, finding my lips with his. They melted into mine. All of my lips were covered by all of his.

My breathing stuttered, and I found it difficult to draw air. "How is it that kissing can be this good?

Why didn't I know this before?" I said when my lungs found the ability to fully inflate.

"You've just never found the right fit," he murmured against my mouth and let his lips enclose mine again.

"You know why I crashed my car that first day?" I said when we broke for air.

Anaru pulled away and grinned. "You were checking me out."

"Just think – if you weren't so hot, we might never have met."

"And I wouldn't be able to do this to you." He raised himself up on one elbow, his other hand cupping the back of my head, and he brought his mouth to mine, his lips parting and his tongue tasting. As it touched mine, a surge of electricity crackled across my skin, and I made a noise like a dolphin squeaking. I hoped it sounded sexy.

His tongue dipped deeper, his lips pressed more heavily, and all other thought evaporated except for that image of him working his way down to my inner thigh. I quivered.

He kissed my jawline, then just below my ear, and when he dropped his mouth to my throat, all the blood in my body rushed to my clitoris. If I hadn't already been lying down, I would have fallen down.

When he nipped my neck with his teeth, my fingers involuntarily contracted and my nails dug into his back. He hissed and withdrew his head, looking down at me with his brows raised in the middle.

"God, sorry," I said. "I'm not doing well at controlling myself right now."

I was given a slow smile. "I can't wait to see what you do when I get to kiss you below your neckline."

I moaned, and he placed his lips in the hollow at the base of my throat.

I pulled his shirt out from his waistband and ran my fingertips up his spine before sliding the flat of my hand all the way back down to his belt line.

He breathed in sharply and moved his lips back to my mouth, kissing me with an energy that left me gasping for breath. Then he rolled on top of me, and I hooked my legs around his, using the hold as leverage to raise my hips and feel how fully aroused he was. He pressed back into me, allaying any doubt as to how much he wanted me.

The hood crackled beneath us, and we froze.

"Do you wanna...?" I asked up at him.

He gave a single nod. "My place."

We sprang apart and leapt down from the bonnet, jumping into the front seats and slamming the doors.

I sat back in my seat, letting my breath return, and looked across at Anaru.

He appeared just as stunned, gazing out the windscreen at the lookout railing and breathing heavily. Then he swivelled his head towards me and held my eye.

We panted in unison once, twice. Then I scrambled over the gear stick and leapt into his lap.

I found his mouth and slid my tongue against his, my pulse frenetic, my breathing ragged.

His hands slipped under my t-shirt, ranging feverishly over my back and shoulders.

"No bra?"

I shook my head. "This weather. Too hot." My brain was too overloaded for full sentences.

"Holy shit. Sexy," said Anaru, apparently plagued by the same mind fug.

From somewhere underneath us, the faint sound of crunching drifted into the cab.

"What's that noise?" Anaru whispered.

"Sounds like tyres on gravel," I mumbled into his lips.

We turned our heads slowly and peered out the window.

The branch of a bush scraped across the glass as we rolled by.

"Shiiiit!" I yelled, bracing for the impact of a cliff plunge by wrapping my arms around Anaru's head and pulling it into my chest.

Anaru muttered "Fuck" into my breastbone and yanked on the handbrake.

With a jerk, the car stopped.

I waited, listening.

"Ah, Em?" Anaru's breath was hot between my breasts. "I can't breathe."

I unclamped my arms, and he fell back into the seat, rubbing his nose. "You didn't put the handbrake on?" he asked.

"No," I said, my voice that of a child expecting a thorough chastening. "I left it in gear."

"Temporarily."

I looked at the gear stick. "I must have knocked it on my way over."

"Yeah. That'd be my guess, too."

I looked down at him, waiting for him to register the humour of the situation, for his smile to appear.

It didn't.

"I'll just..." I climbed back to my side of the car.

"Wow," Anaru said, running a hand through his hair and looking grimly out the front windscreen. "Talk about a cold shower."

I placed a hand over my still-thundering heart and allowed the enormity of my mistake to sink in. "Jesus. I nearly killed us."

"Yeah," Anaru said, still gazing out the windscreen, his mouth slightly ajar.

After a moment I said, "I'll take you back to your car."

WHEN WE PULLED up at my house, I killed the engine and turned to him. "I'm sorry I nuked the moment." I put a finger gun to my head and fired.

"Hey," he said, "we've got plenty of time," and he leaned over and kissed me slowly before climbing out of the car. Before he closed the door, he said, "Tomorrow, we'll laugh about it."

"You want to see me again so soon?"

"I want to see a lot more of you soon."

I had to restart the engine and put the air conditioning on full before I felt composed enough to venture inside.

WOLF WAS in place at the store the following day. He said, "Em," as I walked in without any suggestion of either resentment or smugness.

As much as I wanted to rain a load of the ugly truth down on him, I decided it wasn't worth further aggravation. I wasn't interested in risking more alienation from the community, and I desperately wanted my trapping scheme to stay afloat.

So I said, "Wolf," without any suggestion of smugness or resentment.

Kevin was already in place under the table, and as I sat down, I shook my jandal off and stroked his head with my foot. "No licking my toes," I told him sternly.

When I started the computer and opened my apps, a call came in on Skype immediately.

I was late for my weekly catch-up with Warren.

I picked up the computer and headed outside, answering the call en route.

"Em," Warren said, "you've got so brown."

"Happens in summer."

"It suits you."

"I hope so, 'cos there's not much I can do about it. I just have to look at the sun and I tan."

"Your cheeks are filling out. You feeling good?"

"Yeah, I am. I *am* feeling good." I smiled. I hadn't really thought much about it, but I felt more energetic and more at ease than I had in a long time. "Thanks for asking, Warren."

"I'm really glad. It's what you moved there for."

Something shifted then. An easing of tension between us, or at least a lowering of the wall I had built.

"Yeah," I said, "it is."

He smiled at me a moment longer then asked if there was any huia intel.

"No. I managed to get inside the fence the other night, but I didn't see or hear any evidence of huia." Technically this was correct, given that the evidence came to light outside of the sanctuary. But I still didn't trust him enough to let him know about it.

"How long were you there for?"

"A few hours." I didn't need to tell him most of those hours were spent indoors.

"Doesn't mean anything. The area's huge. You need to gain the trust of a ranger and get them to talk. Is there someone you can get cosy with?"

I thought about Anaru's full, soft lips against the skin of my neck. "Perhaps."

"Good. If not, find someone quickly."

Four rangers walked behind me and headed for the entrance to the store.

"Go and talk to them," Warren whispered.

"Sure," I said, seeing the opportunity to end the call. As I reached to move the mouse, the radio on the lead ranger's lapel crackled into life. "Attention all units. We have a Code Pegasus. Repeat. A Code Pegasus."

The rangers turned and ran for their Department of Conservation branded ute, reversed blindly onto the road, and accelerated towards the island interior in a cloud of road dust.

Three seconds later, a second ute sped past.

"What's going on?" asked Warren.

"Dunno. A Code Pegasus, apparently. The rangers are in a total flap – driven off in a great hurry."

"Follow them! You have your car, don't you?"

"Yes. And no, I'm not following them."

"This could be our big break, Em! You have to find out what's going on."

"And I will. Just not by rubbernecking. A tūī's probably broken its wing or something."

"You know it's much bigger than that, Em. God, you're frustrating. If I wasn't so busy here, I'd be over there myself."

And just like that we were back in our old contrary roles.

"And do what? Dress up in camo gear and stake out The Facility?"

"No. I'd make a proposal and see if they were forthcoming."

"Not a good use of company funds if it turns out to be a dead end."

"Right. Which is why I need you." He leaned closer to the screen, his eyes shining. "Can't you see what this might mean if they *are* breeding them?"

"No. I don't have your nose for economic exploitation. Why can't you find an investment opportunity, like the rest of our portfolios, that doesn't involve bullying?"

"Mutual benefit, not exploitation."

"A beautiful symbiosis?" I mocked.

"Exactly."

"If you weren't now my boss, I'd say you were full of shit."

"*Em*. You need to tread more carefully. The company's well aware that our past relationship could complicate our working relationship. They *are* watching."

"Well, you'd better stop mentioning words like 'miss' and 'you' in the same sentence, then. I'd better get back to my tasks." I signed off and sent Anaru a text:

What's a Code Pegasus?

I didn't receive a reply.

I DIDN'T SEE or hear (much) from Anaru over the next couple of days. It was obvious that Code Pegasus was obviously a) a serious one, and b) difficult to deal with.

I understood the focus and commitment an emergency was likely to take, but the lack of contact left me steaming in a pathetic cloud of lust. I couldn't stop thinking about the other night, and it bugged me that he was likely far too busy to be as preoccupied with thoughts of me. Unreasonable? Yes.

So what was the best thing to do about it? Force him to think about me.

I sent him a text telling him I hoped everything was OK and nobody was hurt, any species under threat, or their infrastructure compromised. It wasn't in the least bit sexy, but it covered all possible high alert bases and let him know I cared.

I waited eight hours, then I sent him a text asking if any heavy petting couples needed rescuing from the bottom of the lookout. It had the dual effect of being funny and reminding him of the steamy events of the other night.

That one got a reply. A smiley emoji. It wasn't much, but it was something.

When I'd waited sufficiently long enough to send another text without seeming needy, Janey walked past and said, "For heaven's sake, Em, leave the boy alone. He's busy."

I swear that woman is omniscient. It's awe-inspiring and very frightening.

EXACTLY FIFTY-SIX HOURS after the Code Pegasus was declared (and sixty-eight since I'd last seen Anaru), something rather remarkable happened.

I sat at the outdoor table, enjoying the quiet after Ruben had finished gibbing the new ceiling in my bedroom, and reading my book.

The afternoon air was filled with the hissing of cicada clicks and the usual cacophony of birdsong.

Gradually, like a free diver rising to the surface, my awareness was pulled from the world of the book by the repetition of a stuttering whistle that ascended to a high, clear note. It was unlike any bird I had heard before.

The song came from the direction of Ted's backyard.

I put down my book, swung my feet down from the chair they were propped on, and headed for the gap in the hedge.

Ted stood on his patio. He glanced at me, raised a

finger to his lips, and turned his head in the direction of the song.

There, in the bush beside Ted's shed, and foraging in the trunk of a fallen fern, was a large, dark-feathered bird. It had white tips to its tail feathers and bright yolk-yellow wattles on either side of its beak.

A huia.

PART 4

CHAPTER TWENTY

I GASPED.

"I told you I saw one in my garden," Ted said in a low voice.

"That's not for fucking real. Is it for real?" I whispered, glancing at him and noticing Janey standing in the shadows just behind him, a glass of Ted's red wine in one hand, a cigarette in the other, and nothing on except a pair of sparkling jandals.

"It's for fucking real," she said.

Mesmerised by the extraordinary sight of an extinct bird very much alive and well, I crept over to where Ted stood and slid my phone out of my back pocket. My blood fizzed in my veins, its energy humming beneath my skin.

The call did not come from the bird on the

ground, but from a second one with a longer, curved beak on a branch above.

The bird on the ground chiselled into the prone fern trunk with several taps of its beak, drew out a small grub and ate it, then it hopped further down the log and began to peck at the wood again.

With an excited-sounding whistle, the bird in the tree flew down and probed into the hole the first bird had created with its long beak.

I took a photo and put the phone back in my pocket to watch as the second bird extracted something small from the hole and slid it along its beak into its mouth.

"They're different," said Janey.

"I believe huia are dimorphic," said Ted. "Their beaks do different things, so they rely on each other to get food."

"It's almost romantic," I said. "Which is which — male and female, I mean?"

"I don't know."

We watched while the bird with the shorter beak pulled a fat grub from the tree trunk and, flying to the ground, offered it up to the other. It worked the grub to the tip of its beak where the curved bill of the second bird could grab it more easily, but before it did, the bird with the grub leapt around the other one, its tail fanned and its wings extended, in what seemed like a display. The other bird chittered and plucked the proffered grub before hopping back up a tree trunk, its claws anchoring it to the bark like a cat. Or a sloth.

"They look like they're dancing," I said. "Look at them. It's like a carefully choreographed waltz."

"Huh," said Janey. "I bet my blackened lungs it's the male feeding the female."

"Rightly so, my dear," said Ted.

"Do you think they mate for life?" I asked.

"I reckon that's a good possibility," said Ted.

We watched for another minute before I said, "I guess this is the emergency."

Janey nodded. "You'd better call Anaru."

His phone rang and went to voicemail. The only thing I could do was text him and hope that if he was too busy to take my call, he could spare a second to glance at his phone.

Come to Ted's immediately, I wrote. **We have what you're looking for.**

IT TOOK Anaru ten minutes to arrive. He parked at the front and appeared around the corner of the house on foot, Mel in tow.

I pointed at the two birds who were now up higher in the trees beside the garage, but Anaru had already spotted them.

"There's the little fullas alright," said Mel. "You want me to call for back up?"

"Yeah," said Anaru. "Best get the experts in. You

three," he said, turning to us and pausing as he registered Janey's state of undress. He flicked his eyes back to me, a glimmer of amusement in them. "Don't go anywhere."

"Wouldn't dream of it, my son," said Ted.

Mel walked back towards the ute, her phone clamped to her ear, and Anaru stood in line with me, turned towards the bush. The four of us formed a shallow semi-circle, our arms crossed, watching the birds foraging for their afternoon tea.

"Anaru?" I said.

"Yeah?"

"What the fuck?"

"Funny thing," he said, still looking at the birds. "Turns out we *are* breeding huia."

"No shit?" said Janey.

"They're terrible flyers, but occasionally one, or two, escapes."

"You lied to me," I said, more in wonder than in hurt.

"No, I discouraged you from a particular line of thinking. I never said we weren't breeding them – a tactic you're familiar with." He turned to us then. "I can tell you this because when this is all over" – he waved his hand over us and dropped his voice – "you will remember nothing."

"U-huh," I said.

He turned back to the birds. "Or at least I trust you enough to pretend to remember nothing."

I thought of Warren and swallowed. The noise washed out all other sound for the briefest of moments, and I wondered if the others noticed.

"Alright, Em?" asked Mel, who had re-emerged from around the side of the house.

I wasn't sure. This revelation potentially put me in a rather hot spot. How long would I have to discourage Warren from pursuing his theory before he lost interest? And now there was the added complication that I would have to lie. And do it very well.

"I know what you suspect," Anaru said, "but we haven't genetically engineered them. There was a remnant population discovered deep in the Ureweras. They were brought here, and we've done our best to protect them and increase their numbers ever since."

"And that means protecting them from humans?" I asked. "Why are they secret?"

Anaru nodded. "Humans are their biggest predator." He looked at me. "Did you take any photos, any footage?"

"Yeah," I said, as if I had no other option but to take photos.

"Delete them. Show me while you do it."

I looked up at him, my mouth slightly ajar, but I had no choice other than to accept his request. I pulled out my phone and said, "I will do this, but I want you to tell me everything, especially why this is all so covert."

Anaru considered me for a moment, then said, "OK. Dinner at mine tonight."

My disappointment at having to remove the record of, most likely, my one and only chance of seeing huia was replaced by a tingle that gently ebbed in my gut. Dinner at his place sounded like a date, whatever the context. And we had unfinished business to get on with.

I opened my photos app, showed him the image, and removed it.

"Do you have any shared albums?" he asked.

"Ah..." I remembered that Warren and I shared all our photos. The tingle was crushed by a block of ice. It melted under my ribcage, the cold spreading down into my gut. I took so few photos, I hadn't thought to turn off the sharing function after things ended. "It won't matter, I'm not connected to Wi-Fi."

"You're on a mobile network, Em. Check the shared album and get rid of them."

I opened the folder. Sure enough, the photo was there. I stifled a squeak and deleted it. Then I turned off the sharing function and deleted the entire album. It was, what? Only five, ten minutes since I took the image. Surely Warren wouldn't have seen it. It would be incredibly bad luck if he happened to be looking at the album. Even worse luck if he had a notification set up. Oh Christ.

I pocketed the phone and ran a hand through my

hair. Then I looked up at Anaru. He watched me, his mouth set in a grim line.

I offered him a smile and said, "It's OK. Secret's safe."

The crunch of tyres on gravel drew his attention away from me, and he walked back down the driveway with Mel.

"You don't need photos, Em," Ted said. "Store them in your image vault." He tapped his head and turned to beat a retreat into the house before the strangers arrived.

"Or wait for the next breakout," said Janey. "Ted's seems to be a bit of a huia hotspot."

"Holy shit," I said, struck again by the enormity of what I was seeing. "This is huge! How can you be so calm and nonchalant about this?"

Janey shrugged. "Cabinet Sauvignon downer."

Two rangers trudged around the corner, followed by Anaru and Mel. One carried a pole, and both carried nets and wooden boxes, which presumably would house the birds once they were captured.

The rangers briefly shifted their focus away from the birds to us, giving quick nods in greeting, then stopped several feet away from the tree the birds were in.

The huia watched the pair, one ranger crouching and unscrewing a jar, while the other imitated the call I had heard earlier.

Both birds descended to the ground and approached the rangers, their heads turning from side to side as if listening intensely. Once the birds were two feet away, the crouching ranger emptied the jar onto a flattened head on the pole and offered it to the long-beaked bird. Grubs wriggled on the tiny platform, and the bird hopped closer.

"The female is always caught first," Anaru whispered. "The male is easier to catch once the female is taken."

As soon as the bird extended its neck to pluck one of the offered insects, the second ranger, who had positioned the net to rest on the ground beside the bird, swept her up in a well-practiced manoeuvre. She gently removed the huia, placing her inside the box and sliding home the door.

The male, offering a high-pitched whistle, hopped into range of the net and was just as quickly secured.

"Right, you two," said the net-wielding ranger, "adventure's over. Time to go home."

"Nice work, team," Anaru said, as the troop walked past him towards their vehicle.

Mel waved goodbye, and before Anaru moved to join her, he turned and grabbed my hand, giving it a little squeeze. "See you tonight. Come at six." His eyes slipped to my mouth, then he looked over at Janey and a re-emerged Ted. "Ka kite," he said to them, and with a smile, he tapped his nose and winked.

"See you, my boy," said Ted. "You have nothing to fear."

My phone began to vibrate in my pocket.

I smiled at Anaru and held up a hand in farewell, before turning away from him and checking the incoming call. In the sunlight, it was hard to read, and I had to shield the screen with my hand. I groaned and let both hands drop to my sides.

Chron, it read.

"I WAS RIGHT," were the first words out of Warren's mouth.

"What about?" I said, feigning ignorance and scampering off through the hedge with the phone clamped to my ear.

"You know what, Em. I saw the picture before you deleted it. I didn't get a chance to copy it, unfortunately, but at least we know they're there."

"*Fuuuuuuuck*," I said, wishing the conversation was about anything – his new, incredibly hot girlfriend, the dry patch on my chin from Anaru's stubble – other than this.

Warren was quiet for a moment.

"How long have you known?" he asked, the accusation sharp.

"I didn't until just now. That's the first I've seen them."

"Why do you sound like you're panicking, then?"

I sighed. "I just don't feel comfortable with you pursuing it. I don't think it will be in the best interests of anybody except Chron and their investors."

"So you would have hidden it from me."

"Yes," I said after a pause.

"I see."

"Do you? I really hope you do, Warren. Exposing this project might have a serious impact on it. I mean, there's obviously a pretty important reason why it's so hush-hush."

"We'll work it from all angles. There has to be a way that will be mutually beneficial to all parties."

"I don't get it, Warren. How do you think you're going to convince anyone they should partner with you when they can seek partnership with someone who won't bring any conditions?"

"Do you have any idea how much money is at my disposal? In the last quarter we've become the biggest private equity firm in Australasia. I don't have a figure in mind to put on the table. I can give them any amount they demand. No philanthropist will be willing to do that."

"But it can't be worth that much."

"Imagine if tomorrow you read online that they'd resurrected the Dodo. How much money do you think people would be willing to pay to see it?"

I didn't answer.

"Precisely."

I tried very hard not to sigh again. "Look, I'll find

out tonight why the project's top secret. Please don't do anything until I've reported back. OK?"

"OK," Warren said after a beat. "I want a Skype meeting in the morning at nine."

"Fine."

"See you then."

"Yep," I said, ending the call and closing my eyes. How had I managed so effectively to get myself stuck in a shit-smelling quagmire? And with the two men in my life staring each other down on either side of it, no less. I mentally shook myself. I was being dramatic. It might not be anywhere near that bad.

IT WAS THAT BAD.

Over a dinner of chicken and mushroom risotto, Anaru told me how the birds were relocated with the help of a Whanganui tribe, Ngāti Huia, and Tuhoe, the iwi from the area the birds were found in, how the huia were ceremonially handed over to the guardianship of Ruatapu's iwi, and how the project was struggling under a lack of funding.

"The population's tiny and it's still fragile. We can't afford to risk it by making their existence public. Not yet."

I scraped some rice off my fork, my teeth clinking on the metal. "If you made it public, you'd have money flowing in."

Anaru shook his head. "It'd be a feeding frenzy. Everyone will want to be a stakeholder. These birds are a national treasure, a national fascination. For everyone, not just Māori."

Knowing that I would close tomorrow's conversation down with Warren before it even started, I reached my hand out and took his. "It's not going to stay secret forever. Especially if your birds keep escaping."

He turned my hand over and ran his fingertips across my palm. The feathery touch sent an electric charge to my belly. "No. But we'll try to keep it secret for as long as we can."

"And hamstring yourself in the process? There are plenty of rich, greenie philanthropists out there who'd be happy to back the project."

"But at what price? There's always a catch."

I put my fork down and placed my hand on top of his, stilling his stroking. "I don't believe that. You have to have some faith in humanity."

Anaru shrugged. "They've been nearly wiped out by us before. We can't take that risk until we're ready. Until the population's stable. And they're valuable. There's a chance attempts will be made to steal them. Our best hope is a change in government. It's election year. The left is already promising a large budget for the department. We could get a significant cash injection."

"I'd better get interested in politics, then."

Anaru's eyebrows shot up. "And you call me a barbarian?"

Smiling, I brought his hand up to my lips and kissed it. Then I slipped one of his fingers into my mouth and wrapped my tongue around it.

His mouth went slack, and he took two shallow breaths before saying, "Um."

I slid the finger out of my mouth and nibbled at the next one.

Anaru closed his mouth with a clack of teeth, pulled his hand out of my grasp, and rounded the table before I could push my chair back.

He placed his hands on either side of my face and found my lips with a kiss that was at once ferocious and erotic in its intensity. The pressure of his mouth and the heat from his skin ignited a fire in my belly that pulsed its way to my groin. I was pulled out of my chair and pushed backwards, possibly with the intention of heading to the bedroom, but neither of us were paying any particular attention to the direction we were going. We staggered into the back of the couch, toppling over it, and landing on the wide cushions of its seat, Anaru underneath me.

He grinned up at me. "Not quite what I had in mind, but this will do." His hands ran down from my waist to my buttocks and cupped them. "You look good from down here."

I sat back. Anaru's hands shifted to my waist, and I plucked the bottom of his t-shirt. I lifted it and took a good, long look at the smooth skin, taut with ridged muscle. I met his eye. "You look pretty good from up here." I wiggled my hips, and Anaru groaned, wrapping his hands behind my head and pulling me down for a dizzying kiss.

"Are you bra-less?"

"You didn't check me out?"

"Tried," he said, placing his lips against mine. "Couldn't tell."

I slid his hand under my shirt and guided it up my belly to the soft material of my sports bra.

"Oh," he said.

I leaned forward and nipped his ear. "It's just one more thing to pull off with your teeth. I reckon you're up for the challenge."

Anaru grinned and rocked forward, pulling us both upright so that we sat facing each other, chest to chest, groin to groin.

He kissed my neck and tugged my t-shirt upwards. When it came free, Anaru locked eyes with me and threw it across the room with a flourish. As he bent towards my bra, I pushed him away.

"Not so quick, buster. I get to see you now."

He crossed his arms over to remove his shirt, and I slapped his hands away, peeling the material towards his neck. He pulled his arms free, the shirt covering his face.

"This is good," I said, running my hands across the muscles in his chest.

"Not for me."

"You don't like this?" I said, sliding a finger between his pecs and down the line of hair emerging from his shorts.

He inhaled sharply and flinched. "No. Horrible."

I laughed and tugged at the t-shirt, the tight neckline catching on his nose and pulling him backwards. "Ow!"

"Sorry," I whispered, enclosing a nipple in my mouth, leaving him to free himself.

I took the t-shirt from him and twirled it around my head, releasing it and flinching when it knocked over a wine glass on the dining table.

He laid his lips on mine and said, "Don't worry about it. Don't care."

"Good," I mumbled back. "It's your turn."

He pulled away from me, running his eyes down my front. He raised them briefly before bending down and nuzzling into my breast, his mouth hot through the tight fabric, his tongue running a lazy circle around my nipple. It ached to be sucked, for him to take it into his mouth and pull against it with his tongue.

"Immff," I said.

"What was that?" Anaru asked, shifting to the other breast and unbalancing me. My right buttock slipped on the edge of the couch, and my momentum carried me over. I landed on the floor with an *oomph*, my left foot connecting with Anaru's chin.

He clasped it and looked down at me with watery eyes. "You OK?"

I sat stunned for a moment, then a ball of laughter surged up from my stomach and burst brightly into the room. "We are so shit. Talk about a comedy of errors."

Anaru chuckled and climbed down from the couch. He pushed me back onto the floor with a kiss and said, "Let's just stick to horizontal. We should be safe at ground level."

While he took my bottom lip gently between his teeth, he pushed the coffee table away with his hand. "There. No obstacles. Now," he said, peering down at my bra, "back to releasing these into the wild."

HOLY MOTHER OF GOD. I had no idea sex could be that good. That it could create a whole new awareness of the deepest, most secret parts of me.

It wasn't that sex with Warren was bad. It was just...adequate. Anaru opened a door to an unfamiliar and very welcome realm of pleasure.

When he had freed the beasts and tamed them with his tongue, his lips, his teeth, his fingers, he ran his hands up my thighs and traced their path with his mouth, pressing a light kiss on the soft junction between leg and groin, then moving to the other side and doing it all over again. My skin turned to goose flesh at the butterflying of his lips against my inner thigh, and the nerve endings between his mouth and my nipples tingled with the energy of our needy touching.

I slid my skirt up my body and over my head, allowing him to kiss the skin beneath my belly button and slide his way back to my mouth with his lips.

"I thought you'd insist on your turn," he said, touching his tongue against mine.

"Fuck the rules," I panted. "Can you do that thing again?"

"What? This?" he said, running a finger from the waistband of my underpants to the wet patch between my legs.

"No. Yes," I breathed.

"Or perhaps this." He dipped his head, pulling my knickers down to reveal my throbbing flesh and blowing air across my clitoris. The abruptness of the cool air on my feverish skin sent an electric pulse through my body, and my fingers and toes splayed and curled, my right hand grabbing a fistful of his hair.

Anaru hissed, and I relaxed my hand with a "Sorry" and an insistence that I couldn't be responsible for my actions if he did things like that to me. He pulled my pants back up and levelled his head with mine, pressing his body down onto me and letting me feel the fullness of his erection.

"You want me to stop?" he asked, smiling down at me.

"God no," I gasped. "I want all of it. Right now."

"All?"

"Yes!" I fumbled with the buttons on the front of his shorts. "Aaarh," I said, wrenching at them. "What's wrong with a zip?"

"Would you like some help?" Anaru asked, his voice a rasp.

"Get naked!" I said between gritted teeth, and popped them open with a tearing of fabric. I felt for an underpants waistband and was met by flesh. "Commando. Sexy," I said, sliding his shorts over his buttocks and wrapping my hand around his penis, feeling his girth.

Anaru moaned and said shakily, "We can take this slow."

I slipped my pants down with my spare hand and slid the tip of his penis over my slick clitoris, drawing circles around it. "Next time," I panted. "Right now I want a good, hard rogering."

"Rogering?" he asked with a smile and raised eyebrow.

"Yeah. Reckon you're up to the task?"

Anaru looked at me for one second, two. Then shucked his shorts off and rummaged in a pocket, pulling out a condom.

I laughed. "That sure of yourself, were you?"

"That hopeful," he answered, raising himself on his knees and sliding the condom on. I looked up at him, towering over me from between my splayed legs, and never had the act of sheathing an erect penis seemed so erotic. A new wave of heat swept through my body and settled in my groin.

I reached up and pulled him to me by his hips. Then I ran my tongue over his bottom lip, wrapped my hand around him, and slid him in.

We let out a collective sigh as our bodies moved into each other.

Anaru looked down at me once he had filled me and asked if I was OK.

I placed my hands in his hair and pulled him down to kiss me. My tongue made it very clear that I was indeed OK. Very OK. I wrapped my legs behind his hips and tilted my pelvis, inviting him to find a rhythm.

He thrust involuntarily and sucked the air out of my mouth with his gasp.

I smiled against his mouth and lightly ran my fingernails down his back, sliding my hands over his buttocks. They were almost out of my reach, and I had to curve my body into him, my face level with his neck. I nipped his skin and pulled at his bum, inviting him to roll his hips a second time.

He didn't need any further encouraging. He slipped a hand under my bottom, pulling me closer and tilting my hips upwards, so that with each slow thrust, he hit my G-spot with perfect precision.

I clamped my lower lip between my teeth and

arched my back, the pleasure a delicious ache from deep within me.

Anaru nuzzled my ear. "Jesus, you're sexy when you do that," he whispered.

I wanted to tell him that it was him making me do it, but my voice had been sucked out with my breath. All I could manage was ragged sips of air every time his tip pressed into my sweet spot.

"Faster," I managed to croak, urging him on with a slap on his buttock.

He laughed and slid his tongue across my throat. "I can't."

"You can," I panted.

"Carpet. Knees," he said, closing his mouth back over mine.

I shifted my weight, pushing against him until he rolled over. I sat above him, very still, feeling the pressure of the lovely hardness of him completely filling me.

Anaru reached up, wrapped a hand around the back of my neck and pulled me down towards him, kissing me long and slow.

I moved against him, rocking into him. His hands traced my neck, my clavicle, my shoulders. They mapped my shoulder blades and my ribs and came to rest on my hips. He bore me down on him and raised his pelvis, our flesh meeting in a long, hard grind. Then he released me, and I sat upright, still again, looking down at him. Running a finger down his cheek, I traced his jawbone. He turned his head and caught my finger in his mouth. Watching me from the corner of his eye, he sucked his thumb then ran it over my clitoris, drawing it lightly back and forth.

I moaned and arched into his body, eliciting a groan from deep in his throat. "If you keep doing that, I won't be able to control myself," he growled.

I raised my eyebrows, tugging on his arms and pulling him towards me so that our bodies met, our legs encircling each other.

"That's better," I said, running my hands down his chest. "I could hardly see you from way up there." I wrapped my arms around his neck and pressed my breasts against the warmth of his chest.

"Way up there?" he smirked. "The dizzying heights of two-foot-nothing?"

I dropped my hands and tweaked his nipples.

"Hey!" he said through a laugh. "You can't abuse a man in such a vulnerable position. I might be forced to do this." He slipped his hands under my buttocks and pulled me into him as he thrust upwards with his hips. He hit my G-spot as my clitoris connected exquisitely with his groin, and I emitted a "Hoh" and on the next pull and thrust, an "Oh my God."

When I *ungh*-ed, I knew I had lost all control.

I rode with his pull and urged him to up his rhythm, meeting his body with a flick of my hips and a soft grunt. As the pressure built between my legs, I arched away from him, exposing more of my clitoris to his hot skin.

One of Anaru's hands shifted to my upper back, holding me upright while his mouth captured a nipple. A line of heat rippled from it down to my groin, and I no longer had control of the noises that came from my mouth. Their rising pitch matched the sweet swelling of pleasure between my legs, and as I cried out with more urgency, Anaru mumbled a series of curses against my breast. He pulled away and shifted his hands to the back of my head, pressing his mouth hard against mine and grunting with our rhythm. His eyes went very wide as I squeaked my final cry, my orgasm rolling from my centre and out my extremities. I slumped against him, and he bit his lip, held his breath, then let it out with a wheeze as he shuddered and gave a final thrust.

He collapsed backwards, pulling me down onto the floor next to him. I lay cradled in the crook of his shoulder, my breathing slowing as I watched his chest rise and fall with his heaving breaths.

Eventually, he gave me a squeeze. "You OK?"

It took me a moment to connect thought with tongue. "I have never. Ever. Had sex like that."

"Never?"

I shook my head. "I've only ever had pathetic teenage fumblings. Or Warren."

"You've never tumbled over the back of a couch with Warren?"

"I can't remember ever doing it outside of the bedroom."

Anaru ran his fingers through my hair, brushing it away from my face. "Sensible man. Way less chafe-y."

I laughed and looked up at him. "How are your balls?"

Anaru's smiling mouth met mine. "Regrouping." He kissed me slow and soft as if nothing else existed but for our mouths and our shared breath.

My stomach revolved on its axis, and I brought my leg over his hip, my groin stirring as he ran his hand down my body and stroked my thigh.

"As much as I'd like to do you in every unconventional part of the house," Anaru said, "I prefer to keep my skin on my body."

I ran my finger down to his belly button and circled it. "You want to show me your bedroom?" I lowered my leg and walked my fingers beneath his navel.

He caught my hand and kissed it. "With pleasure."

BEFORE ANARU LEFT for work early the next morning, I assisted him with scrubbing his hard to reach places in the shower. Anaru, in turn, introduced me to the exciting new world of lovemaking in a tiny, wet and steamy cubicle. Turns out confined spaces make for inventive and somewhat acrobatic coupling. How had I gotten through thirty years of life without discovering this? Until now my sex life had been a monochrome dock and grunt. Anaru had shown me a rainbow in one night.

I rushed home to change into fresh clothes before the dreaded nine o'clock with Warren, walking in the back door with a mild waddle.

Janey eyed me from the kitchen as I headed towards my bedroom. "You obviously had a good night. We call that the cowgirl stagger in the trade."

"You were never in the trade, Janey," I called over my shoulder. I paused outside my bedroom door. "Oh God, were you? You know what? I don't want to know."

I hunted out my power suit. It didn't have shoulder pads, but it had a matching tailored jacket and sailor-leg pants and was the most business-y outfit I owned. And I meant business today.

I had already decided during Anaru's explanation of the project's need for concealment that I wouldn't act as an agent for Chron. I didn't necessarily agree with his reasons, but I couldn't allow the project to be leveraged for exploitation.

Yes, I was responsible for Warren seeing the evidence. So it was up to me to make sure things went no further.

I ordered a triple-shot espresso when I arrived clip-clopping on my stilettos into the store.

"What's with the mean-girl heels and the face?" asked Wolf.

"I presume you mean my lipstick?"

He grunted.

"I have a very important meeting this morning. I want to look badass."

"You look very professional, Em," said Trace. "It's a shame they won't see most of you."

"Doesn't matter," I said. "It's about mindset. I *know* I look killer. Which means I will act killer."

I took the computer outside to the picnic table, plugged my earphones in, and opened the Skype app.

"Em," said Warren. "You are positively glowing today. Ruatapu must really suit you."

"Thank you," I said with only the mildest touch of smugness.

"Seriously. You look really happy."

"I've been doing a lot of exercise lately. Good for the serotonin."

"Good for you, Em," Warren said in a lowered voice.

Anticipating he might be about to reintroduce the Miss You topic, I suggested we get down to it before he became all dewy-eyed.

"Right," said Warren, and opened his mouth again to pitch his plan.

"No," I interrupted.

"I haven't said anything."

"I don't care. It's not within the project's interests

to enter into any partnership, especially not one that seeks a financial return."

"Em, you need to hear me out."

"No, I don't. Ultimately, it will be taken advantage of by Chron. I won't allow that to happen. Find another investment opportunity, Warren. This one's not for the taking."

"I don't want to find another one. This one's huge. An extinct bird? An extinct bird already entrenched in the hearts of the nation? The ecotourism will be off the chart! The whole island stands to win from this. I bet if I put it to the community, they'd jump at this opportunity in a heartbeat."

"It's not up to the community to make that decision."

"It could be. If they exerted enough pressure."

"They won't have an opportunity to. How can they if they don't know?"

Warren's face settled into expressionlessness, and he sat back in his chair.

"You wouldn't," I said.

"That would be plan B."

"Jesus, what's plan A?"

"I want you to meet with the project's head and make a proposal."

I laughed, then resumed my game face. "No."

"You're going to do this, Em. You've been given a directive from your superior, and you need to carry it out."

"Not if I feel the directive is misguided and unethical."

"Christ, Em, don't make me do this."

"Do what?"

Warren ran a hand through his hair. "Either make the proposal or find a new job."

I was quiet for a moment, then blew air out between my lips. The man had gall, I'd give him that. But he'd forgotten one thing. I had enough money to comfortably carry me through a period of temporary unemployment.

I shrugged. "OK. I resign."

"Em!" Warren leaned into the screen, his features large and distorted. "You can't seriously hold the interest of a few birds ahead of your own financial security."

"Ah. Yes, I can. Is this conversation over yet? I have a letter of resignation to type."

Warren pulled at his tie, loosening it with a series of yanks. Then he took a deep breath and said, "OK, look. I don't want you to resign. I need you over there. And I want us to be OK. More than OK." He gave me a small smile. "You need to understand the incredible pressure I'm under to find new investment potential, especially ones that tick the environmental sustainability box. Clients are demanding that. *Carbon neutral* and *conservation* are hot words right now in the sector and this " – he clasped his hands together and shook them in a gesture that I could only take as pleading – "is exactly the kind of thing I need to deliver. I have key performance indicators that ensure I put in ten hours a day. And work most weekends. I've lost seven kilos due to the stress." He knitted his brows together and said, "Will you help me, Em? Will you please help me?"

I pursed my lips, counted to five, then said, "I'm sorry you're stressed. I really am. But the thing is, Warren, if you'd listened to yourself just then, you'd have heard that this entire thing is about you – *your* need to enter a partnership, *your* pressures, *your* stress. Bugger anyone else's interests. So, no, I'm not interested in helping you. If you insist on pursuing this, Warren, I will warn the project leaders and make sure they never answer an email or take a phone call from you. I will dead-end this."

Warren looked at the screen for a beat then threw his hands up in the air. "Fine. Let's do this the hard way."

CHAPTER TWENTY-ONE

IT TURNED out Warren had a game face, too. And he affected it with the ease of a well-trained actor.

He straightened his tie, smoothed down his hair, and looked at me with an expression of calm calculation.

"You've been doing a lot of renovations to the house."

"Yes?" I said, completely baffled by this sudden change in direction.

"Costing you a pretty penny?"

"Sure."

"How much money are you down to?"

"I'm getting pretty low, but that's not much of a concern given *the amount we're splitting*," I said, leaning into the screen and raising my voice.

"You checked our joint account lately?" he asked.

"No." I sat back abruptly. "Why?"

"Do it now."

I opened the app on my phone and saw that the account held nothing. It had been cleaned out. I looked up at him. "What the fuck? Where is it, Warren?"

"It's safe. I've just got it in a holding facility for the time being."

"Jesus, Warren. What is going on?" I said, the notion of how he might use the money as leverage already coming into focus.

"Oh, and I lied about the conveyancing lawyer. I haven't actually sent any paperwork to her, so I am still an owner of that delightful shit box you call a home."

Ice slid down my spine and settled into a cold pool in the pit of my stomach.

"You will make that proposal, or I will drag the division of our assets through the most expensive legal process you can imagine. And right now, you don't have much to secure a decent lawyer with."

I opened and closed my mouth. "You fucker. You dickless, son of a –"

"Set up a meeting by the end of the week," Warren interrupted.

"But that's tomorrow!"

"You better get a move on, then. And make sure it's somewhere where there's Wi-Fi. I want to be there, too." And he ended the call.

I reached out a shaking hand and closed my laptop, then I shut my eyes against the roar in my ears. My stomach heaved, and my eyes flew open. I stood up, managed one step away from the table, and emptied the watery contents of my stomach onto the boots of the ranger walking towards the store.

When I wobbled back inside, perspiration tracking down my cheeks and soaking the armpits of my shirt, I received a snort from Wolf. "Arse kicking went to plan then?"

I WAS FUCKED.

I was royally – hell, I was galactic-ly screwed. My financial situation was fairly dire and was likely to be so for a long time yet if I chose the lawyer route. It was hard not to believe the whole thing was my fault – foolishly making Warren deal with the asset splitting as punishment for desertion. I should have known that if he had it in him to betray me so completely at the beginning of our new life on the island together, he would continue the pattern of treachery further down the line.

And then there was the big one. If I gave in to Warren's blackmail, I would ruin my relationship with Anaru.

I couldn't pretend to give the proposal and keep Anaru out of the whole thing. Warren was obviously too smart to let me do it on my own. And the sad thing was that all of Warren's desperate efforts would be for nothing. DoC and the hapū would never agree to a partnership with an investment company.

I needed time to think of a counteroffensive. I needed a way to let Anaru know the secret was out – *and, guess what? It's in the hands of the worst person possible* – without him never wanting to see me again. A bit of a hard ask on an island the size of a postage stamp.

And besides, I rather liked spending time with him. In fact, the idea that he might no longer want to spend any time with me, let alone look at me, clamped the sides of my empty stomach together with such force, I had to lay my head down on the table to gather composure.

When my blood rose enough for me to lift my head, I opened the Messenger app on my phone and typed to Warren: If I deliver the proposal, will you divvy the assets without any fuss?

His response was swift and brief: Yes

I closed the app and put my head in my hands.

I didn't know what to do. I had little reason to trust him to be good on his word, but I still had to make a decision within the next few hours so that I could set up the meeting, if that was the course I took.

For the first time in my adult life, I needed my mum.

"WELL, you're a tit for taking the photo in the first place," was the extent of Janey's sympathy when I told her the whole sorry tale.

"I know."

She pushed a packet of biscuits towards me. "Did you record your conversation with him?"

"Sadly, no. I didn't think I'd need to."

"Could've dobbed him in to the bosses with it."

I took a bite of chocolate chip cookie and said, "Yep."

"You could try again. Get him to incriminate himself."

"I think he would be well wise to that. I won't get anything written or vocal now. He's already made his point clear."

Janey took a sip of her tea and held the mug just below her chin, gazing across the room in thought. "So there's no way Anaru, or whoever the decision maker is, will say yes to Warren?"

"No."

"Then you have to convince Warren it's a dud plan."

"I can try. He'll want to hear it from the horse's mouth, though."

"Can you have a phoney Anaru – a stand-in? Warren won't know."

I chewed my biscuit and thought about it. "It would have to be someone convincing, someone who sounded authoritative about the project. They would then have to keep the project secret. It's a big ask. And what if Warren doesn't take no for an answer, wants to keep pursuing them until they give in?" I blew across the surface of my tea and said, "At the end of the day, if Warren is ruthless enough to force me to do his bidding, then my saying no to delivering the proposal won't stop him. He'll pursue it anyway."

My phone began to vibrate in my pocket. I pulled it out and grimaced. "Anaru." I looked at Janey and whispered, "I have to answer. What do I say?"

She rolled her hand over in a "get on with it" gesture. "Just see what he wants first."

"Hi," I said, somewhat breathily. I hoped I sounded like a nervous and excited woman greeting the man she just had a twelve-hour sexfest with, rather than a guilt-ridden stupida who documented a top-secret project and sent the photo to her conniving ex.

"Hey," he said, sounding flat. My sphincter clenched. Had he found out about it already? Had Wolf interpreted my one-sided conversation, and now everyone on the island knew what a tool I was? "Fancy a drink?"

"Um." I looked at Janey, frowning. "OK. What's up?"

"Another round of cuts. I just lost four staff."

"You're kidding." I slapped myself on the forehead. This news put the project in a more vulnerable position. My proposition, should I deliver it, would seem vulture-like.

"Nah. It really sucks."

"I'm so sorry." Little did he know how much.

"Come to mine? Five-ish?"

"Sure. I'll bring a bottle."

After we'd hung up, I looked at Janey. "They've had another budget cut. Four rangers gone."

She sighed and patted my hand. "I think you just need to come clean and take it from there."

"But he'll hate me."

"He won't hate you. He might withhold sex for a decade or two, but all you're guilty of is being a prize idiot. He'll get over it."

I rubbed my face. "Oh God, we've only just started. Less than twenty-four hours into some kind of romantic thing, and I'm already making it incredibly difficult."

"Then you need to redeem yourself."

"How do I do that? I'd murder Warren, but he's not easy to get to right now."

Janey stared out the window at the view, one arm slung along the back of her chair. "So the reason the project's seen as something that's ripe for exploitation is its lack of funding?"

"Yeah."

"Well, we'll just have to do something about that, then. Make it impervious to any outside players."

I snorted. Then wished I hadn't and wiped my

damp upper lip. "How do you suggest we find several million dollars? At such short notice, and all?"

Janey smiled at me like an underworld queen-pin about to bleed her minions for all they were worth. "You worry about Warren. I'll sort the money."

JANEY WAS RIGHT. I had to come clean and face the consequences. With a churning stomach, I drove to Anaru's house through a heavy downpour, running the short distance between my truck and the front door with a raincoat thrown over my head.

Anaru sat on the covered back deck watching the rain wash the bush clean of its dust. A beer bottle was nestled between his thighs.

He looked up at me and smiled. It was at once sad and full of delight at seeing me, and my heart rent in two. He put his bottle on the table, reached out his arms, and pulled me onto his lap. After delivering a long kiss, he told me how glad he was I was there.

Not for long.

I made the excuse of needing wine glasses and pushed myself off him, returning thirty seconds later to watch his knee jig up and down like the needle on a sewing machine.

Oh boy.

"How you doing?" I said.

"Feeling the strain a bit. We're already stretched

as it is. It's not just about the huia — we have several other critically endangered species we're running programmes for. The sanctuary's not massive by chance." He pulled on his beer, finishing it. "I just have to hope our remaining staff are willing to donate extra time."

"Can you use volunteers? Locals?"

"Not without revealing the huia project."

I pulled my chair around to face him and placed a hand on his leg, stilling it. "About that. I need to talk to you about a complication that's come up, and I know the timing couldn't be worse."

Anaru shifted in his chair. "What do you mean?"

"Well." I forced myself to look up from my hands and meet his eyes. "You know how I work for an investment company?"

"Yeah."

"And Warren does, too? That Warren is a manager in the private equity arm, and I report to him?"

Anaru's brow furrowed and his "Yeah" sounded more uncertain than the last one.

"And you know how I unthinkingly took a photo of the huia?"

Anaru didn't say anything. He closed his eyes for a couple of seconds, presumably wishing himself back to the day he met me and had made the choice to keep running.

When he opened his eyes again and looked at me, I couldn't face the certain knowledge in them that I had created a shitstorm big enough to be tracked by satellite. I shifted my gaze to my glass of wine and twisted the stem back and forth. "It turns out I had forgotten that my photos get automatically sent to a shared folder with Warren, and he saw the photo before I deleted it. He doesn't have a copy of it, thankfully, but..."

Anaru sucked a loud breath in through his nostrils and said on the exhale, "Em, what are you telling me?"

I placed my thumb and forefinger on either side of my nose and pinched it, then said in a hurry, "He wants to invest in the project. He wants to give you the money you need to make it successful, and I imagine that in return he'd want you to give the company exclusive rights to an ecotourism venture. He's attempting to bully me into presenting the proposal to you." I put my hand over his and said, "Anaru, I am so, so sorry. I can't believe I didn't use my brain before taking that shot. I've tried talking him out of it, but he's a greedy arsehole."

Anaru pulled his hand out from under mine and stood up. He took two steps towards the back door, then turned and placed his hands on the back of his chair, his knuckles paling. "This, Em, is exactly why we've gone to extreme lengths to hide this remnant population from the world." His voice was quiet, but his anger was clear. "The secret gets out, and what's the first thing that happens? Someone looks for an opportunity to exploit it."

"I know."

"How could you be so...?"

"Stupid? I don't know. I got carried away in the moment. I mean, I was watching birds that were meant to have died out a hundred years ago. My brain flipped."

Anaru's eyes narrowed. "How does he know we're short of funding?"

My shoulders hunched involuntarily. "I told him. Way back before I knew you properly. You didn't hide the fact, and I had no idea huia were implicated. It just came up in conversation, probably as a passing comment about how many DoC staff there were on the island despite the budget cuts."

Anaru straightened and turned away from me again.

"How could I know he would use that information later?"

"Who else knows?" Anaru asked, his gaze on the ground.

"No one. He doesn't have any evidence to make a presentation to those above him. He'll want to seal the deal and then hand it to them in a big shiny bow, get a pat on the head for being a good boy. He's desperate. He's overworked, feeling scrutinised, and he wants to pull in a big one and prove his worth. He doesn't see failure as an option, even though I've painted a vivid picture of it for him."

Anaru's hands clenched then relaxed. "So he's a liability. We're at the mercy of his desperation. Shit, Em. He could go public."

"I doubt it. He has nothing to gain from doing that."

Anaru reached for his glass, and with his back turned to me, downed it in a series of loud swallows. He set the glass down on the table with a *clunk*, and I flinched.

"He, um, wants to meet with you tomorrow. Over Skype."

Anaru whirled around. "I'm not meeting with him. I'm not interested in anything that he might have to say. He might be able to bully you, but he has no power over me."

"I haven't given in to his bullying. I'm just telling you what's happened. How could I keep this from you? It would always sit between us, a big black lump of dishonesty."

"I don't think there can be an 'us', Em. Right now, this is too much. It's taken me a while to sort my feelings out about you, but I gave you the benefit of the doubt, and now you land this pile of teko at my feet?"

My guts turned to liquid. "Benefit of what doubt?"

"You're a snob and you're a bit racist."

"I...I'm not..." I stuttered. I wanted to categorically refute his accusation, but I wasn't sure I could.

"You're embarrassed about your upbringing to the point of lying about it."

"I didn't lie."

"Of course you did. You maintained a pretence. It's as good as a lie. And that whole 'can I call you Andrew anyway' thing. Can you imagine how disrespectful that felt?"

"Yes," I said, without any doubt that I'd behaved very badly in that moment.

"Not to mention asking Mel where she comes from, like she's not New Zealand-looking enough or something."

"I know," I said, my voice small. "Not my best moment."

"And don't think I don't know about the xenophobic attitudes towards DoC in that shop. The suspicion about our motives, watching our every move in case we steal something. Have you any idea what that feels like?"

"I don't think that. Why are you pointing the finger at me?"

"Because –" Anaru let out a long breath and lowered his voice. "– has it ever crossed your mind to challenge them about it? Silence makes you complicit, Em."

I said nothing. He was right and there was nothing I could defend myself with.

"We're not the same. You might think we are, but I'm not ashamed of who I am, and I'm not prejudiced against who *you* are."

I nodded. "I see that," I said in a low voice. "I think I've come a long way since I got here. I'm not the same Em that arrived a couple of months ago, but I see I still have some growing to do." I stood up and met his eye. "I'm sorry, Anaru. Not just for jeopardising the project, but for not being the person we both wish I could be."

I turned to leave, then pivoted back. "I think I should warn you that this won't be the last you hear from Warren. But I want you to know I'm going to do everything in my power to get him to lose interest. Whatever the cost."

Anaru didn't acknowledge me. He stood, a hand supporting him on the back of a chair, face turned to the bush.

I stepped out into the rain and headed home.

"HOW DID IT GO?" Janey asked when I walked in the door. I didn't need to vocalise it to give her an answer. She took one look at me and enveloped me into her bosom. I wrapped my arms stiffly around her. As this was a position we hadn't assumed since I was eight, I was rusty. She smelled the same as she always had – cigarette smoke and rosehip oil – and it brought me back to those times when I really needed her and she was always there, before I started to look critically at who the woman I called 'mum' was.

I relaxed, sinking my head into the cushion of her cleavage and, assuming my eight-year-old self, I began to cry.

I couldn't remember the last time I had, and I wondered if I'd ever allowed myself that outlet as an adult. Even Warren's desertion and my fear of being alone on the island had produced no more than a lump in my throat and a stifled sob. Not a single tear had rolled down my cheek.

"I'm a terrible person," eight-year-old Maxine said.

"No you're not, my love."

"I am. I'm a snob, I'm racist, and I don't even let myself cry."

Janey stroked my hair and said, "You're a bit of a snob, but I'm working on beating that out of you." She squeezed me. "I know I don't make it easy for you. I think your snobbery is part of your rebellion against me."

"You're pretty scary sometimes."

"I know, love." Her voice was soothing, but I thought I detected a hint of pride in it. "And what's this shit about you being racist?"

"I have white-person cultural obtuseness."

Janey snorted. "You're not white."

I laughed despite my tears. "OK then, I'm red and brown and freckly. But I'm still 'white'."

Janey pushed me away from her and stared at me for a beat. "Your father was Ngāti Porou. You know this. I've told you. Your red hair sure as shit doesn't come from me."

"But..." I couldn't remember ever having any other conversation with my mother about my father other than the "wanderer" one.

My brain took two, three seconds to recalibrate. "I'm Māori?"

CHAPTER TWENTY-TWO

IT WAS fair to say I'd had a pretty rough day.

I'd been served by my ex, the new man in my life thought I was little more than the algal scum floating on the tepid pool of humanity, and to top it off I wasn't who I thought I was.

There was only one thing for it.

I needed to get very drunk and pretend I was a happy person. That moving to Ruatapu was the best decision I had ever made. That Anaru hadn't taken a scalpel to my heart when he'd said "there's no us".

Mum and I finished off one goon bag, and when Ruben got home from an afternoon playing with Mel, we did our best to polish off another.

Ruben suggested a game of wine pong. I didn't own any ping pong balls, so we played with Skittles.

They didn't bounce very well, and the wine ended up brown from the food colouring, but it didn't dampen our merriment.

When the rain stopped, Janey brought out a large paper bag from her bedroom and said she'd been saving it for a special occasion, and seeing as I'd finally connected with my roots, tonight was as good a time as any.

I opened the bag and looked up at her in excitement. "Fireworks!"

I ran outside and called over the hedge, "Ted. Ted. We've got fireworks. Come and watch." Then I whipped around to Janey. "Can we start with the sparklers?"

RUBEN WROTE MEL-LOVES-RUBEN to a sing-song chorus of "oo-oo-ooh"s.

Ted wrote NUDITY-IS-THE-GREAT-LEVELLER.

Janey wrote MY-WORDS-CREATE-MY-WORLD.

I wrote WARREN-IS-AN-ARSEWIPE.

Ruben tapped a nail onto the shed for a Catherine Wheel, and we watched it spin and fizz and squeal, and then I pulled out the big boys.

"This one's for Saxon," I shouted, lighting a Roman Candle and holding it to my groin. As each star released from the tube, I thrust my hips and shouted "Pyew!" peppering the night sky with shots from my dick laser.

Janey "planted" a line of sky rockets in the garden and lit them in succession, the crack of each explosion echoing above the valley.

By the time the last one crackled in a blue shower, lights swung into the driveway.

"Uh oh," I said, taking the last firework out of the bag – a layered cake of assorted aerial shells designed for maximum show.

Anaru rounded the corner and stared at us open-mouthed.

"This doesn't look good, does it?" I asked.

"What on earth are you guys doing?" he said. "It's the dry season. You could start a bush fire."

"We're celebrating," I answered, as if it should be obvious.

Anaru stared at me for several moments, presumably wondering what on earth I, of all people, had to celebrate. "Find another way to do it."

"Sure," I said, flicking Janey's lighter and lighting the cake's fuse. "Oops," I said, as the first set of shells burst above our heads.

I DIDN'T MAKE it to the shop until eleven. I sloped in, cap and sunglasses on, and asked for a full, king-sized, greasy breakfast.

Trace called me "poor love", Don tutted, Wolf smirked, and Kevin nosed my hand sympathetically.

"Big night?" asked Wolf.

I groaned in reply.

"On a school night, too."

"It was necessary," I said.

"No doubt." He waited until I opened my computer and said, "Not looking too kick-arse today."

I jabbed the power button and waited for it to boot up.

"Did you hear some stupid buggers let off fireworks last night?"

"Yeah," I said resignedly.

"Not very smart." He waited a beat before saying, "Was it?"

"It rained yesterday," I answered in my best teenager voice.

Wolf's face rearranged itself back into the smirk he was wearing when I came in.

I opened my emails and saw that Warren had sent me one with no body, just a subject line: What time's the meeting?

I wrote back: No meeting. I couldn't persuade the project head that your proposal was in their interests. You can give me my money now. I've done my bit.

I received a reply immediately: I'm not convinced you did your bit convincingly. I'm coming over.

I shut the lid of the laptop and collapsed on top of it, my head buried in the crook of my arms. My worst fear had been realised.

When Warren got here, there was no doubt he would pull out all stops to gather his own evidence. And then the project would really be in the shit.

I SPENT THE WEEKEND PACING. I tried to push Janey's revelation about who my father was — who I was — aside while I focused on the more pressing matter of how to deal with Warren's imminent arrival. But it sat, hulking, at the back of my mind, waiting for the attention it deserved. When I did bring it forth for a chat, I wasn't entirely sure I liked the conversation, so I pushed it back again and put my mental energy into The Situation.

Warren would arrive on the next ferry, which gave me four days to come up with a plan that would convince him it wouldn't be to his advantage to make any proposal.

He'd informed me that, as co-owner of the house, he expected to stay and would do so until he had reached a satisfactory conclusion to his business trip. I would oblige him, but I sure as hell wouldn't make his stay comfortable. Neither would Janey.

. . .

ON THE SUNDAY, after several hours of redundant brain busting, I received a visit from Anaru.

He appeared at the back door just as I'd sat down for an afternoon cuppa and gave me such a fright that I spilled the tea over the dining table.

"Shit," I said, leaping to my feet and running into the kitchen to grab the dishcloth. I frantically wiped at the spreading pool, my dabs having little effect after the second swab.

Anaru walked into the room, took the cloth from my hand, and rinsed it under the kitchen tap. Then he placed a hand on my shoulder, pushed me down into my chair, and wiped up the remaining tea. "Can I have a seat?" he asked when he had finished.

"Of course," I said, placing my shaking hands between my thighs.

He took a deep breath and said, "I've come here to say that I've calmed down since the other day, and I've got a little perspective back."

"OK," I said, unsure of myself and most definitely unsure of him.

"Your...news was the last thing I needed on top of the bombshell I was delivered that day, and I didn't handle it well. I shouldn't have turned it into a personal attack, and I'm sorry about that."

"Um," I said.

He held up his hand and said, "Let me finish. I really want you to know that you were right. You have come a long way since you first arrived, and I actually admire the way you've sought to change your attitudes."

"Oh."

He turned the dishcloth over, folding it into a rectangle and then a square. "And I also want to say that while the photo thing was the most thoughtless thing you could have done at the time, you're not responsible for your ex's decisions."

"Wait," I said. "Are you...forgiving me?"

He smiled and finally raised his eyes to look at me. "Maybe. We'll see what move your ex makes next and depending on how you – how did you put it, 'Do everything in your power to make him lose interest'? – I might find it within me to forgive you."

"No pressure then, 'cos he's coming on the next ferry."

"Right. Well you have a few days up your sleeve. I have every faith you'll see him empty-handed onto the return ferry. There's no other option." He got up to leave.

"Wait." I reached out and grabbed his hand, then I dropped it when he turned back towards me. "Just in case you were confused about the fireworks the other night, the reason we were celebrating was because when I came home and confessed to being a white ignoramus to Mum, she laughed at me. Turns

out the wandering penis that impregnated her belonged to a man of Ngāti Porou origins."

Anaru looked at me for a beat. "You were celebrating being a sister?"

"Yeah. Seems red hair is a strong tribal trait."

Anaru sat back down. "It sure is," he said with a
small smile. "But, Em, that's some pretty big news to
process. How are you feeling about it now?"

"Now I'm sober?"

That smile again, encouraging.

"Um," I said, knowing exactly how I felt but not
the best way to vocalise it. Pushing things to the back
of my mind hadn't stopped my brain from sorting it
out without my conscious effort.

"I imagine it's a bit unsettling," Anaru said, and it
was out of me before I could stop it.

"I feel like a fraud."

"A fraud?"

"Yeah. Half of me belongs to this big, rich culture
that I know nothing about, but that I feel I should
claim and be proud of. But I'm not magically Māori
just because I now know I have Ngāti Porou blood in
my veins." I took a deep breath. "I just...I don't know
what to do with this new identity. I'm not comfortable saying I'm Māori, because I don't feel it." I offered him a weak smile. "Pretty terrible, right?"

Anaru shook his head. "You don't feel it *yet*. That
can change if you want it to. Do you?"

It took me a moment to root through the complexities of everything I had been feeling over the last few days. "Yeah, I think so. But where do I start?"

Anaru stood and said, "Come on. Let's check out your standing place."

ANARU and I leant against the barrier at the lookout where we'd first kissed and looked across the heaving blue at the east coast of the North Island.

"That's my tūrangawaewae."

Anaru nodded and said, "Did you realise this island's in your rohe, your tribal region?"

I ran my eyes up the coast, tracing the outline of the land against the skyline, and came to rest on Hikurangi, the sacred mountain Iwa had pointed out to me. It was clearer today, the mountain's double peaks defined against the haze-less sky. I looked up at Anaru. "So, I've come home."

He smiled and clasped my hand. "You've come home."

I turned back towards the view. Maybe my decision to make a radical life change wasn't as ill-conceived as it appeared to be. Maybe there were larger forces at work. I took a deep breath in, and when I'd let it all out in a long exhale, said. "I'm meant to be here."

Anaru said, "You sure are," and pulled me into a hug. He held me for a minute, then released me, placing his hands on either side of my face and kissing me on the forehead. "Whakatau mai ki tō āhuru mōwai ki tō whānau whānui."

"What does that mean?"

"It literally means, 'Welcome to your place of safety and your larger family', but I mean it metaphorically as well – you've found where you belong."

"Thank you," I said softly, then I closed my eyes and shook my head. I tried again, "Kia ora."

I WOKE up on Monday morning with a fully formed, if rather audacious and presumptive, plan for taking down Warren. I called it Mission Improbable.

My first step was to meet with Anaru and convince him he needed to reveal the huia project to the island community. I didn't expect it to be an easy task, but I had a much harder one ahead of me. Anaru's complicity was small fry compared to the feat I had decided to tackle.

Anaru, Mel and I met in the car park down at the beach. I climbed out of my car, put my sunglasses on, pulled my baseball cap low, and stole into the back of their departmental ute.

"It's not going to work," Anaru said when I had finished telling them the plan. "No one will agree to it."

"Not at first, maybe, but they'll come around.

We've got a pretty big card up our sleeve. I mean, how can you say no to *huia*."

"The plan has merit," said Mel. "It's a bold move, but I think it's gutsy enough to work."

"He won't fall for it," said Anaru.

"He doesn't have to," I said. "He just has to know he's not only taking on the key stakeholders – he's choosing to fuck with an entire island."

Mel nodded. "Intimidation tactics. Very effective."

I agreed. "The message will be loud and clear."

"How are you going to make sure the whole island turns up to the meeting?" asked Anaru.

I looked between the two of them and issued one word.

"Wolf."

WHEN I EXPLAINED the situation to Wolf and said one of the sanctuary's projects had been compromised by outside interest from a commercial party, he nodded and said, "Huia. Only a matter of time."

I stared at him, then mentally shook myself. Of course he knew about the huia. He lived inside the sanctuary walls. He wasn't blind or stupid.

He promised to make sure everyone was there.

. . .

THE EMERGENCY COMMUNITY meeting at the Port Keulemans Hall was called on Tuesday evening. While it didn't give the islanders a lot of time to think about whether they wanted to be involved in the plan or not, it also didn't give them much time to back out if they agreed to help.

DoC staff manned the doors, getting people to sign a non-disclosure agreement, while Wolf assisted in persuading any islander who balked at the legal requirement for something they'd been, so far, kept in the dark about.

By seven, the ferry terminal-cum-hall, which was rather generous for the size of the community, was a quarter full. Every able-bodied adult within a twenty-minute drive was there.

"What's this all about, Em?" asked an excitable Trace. She looked around her. "It feels all" – she lowered her voice – "mysterious and covert."

Don placed a hand on her shoulder and looked at me. "I don't feel at all comfortable about this. I don't like being in the dark."

"You won't be for long," I said. "You're about to learn something that will blow your mind."

"Blow my mind good or blow my mind bad?"

"It's good, Don. It's really good."

Taiporutu, who Anaru and Mel had worked on to convince the existence of huia on the island had to be shared knowledge, opened the meeting with a karakia, his lowered voice filling the room with the words of his prayer.

Anaru stepped forward to address the assembly, but Janey, clad in her Doc Marten boots, a black short-sleeve shirt and a leopard-print miniskirt, strode to the front and said, "I have something to say before you begin." She reached into her bra and took out a folded piece of paper, flicked it open, and placed her reading glasses on the end of her nose. "This is called 'Portrait of an Investment Wanker'."

I held my breath and willed her to have written something that wouldn't offend or shock half the room. Though judging by the title, the audience were about to experience a rather colourful Janey special. Hopefully what she had to say would at least have some poetic merit. My mouth ticked with the beginnings of a grimace.

"A silver-mouthed bankshaft,
Driving the 'mutual' out of funding
With rapacious rapture.
Fingering assets with glistening digits.
A cuntivorous snake,
All slither and quiver and sigh."
Janey punched the air with her pointer finger.
"I'll give you some hard currency –
Neither legal nor tender.
The buck
Stops
Here."

She ripped open the domes on the front of her shirt, revealing a black lace bra and NOT FOR SALE written over the exposed flesh of her 'assets'.

Ruben said, "Boom!" and clicked his fingers in frenzied applause.

There wasn't another sound in the hall.

I peeked out at the crowd from between my fingers. Expressions varied, though most were weighted towards bemusement rather than outrage.

Janey walked over to me and said in a voice that was far too loud in the silence, "That should get them lubricated and pliable. Right, gotta go. Things to do." And she walked out.

"Ah," said Anaru, looking between the back of Janey's disappearing head and me. "Kia ora, Janey, for those...provocative words. We'll just, um, huri atu ki te kaupapa ō te pō nei." He cleared his throat. "Nau mai koutou. You've been asked here today because the Department of Conservation and Ngāti Wherereitanga ō te Rā Hou partnership, and the birds of the sanctuary, need your help. In fact, there is a particular species in an acutely vulnerable position that needs you. They need all of us." He stepped aside so that the screen on the stage behind him was unobscured and raised his eyes to the back of the building. "Iwa, lights. Tama, video."

The room was pitched into blackness and a beam of light streamed from a data projector set up in the middle of the floor. The picture showed forest, dappled in sunlight and accompanied by a riotous chorus of bird song. One bird's call became progressively louder. It wasn't a familiar, everyday song – a tune that blends into the background because of its normality. It was a simple tune, like that of the kōkako – a grey songbird with blue wattles – and just as haunting with its bell-like resonance.

The atmosphere in the hall shifted from a curiosity that was confused and somewhat suspicious, to one that was full of wonder. People leaned into the screen as if they could see around the leaves and branches.

And then the huia took centre stage. The camera swung towards a group of four – two pairs – feeding off the bark of a fallen tree. The wood was rotten enough that the different roles of the two beaks were clear. One probing, one tapping and prising.

When a pint-sized pīwakawaka flitted into view with its fan-like tail outspread, it was obvious just how big the huia were. With their long tail feathers, they were much larger than any other native songbird.

Gasps echoed around the hall and whispers of "huia" could be heard above the muttering.

"It can't be," said Trace.

"It's a hoax," said Don.

"Kill it, Tama. Lights, Iwa," said Anaru. "It is real, folks. If we don't have a budget to keep our staff, we definitely don't have one for CGI. In 1998, five huia were captured in the Urewera forest and brought here. We now have eleven breeding pairs. The project has remained secret to ensure the tiny population has a chance to flourish without risk of political or cultural interference. The temptation to take advantage of the miraculous recovery of this species will be very high. In fact, it's already happened. And that's why you're here tonight.

"An investment company has gotten wind of the project and they are coming to the island in two days' time to secure evidence of the huia's existence. They intend to use that as leverage to enter into a contract with us, so that they can have exclusive rights to financial gain from the huge amount of public interest these birds will create.

"The population is incredibly fragile. The gene pool is very small, and we've struggled to get them to breed successfully. They're not ready for the world to know about them yet.

"By sharing the knowledge of these birds' existence with you, I am inviting you into tiakitanga. I am entrusting you with the guardianship of these birds. They're *ours* to protect."

Anaru paused, and in the lull, someone said, "But we'll make money off it. We'll be a tourist mecca."

"I don't want to live in Queenstown," said Wolf. "Wouldn't have moved here if I did."

A woman near the front said, "This place'd change. We wouldn't recognise it."

"I could do with some extra money," said Macca.

"Didn't you hear?" said Trace. "They're still recovering."

"Yeah," said Tama. "I don't want to be responsible for their *actual* extinction."

Above the hubbub, Wolf said, "So what do we do about this company?"

Anaru waited for the cross-talk to die down and said, "We have to convince their agent that it's not worth their while taking us on. That we'll do anything to protect the status quo. And we have to do it before they find the huia." He turned to me. "Em has an idea about how we might go about that. Em?"

I walked to where Anaru stood, swept my eyes around the hall, and smiled at the expectant faces.

When I had finished outlaying the plan, I waited for the debate to begin. I didn't expect it to go down well.

"You have to be kidding," someone near the back said.

"No way," another person added.

"That's the best plan you've got?"

Then Wolf stepped forward, and the hall descended into silence. "I'll do it."

Trace looked between him and me and put up her hand. "I'll do it, too."

Tama said, "I'm totally doing it."

"I think you're all completely bonkers," said Don, "but I'm in."

From then on, the reluctant islanders fell one by one. Those that weren't comfortable in taking on a role on the front line volunteered as support crew.

"Awesome," I said. "We've got a day and a half." I clapped my hands and rubbed them together. "Let's get busy."

PART 5

CHAPTER TWENTY-THREE

JANEY WAS MISSING.

She hadn't been seen or heard from since she shocked most of the island with her first foray into poetic oration.

Rumour had it that a chartered plane had left the island that very evening, but since pretty much everyone who lived in the vicinity of the airstrip was in the Port Keulemans Hall, nobody could confirm it.

I was fairly sure she wouldn't have the kind of money required to hire a plane, but considering her bag and most of her stuff were also missing, it was looking more and more likely.

I asked Ted if he knew where she was, and he answered, somewhat enigmatically, "She's on her own mission."

"Do I need to worry?"

He shook his head. "That woman is a force of nature. She'd part the ocean to get back here."

I wasn't entirely sure that statement was comforting. Janey was obviously up to something. Something big. Ted wasn't about to tell me, so I let it drop and tensed myself for when all would be revealed either by Janey herself when she came back, or the six o'clock news.

WHILE MEL and Wolf were left in charge of the Mission Improbable headquarters, Taiporutu, Anaru and I donned responsibility for delivering Warren to the front line.

"You lived with this man?" asked Tai as we watched the ferry dock from inside his Honda Civic.

"For thirteen years," I said on a sigh. "I should have seen it. He gets an idea and has this dogged determination that pushes everything else aside. He doesn't stop until he's reached his goal, and then he loses all interest. Two years ago he ran a marathon. Now his only exercise is lifting another champagne cocktail to his lips."

"So if we can get him to lose interest..." said Anaru.

"Unlikely. He's never not gotten what he's gunning for before."

Cars began to roll out of the belly of the ferry,

and the first of the few foot passengers disembarked. Warren, clad in an expensive-looking suit and carrying laptop and overnight bags, left the ship last.

"Just like the fucker to make us wait. Remind us how important he is," I said, opening my door. "Sorry, Tai. He brings the expletive out in me."

Warren spotted us and split his face in what he presumably believed to be his most charming smile. His mouth was wide and his teeth small, so the effect was less princely and more shark.

"Em. Lovely to see you," he said, stepping into me to deliver a kiss on the cheek.

I leaned backwards out of his range, and he laughed. "Inappropriate staff relations. Quite right."

I gestured towards my companions. "This is Taiporutu Carter, the hapū's representative for the sanctuary, and Anaru Waaka, head of several breeding and research programmes."

Both men greeted Warren with a "Tēnā koe" and hongi, pressing their noses against Warren and breathing in deeply. Warren didn't miss a beat, mirroring their formality with confidence. He then eyed Tai's small, two-door hatchback. "No official vehicle?"

"No," I said.

"Ah. I see I'm being put in my place. I shall have to work doubly hard on making a proposal you can't turn down. I'll be sitting in the back, I take it?"

"You got it. Put your bags in the boot and squeeze in next to Anaru."

Once Warren had climbed in, I levered the seat to its upright position and pushed it back as far as I could on its tracks. Warren had to turn sideways to fit into the space, and with Anaru's long legs splayed to fit around Tai's seat, he was forced to sit upright, his knees almost touching his chest. "This is cosy," he said.

"So," said Tai, starting the engine and heading for the car park exit, "I understand this is your second time here?"

"That's right."

Tai nodded. "You chose to make this special place your home, and in less than twenty minutes, you turned your back on it?"

Warren attempted to shift position but was forced to settle back into his original one. "I did."

"And left Em to run after you all the way back to the ferry because you left her with nothing," said Anaru, his voice surly.

My heart expanded for a beat, then just as quickly collapsed at the sound of Warren's voice.

"Not my finest moment."

"No," said Anaru.

"You know, Warren," said Tai so quietly I had to lean towards him to hear him properly, "it's hard to respect a man who would do that. If you expect to have any kind of conversation about having an involvement with the sanctuary, you are going to have to work very hard to prove yourself."

"Yes, I know. I completely understand how you feel. Let me assure you that I will make every effort to be an active and valuable member of this community."

"What?" I said, whipping around to face him.

"I own property here. I want to be involved."

"But you gave the house to Em," said Anaru. "You washed your hands of her and this place as fast as you could."

"You arsehole," I said. "You're keeping it as a foothold here. You don't intend to negotiate a buyout at all, do you?"

Warren opened his mouth to speak, but Anaru got in first. "What do you mean, 'a buyout'? He didn't buy you out?"

I turned back around in my seat and offered a humourless laugh to the passing bush. "This is not a good start, Warren. Are you going to tell them, or am I?"

When Warren issued a strangled sound, I figured the floor was open.

"Warren has attempted to hold a gun to my head. Not only has he not signed over the house to me, but he's refused to split our assets. I have three thousand dollars to my name, and he's threatening a very expensive legal battle to reach settlement if I don't come to the party and push his agenda."

"Now, Em," said Warren, "that's a gross exaggeration of the truth."

"No, it's not. And every one of us in this car knows it."

Warren laughed. "I'm afraid you're misrepresenting me to these gentlemen. Rest assured, I have no such inclination to make things difficult for Em. She misunderstood."

I turned back to him and caught Anaru's eye. His jaw ticked, and he looked like he was using every ounce of his self-discipline not to pound Warren through the back seat and into the boot.

I glared at Warren. "You are a first-degree shit. You are *very* lucky Mum's not here anymore."

Warren's eyes widened a fraction, and he rattled out, "Janey was here?"

I didn't answer. I enjoyed watching that spark of terror roll through him, and then I turned back to smile at the blur of gravel below my window.

Nobody spoke for a minute. I imagined Warren's brain working overtime to try to get things back on track, to cast his business acumen in a light that was attractive and persuasive. He'd lost the tentative grip he had on convincing them his character was genuine and sound. His proposal was all he had left.

"I take it from Em you're here without the knowledge of the company you represent?" asked Tai.

"Part of my role is to scout potential investment. I have the authority to carry out my duties without seeking permission first."

Tai grunted and smiled. Warren was a lone liability. If we could convince him there was nothing worth pursuing, the battle was already won.

"So this is an official business trip?"

The car travelled two hundred metres before Warren replied. "I've taken some leave. This is on my own time."

"Ha," I said, as the gates to the sanctuary came into view. "Some authority."

Tai slowed the car, pulling up outside the gates and punching in the pin code. While we waited for the first set to open, he turned around and faced Warren.

"With all due respect to your employer, Mr Barton, we are not interested in entering into a partnership of any kind, let alone with a financial institution. I want to make that very clear."

"And yet it appears you're bringing me inside the sanctuary walls, a privilege I imagine few get to enjoy." Warren's tone was amiable. The happy-go-lucky guy making a gentle observation. "I think you *are* interested. I believe you have little choice but to be. The government has announced another round of cuts I hear. How has that affected the project?"

Tai drove through to the holding area. Neither he nor Anaru answered him.

"Hmm, shame," he said, as if truly feeling the pity of the situation. "Things must be getting pretty difficult. You'll be making compromises you're not really in any position to make, being as resourceful as you can to keep this place from floundering. Well," he said, with the calm smugness of the disingenuous benefactor, "I can make it so that you don't ever have to worry. In fact, I can make it so that you can have everything you need, anything that would bring the programme forward – expertise, technology, facilities, you name it."

"Sounds good," said Anaru, "but at what price?"

"You make it sound like we would interfere with the project. You'd still have autonomy. You'd just have to be willing to let the secret out and allow people inside the fence."

Tai accelerated away from the gate and said, "You're right, Mr Barton, we do have a secret." He paused, changing down as he approached the first corner. "But you're wrong about one thing. We're already allowing people inside the fence." We rounded the bend, and a group of tents scattered about a large glade came into view. "You see, this area is no longer just a bird sanctuary. We've decided to draw extra income from protecting a particular way of living, a lifestyle that is under threat from the judgement of normalised society."

Tai brought the car to a halt just as a gloriously naked Wolf stepped out of the nearest tent and waved at us.

"Welcome to the Ruatapu Nudist Colony."

CHAPTER TWENTY-FOUR

BEHIND WOLF, an elderly couple played a vigorous game of swing ball, the woman's breasts clapping against her ribs as she lunged for the ball.

To their left, a pair of wide bottoms spilled over the edges of a picnic table bench seat, their male companion and lunch chef bravely turning sausages on a groin-level grill.

Wolf walked over to a cluster of sun loungers draped with naked bodies, spread a towel on a vacant one, and then with his backside to us, bent over to release the hinging mechanism.

A strangled splutter issued behind me.

I got out of the car and turned to slide the seat forward. Warren stared out the window, his lips turned down in distaste.

Anaru looked at me, his nostrils flaring with the

effort of holding in laughter, and I had to turn away and bite my lips together.

"Warren," I said, once I had regained composure, "close your mouth and focus. You need to get out of the car."

He emerged with a stumble and blinked rapidly as if exposed to bright light after a period of dark. Then he walked up to me and stood very close. "Em," he said under his breath, "what the fuck is going on?"

I didn't have an opportunity to answer him, because a vision stopped us all in our tracks. Mel walked out from behind a tent and strode towards us. Her long limbs exuded an athleticism and grace I could only dream of, her breasts were full and round, and a lean belly curved down into a perfect V of pubic hair. She was a goddess.

I stifled my "Phwoar" and thought of Ruben. He was one lucky bugger.

She stopped in front of Warren and said, "Is this our special guest?" Then she took his hand, shook it, and looked him up and down. "Bit overdressed for the occasion."

"Ernff," said Warren, trying and failing to look her in the eye.

She adopted her usual casual/aggressive pose — legs astride, arms behind her back. "I hear you want to bring in perves posing as tourists. That's rather disrespectful to our chosen way of living. Makes a mockery of us."

"No, I...Um. No," Warren stuttered.

"Good. Any form of exploitation is not acceptable. It would, in fact, be in direct violation of the Human Rights Act 2004 in which no commercial enterprise can benefit from the freedom of expression of a group or individual without first entering into a legal agreement." She took a step towards him, and he attempted to move backwards but was hampered by the Honda Civic. Given Mel's height and Warren's lack of it, she met him eye to eye. She moved her face close enough so that her nose nearly brushed his and said, "Do these people look like they deserve the disrespect of being made into a sideshow?"

Warren squeaked and vigorously shook his head.

"Good. You look like a law-abiding citizen, Mr Barton. It would be very much appreciated if you fucked off." She tilted her head slightly to one side. "Have we made ourselves clear?"

Warren stumbled sideways and grabbed my arm, pulling me after him. He stopped dragging me after a few metres and turned to face me.

"You're taking the piss," he whispered furiously. "This whole thing is a set-up."

I affected a look of confused innocence. "Set up for what?"

"Don't give me that shit, Em. You and the rest of these island mongrels don't want Chron moving in and making money from their best kept secret. Why you're not already milking it is beyond me."

"Milk what?"

Warren stood back from me and put his hands on his hips. "Oh I see. You're playing the dumb game." He raised his eyes to the heavens and said, "Fine. If that's what it takes, I'll play along." Then he put his face close to mine and said, "Milk the fucking fact you're breeding a supposedly extinct bird. How can you not want to make money off that? I mean" – he threw his hands in the air – "huia! Fuck's sake."

"Huia? That's crazy talk, Warren. Are you on something? They working you a bit too hard?"

Warren looked at me a moment, his forehead wrinkled in disbelief. "Alright. If you're going to play hard to get, I'll just bide my time. Take me back to our home, will you? I've got all week to gather evidence."

I folded my arms. "I don't think you're hearing us. Nobody here, *nobody* wants to discuss any sort of partnership proposal. We've gone to extreme lengths to demonstrate that to you." I gestured to the "colony". "You think we're prepared to stop here?"

"No. But I'm sure you can convince them to back off. You don't think I was serious when I said I'd drag our settlement through a lengthy legal process? How long is your remaining money going to last, do you think? Fancy being destitute in this armpit of a place?"

"And that, folks," I said, addressing the crowd and pulling out my phone, "is a wrap." I touched its screen and tossed it to Anaru. "Look after that for me. In case he tries to take it off me."

Warren looked between Anaru and me. "Why would I take your phone?"

"Because I recorded you, numbskull. Now I've got proof that you tried to force me to act unethically by means of coercion. I'm sure Chron will be very interested in your highly unprofessional conduct if you don't honour our original verbal agreement for settlement."

Warren paled and opened his mouth, then thought more wisely and closed it again.

I pointed at the car. "Get in."

Warren didn't move.

Mel and Anaru took a step towards him and he scuttled over to the passenger door, leaping in and slamming the door after him.

"Tai?" I said, holding out my hand. "If you wouldn't mind. Warren and I need some alone time."

Tai placed the car keys on my palm.

"Thanks."

"Will you be alright?" asked Anaru.

"I'm the daughter of Janey Stewart," I said, opening the driver's door. "I'm going to be fucken A."

WARREN STAYED silent until we arrived at the sanctuary gates then leant against the window and groaned. I looked over at him. Beads of sweat glistened on his forehead. "I've really messed this up."

"Yep. All that arseholery and nothing to show for it."

"I don't have a back-up, Em. I haven't successfully hunted out a new investment opportunity since I took my new role."

I made a sarcastic cluck of the tongue and drove through to the holding area. "I see you haven't changed. The only person you feel sorry for is yourself."

"Em —"

I swivelled to face him. "Can I ask you something, Warren? All the 'I think I still love you's, the 'you're looking beautiful's and the 'miss you's — was any of that real?"

Warren waited while the gate rolled open and said, "It wasn't...completely untrue. I was, um, banking it in case I needed it." He looked over at me. "I'm sorry, Em."

I put the car into first and said, "Tell someone who gives a fuck," and accelerated off in a cloud of dust and petrol fumes.

"Em?" screeched Warren, as I approached the first bend at speed. "What the fuck are you doing?"

"Getting in touch with my roots, baby," I yelled over the roar of the engine. I spun the wheel, sliding the back of the car out and spraying gravel over a reflective sign that suggested I corner at thirty-five kilometres per hour. I was doing seventy. "Whoo!" I shouted. "This feels *good*."

"For fuck's sake, slow down!" Warren gripped the dash as if to fend it away from the inevitability of it crumpling into him.

"No. I don't want to."

Warren flung his arms over his face as I skidded sideways around another corner. "Fine then," he said, after we'd fish-tailed safely out of the bend. "I'll walk. Let me out."

I laughed. "No way. I'm seeing you safely onto that ferry if it's the last thing I do."

"Em!" Warren yelled. "Stop. The. Fucking. Car." He braced himself for another corner. "Shiiiiiiit."

I ignored him and sped towards the top of a rise, the tyres briefly leaving the road as I reached the apex.

"OK. I'm sorry. I'm truly sorry, Em. Please." His voice cracked. "Please slow down."

"I'll think about it," I said, changing down and accelerating towards a blind corner on the wrong side of the road.

BY THE TIME I arrived back at Port Keulemans and pulled to a stop in the ferry car park, Warren was in a terrified stupor. He had to use his free hand to unclamp his fist from the handle above his door.

I jumped out of the car, unloaded his baggage

onto the bitumen, and marched around to his door. Opening it, I said, "Get out."

Warren looked up at me, pale and wild-eyed. He didn't move.

I reached across him, undid his seatbelt, and pulled on his arm. "Get out!"

As soon as he was out of range of the door, I closed it and got back in the driver's seat.

I did a single donut around him, the smoke from my tyres making him cough, then I thrust my arm out the window and raised my hand in a devil horn salute. "You can stick your job, Warren," I shouted at him. "Money in my account tomorrow, or I release the audio." And I sped off up the Port Keulemans road.

CHAPTER TWENTY-FIVE

THE PUB HUMMED.

Everyone involved in today's subterfuge was there to celebrate, and when Macca walked in and announced that he could confirm the "Shitbag got on the ferry," a cheer went up.

Anaru, Mel, Ruben and I were balanced on stools around a table in close proximity to the bar and therefore within easy distance of ordering subsequent rounds. We sipped our first, savouring the fact that the sanctuary's secret was safe for a while. And we'd only had to share it with a few dozen people, give or take, to make it so.

"You gonna send your recording to the bosses?" asked Anaru after I'd regaled them with the tale of my farewell joyride.

"I don't think so."

Anaru raised his eyebrows. "You reckon he deserves to keep his job?"

I took a sip of beer and considered the bubbles racing to the surface. "It's more the fact I didn't record anything."

"It didn't work?"

"I didn't think fast enough to set the phone up. I bluffed."

Anaru stared at me for a couple of seconds, then threw his head back and laughed. "You have one hell of a poker face. No wonder you played the pants off Wolf."

I looked over at Wolf leaning in customary fashion against the bar, thankfully with his pants on. He raised his glass and winked at me. I grinned at him, and then the flickering of the television at the other end of the bar caught my eye.

The six o'clock news was on, the sound muted. The background behind the presenter was filled with a black and white picture of a young man dressed in clothes that were fifty years out of fashion.

Ted.

I asked the publican to turn the subtitles on, and sentences appeared and refreshed at the bottom of the screen.

The artist relocated to New York in 1974 and after a period of depression, began to withdraw from public life towards the end of the decade. Sloane was last sighted in November of 1983 and following spec-

ulation that he had taken his own life, the value of his paintings skyrocketed. The last Sloane to be sold at auction fetched a staggering 2.2 million three years ago and within two hours of his agent publicising these new paintings, there has been a huge flurry of interest from art collectors around the world.

The five paintings will be moved to a London auction house where they are each expected to fetch between 2.5 and 3 million dollars.

As for the whereabouts of Edward Sloane, his agent issued a statement earlier today in which she said she respected the wishes of the artist to remain reclusive and will not be discussing the circumstances in which she was engaged to represent him. However, there is already a lot of supposition within the artistic community...

I stopped watching the screen and gripped the edge of the table.

"You OK? You look stunned," said Anaru. Mel and Ruben shared expressions of concern and looked at me questioningly.

I looked at their three faces in turn. None of them had any idea who Ted was or what his willingness to risk exposure meant.

I beckoned them to lean into the centre of the table. "You take this to your graves, or I will cut your tongues out."

Mel leant in further, Ruben's eyes widened beneath his frown, and Anaru laughed.

"That artist," I said, pointing at the screen, "is Ted. You all read that, right?"

Ruben nodded, and Mel sat upright. "Ted?" she asked, a little too loudly.

"Shhhh," I said, flapping my hands in a quiet down gesture. "It looks like Mum's spirited several of his paintings off the island to sell."

"Why would she do that?" asked Ruben.

I looked at Anaru. "To, as she put it, 'make the project impervious to outside players'."

Anaru knitted his brows. "She's raising money for the sanctuary?"

"Yep. And there won't be any strings attached. It's Ted," I said, shrugging my shoulders.

"Holy shit."

"How much will fifteen million dollars get you?"

Anaru looked at Mel, his eyes shining. "Anything we need for the next few years. Maybe even a few things we want."

Mel's face split into a grin. She held up her glass and whispered, "I propose a toast to our main man, Ted."

"To Ted," we said, clinking glasses.

Anaru turned to me. "I take it he was your muse for today's plan?"

I smiled. "We've got a lot to thank Ted for."

"But it was you who saw the strength in solidarity. You know what some tribes believe huia means?"

"I thought they were called huia because that's what their call sounds like."

"Yes, but it also means 'the calling together of the crowd'." He sat back and let the significance of his words sink in.

I couldn't have taken a more appropriate action in protecting the secrecy of the bird. A shiver ran down my spine.

Anaru sent me his you-are-the-best-and-only-human-on-the-planet smile. Everything else – the pub, the hubbub, the sharp smell of spilt beer – ceased to exist for several loud heartbeats.

Mel said, "Intense," and the spell broke.

I blinked rapidly in the light and noise of the re-emerged world, and Anaru leaned over, laying his mouth against my ear. "Would you like to help me celebrate back at mine?"

I gripped his thigh and asked how soon we could leave.

He downed his drink and said, "I'm done. Are you done?"

I nodded, and he grabbed me by the hand and pulled me towards the doors, where a series of wolf whistles went up as we pushed through them. Once we were outside, Anaru backed me against the wall and kissed me in a way that left me in no doubt of just how much he wanted to celebrate.

"It's so far to my place," he whispered. "Do you think anyone would mind if we did it here?"

"Probably not. But *I* mind."

"Killjoy," he said, smiling against my lips.

"On the contrary. I'm going to be the creator of a motherlode of joy."

Anaru stepped away from me, his face slack. Then he turned and ran for his car. "Race you."

"You'd lose," I said through a laugh and ran for my own.

TWO WEEKS LATER.

I pulled Mum into a hug and said thickly into her nicotine and rosehip hair, "I'm going to miss you."

Behind her, the ferry idled, its belly already half-full of departing tourists.

"Good," she said, rubbing my back. "I'm glad you've settled all the money stuff with Warren. Weight off your shoulders."

"Yeah," I said on a sigh. "Me, too. You'll come over for Christmas? Sax, too?"

She nodded against the side of my head. "Got to keep an eye on our Ted. Make sure he doesn't regress to shirts and pants."

I gave her a squeeze and released her. "I don't want to go back to an empty house," I sniffed. Ruben had finished the last of the renovations two days ago and had promptly moved in with Mel.

"You'll be fine. You've got so many projects to get

on with. Māori language classes at the marae, coordinating the backyard trapping programme with Don and Trace, and now that your home's completely watertight, you'll be planning its beautification."

"A new kitchen," I said wistfully.

"And organising that work hub thing." As soon as Ruben had hammered in the last nail and we'd drank a toast to the shedding of the house's "shit box" status, I commissioned him to build a glorified shed that could be used as a shared workspace for all the lonely work-at-homers. Don and Trace agreed to have it constructed in their spacious front yard. "And you'll probably want to think about finding a job at some point."

I smiled out of the corner of my mouth. "At some point."

The ferry honked its fifteen-minute warning.

Mum pulled me to her, put her mouth to my ear, and whispered, "I'm proud of you, Em," before stepping away and turning to walk towards the ferry.

I watched until she disappeared up the gangplank, then I walked to my car and pressed my forehead to the chest of the man leaning against it.

Anaru placed a hand on the back of my neck and kissed my hair. "You wanna stay at mine tonight?"

I nodded.

"Excellent. I've been looking forward to thrashing you at strip poker."

I pulled my head back and looked up at him. "You honestly think you have a chance against me?"

"Hey," he said, landing a kiss on my lips, "I don't have to beat you to still be a winner."

I pulled away and walked around to the driver's door. "Will you wear your uniform?" I asked, climbing into the seat.

"Why?" Anaru said in a deep-voiced drawl. "Are you in need of rescuing, pretty lady?"

"Not anymore, ranger cowboy," I said, smiling at the photo of Mum, seven-year-old Saxon and eleven-year-old me dangling from the rear-view mirror.

\m/

THANKS FOR TAKING THE TIME TO READ MY BOOK

I hope you enjoyed it. Please consider reviewing *Bluffing for Beginners.* As an independent author, reviews help support my work so that I can produce more great novels for you to read. If you're not sure where to post a review, try the Goodreads website or your favourite online bookstore.

AFTERWORD

Image sourced from Alexander Turnbull
Library.

Why did I write a book about saving a (extinct) bird species? It's important to point out, to those who have never visited the shaky isles, New Zealand is a nation of birds. Our only other indigenous land mammals are bats and fur seals. It was John Keulemans' illustrations in the 1873 publication *A History of the Birds of New Zealand* (of which the above image is one of) that inspired me to write this book; partly because the drawings are incredibly beautiful and partly because of the tragic way in which they came about. Keulemans never set foot in New Zealand. He drew the birds from taxidermised specimens shot by Walter Buller, *A History*'s author. Buller, believing New Zealand birds were on an inevitable path to extinction, didn't question his right to preserve birds for study. He shot the breeding pair of huia for his book knowing the population was showing signs of becoming critically endangered. Unfortunately, the reestablishment of the magical huia population in *Bluffing for Beginners* is completely fanciful. The last huia was sighted in New Zealand in 1907 and they are not the only casualties of human settlement. Nearly half of our endemic bird population is now extinct and we have the world's highest proportion of at-risk indigenous plant and animal species, which is a fairly shocking legacy. However, I want this story's narrative to ultimately be one of hope, and maybe even one that inspires some to action.

Thanks to the wonderful project leaders of Karioi

Maunga ki te Moana Biodiversity Project, who have introduced me to the very rewarding world of conservation at the local level. It's been over a decade and you never fail to inspire me.

When Taika Waititi said, "New Zealand is as racist as fuck," I was affronted, which isn't a surprise given the aggressiveness of his statement. *No it isn't* I thought. *New Zealand is a progressive, bi-cultural and increasingly multi-cultural country. I'm proud of what we've achieved as a post-colonial society.* And then I realised that my cultural perspective counted for little. I'm a part-Maori-part-European woman who's been raised white and has identified as white for most of her life. *What do I know?* And that's when I started paying attention. Taika wasn't simply referring to the obvious, easy-to-call-out racism of bigots. He also meant the subtle stuff. The casual slights, the jokes, the inability to see that what you say can marginalise others, the institutionalised attitudes that keep white perspectives front and centre. And I started to see it and I certainly heard it. Subtle racism is everywhere and this book is as much about me coming to terms with that (as well as my shift into a bi-cultural identity) as it is for Em. So, Taika, thank you.

Thank you to my editors, Louise Cusack and Sara Johnson, and my first readers who gave me invaluable feedback. My father, John, and my brother, Mathew, advised me on aspects of te reo me ōna tikanga Māori and I owe a lot to their expertise.

I also owe a lot to Dave Snell, whose book *Bogan: An insider's guide to metal, mullets and mayhem* informed me about bogan culture in a wonderfully entertaining way. Bogan is an Australasian term, but is used to describe different cultural groups in Australia and New Zealand. Snell's subtitle might give non-New Zealanders an idea as to which cultural group a New Zealand bogan belongs (as do, hopefully, the characters of Janey, Em and Saxon). And might I add (paraphrasing Snell himself), bogans are highly cultured in terms of the richness of their identity.

A nod to my inner bogan: 1984 will forever stand out in my musical education. It was the year Iron Maiden's *Powerslave* album was released. The cover art and the heavy, gorgeously synchronised, power-chord-based guitar and bass riffs captured my seven-year-old imagination (as did my first exposure to the poetry of Samuel Taylor Coleridge courtesy of the final track).

And then there's ACDC's seminal (in my opinion) *Highway to Hell*. It will forever remain one of my favourite albums.

\m/

ABOUT THE AUTHOR

Merren Tait writes quirky and irreverent romantic comedy about empowered women, and her books have earned a reputation for living up to the laugh-out-loud promise of the genre. *The Year of the Fox*, her first novel, has been optioned for television.

Merren has lived a series of bookish lives. Her first incarnation was as a book-hungry child, then as a mildly pretentious English literature student. Her third life saw her teaching English to somewhat-willing high school students, and her fourth, sharing her love of books as a librarian. Now she has been reincarnated as a fiction creator.

She is of Scottish, Ngāti Apa ki te Rā Tō, English,

Irish and German extraction and attributes her cross-cultural comedic flair to the enthusiastic inter-breeding of her ancestors.

Merren lives in a small house on a large piece of land near Raglan, New Zealand, where she dreams up fabulous names for her chickens, like Princess Layer.

www.ingramcontent.com/pod-product-compliance
Lightning Source LLC
Chambersburg PA
CBHW050901130726
47900CB00015B/1602